BROKEN LACES

Patsy –
I hope you enjoy the
story. Make impact!

Rodney Walther
12/4/10

- Enjoy -

I hope you enjoy the story. Make impact!

is 4 10

Broken Laces

RODNEY WALTHER

Redstone Ranch Press

Cover Design by Laura Wilhelm

ISBN: 0982944608
EAN-13: 9780982944608

PRINTED IN THE UNITED STATES OF AMERICA

To order additional copies, visit the author's website at
www.rodneywalther.com

For Susan, Lisa, and Brian

Acknowledgments

Because this story deals with the importance of nurturing our significant relationships, I wish to acknowledge the people who share a special bond with me.

As a husband, father, and son, I have been blessed to be part of a family that cares for each other. Mom and Dad, you have set a wonderful example with your marriage—thank you for building that legacy. To my wife Susan, who has been my best friend for more than a quarter-century, thank you for making me a better person. And to Lisa and Brian, please know how honored I have been to be your dad. Thank you for your unconditional love.

Writing is both intensely personal and extremely collaborative. For their support of my vision as well as their willingness to challenge ineffective writing when they see it, my deepest thanks goes to the talented writers of my critique group: Stacey Keith, John Oehler, Bill Stevenson, Vanessa Leggett, Rebecca Nolen, and Michelle Devlin. I also wish to thank: Roger Paulding of the Houston Writers Guild for his many suggestions; Dr. Tina Elkins for her medical knowledge and guidance; Laura Wilhelm for designing a wonderful cover that captures my story's theme; and numerous readers who offered their insight and encouragement.

For more than a decade, I had the pleasure of teaching kids how to play the game of softball/baseball. For the girls on the Angels, Wildcats, Red Hots, Tornadoes, Panthers, Wild Things, Tigers, and Rebels, thank you for your unbridled enthusiasm and your love of silly cheers. For the boys on the Rockies, Volcanoes, Pirates, Riverdogs, Diamondbacks, Astros, Aggies, Cubs, and Flames, I am grateful for your hustle and your respect, both for me and for the game of baseball. I get a thrill from seeing how you have grown into fine young adults.

One of the deepest bonds is that between a writer and his reader. My job is to deliver characters worth caring about, story that keeps you interested, and writing that doesn't get in the way. And your job is to suspend disbelief, to disappear into a world described by the author but given full life in your own imagination. Thank you for joining me on the journey.

With the publishing world in the midst of incredible change, I ask you to join me in supporting writers who are truly serving their readers. And the best way to do that is to spread the word when you find a story that engages you, that takes you into a rich world filled with complex characters. If you enjoy a book, email your friends or update your social networking accounts. Stand next to someone in the bookstore and tell them about your latest discovery. And you'll develop a bond . . . between fellow readers.

Of course, I'd love to hear from you. Please visit my website:

www.rodneywalther.com

BROKEN LACES

Chapter 1

I never could hit the curveball. A scrawny teenager named Tate Gillum once ruined my life with that lousy pitch. Twenty years later, as I watched my kid's Little League game, I had no idea that God was lacing up his spikes and preparing to deliver another devastating, knee-buckling curve. The hook. The deuce. Uncle Charlie.

"Jack, get off the phone," Melanie said, lightly punching me on the arm. "It's Kellen's last game."

I covered the mouthpiece. "Just talking to Scott. He's going all Chicken Little on me. Back in a minute." I scooted off the shiny, aluminum bleachers filled with doting parents and found quiet behind the third base dugout.

"I'm back," I said into the phone. "Now explain again why our proposal needs work."

Scott's voice was drowned out by the crowd, and I looked toward the field, where clueless Little Leaguers engaged in an animated rendition of *Where do I throw this?* My view of the action was partially obscured by dugout clutter—metal bats leaning haphazardly and a half-dozen helmets hanging from pegs—and by the flailing arms of Kellen's coach. I watched our pitcher lob a throw over the third baseman, then shook my head as two runners from the opposing team scored.

Scott's voice cleared through the noise, and I replied, "Yeah, I'll help you work on the document. But you owe me."

A chant of "Dee-fense" rose from our stands, and I turned to see Melanie sitting cross-armed, staring at me. She mouthed the word *Now*. I nodded and waved apologetically. "Gotta go," I told Scott. "Mel's giving me the evil eye."

I clambered along the top row of bleacher seats, my shoes crunching the broken shells of roasted peanuts and the empty hulls of sunflower seeds. "See you at three," I said into the cell phone, flipped it closed, and stuffed it in my pocket. Sliding on my finest salesman smile and hoping my eyes said *Trust me, I won't disappoint you*, I turned to face my better half.

Melanie's bottle-blonde hair was pulled back in a ponytail, and a visor shaded her eyes from the June sun. Understated makeup and gold earrings highlighted her flawless face. She could have pursued a career in modeling or acting; instead, Melanie elected to remain a kid-cheering, school-volunteering, bunco-playing stay-at-home mom in our upscale Houston suburb. Sugar Land, "the sweetest city in Texas" as the motto went, was a world apart from the central Texas farm I once called home.

A batter blooped a hit over the second baseman's head and then tripped over first base. Melanie chuckled when the kid stood and turned, revealing a chalk line that ran from his chest to the bill of his cap and dotted his nose white. When the laughter subsided, her head whipped around. "Don't tell me you have to work again. It's not enough that you stay late every night, now you have to ruin our weekend? Thanks a lot, Jack."

"Sorry, babe. Scott needs the help. You know I do this for our family."

Melanie stiffened. "I want you to spend time *with* your family."

"I know. But I won't be gone long." I inched closer and wrapped my arm around her waist. "Forgive me?"

She glared at me and I screwed up my face into a cheesy grin. Her eyes softened and she sighed, "I always do." Then she reached out and tousled my thinning brown hair with both hands. I lifted my arms to block her, and she moved lower, poking me in the ribs. "Sorry," she teased. "Forgive me?"

"I get it," I said, smiling broadly. "I'm a thoughtless goofball."

"Yep."

My seven-year-old son sat cross-legged in the outfield, filling his glove with blades of grass and tossing the contents above his head, where they settled on his Yankees uniform like green dandruff. Kellen's manager, Coach Bob according to the oversized letters on his extra-extra-large jersey, didn't bother to correct him.

"Wake up, Kellen!" I hollered. "Get in the game!"

Melanie shushed me. "Don't embarrass him. He's having fun."

My wife was a smart woman—I absolutely adored her—but she didn't understand the first thing about sports. Baseball wasn't about fun. She couldn't appreciate that hard work and overcoming disappointment built character, that coddling a boy didn't grow him into a man.

Suddenly Kellen stood and threw his cap in the air; his teammates did likewise.

"The game's over?" I said in disbelief. "Only four innings? At least we won."

Melanie shook her head. "Nobody won. Honestly, Jack. It's Rookie ball. We're not supposed to keep score."

The rules in Kellen's Little League were nothing like the ones I had growing up. These days, teams didn't keep score until the players turned eight years old. What kind of wimps dreamed up these rules? Soon all the boys would play baseball in dresses. For the record, Kellen's team won by five runs.

The Yankees stood at third base, and the White Sox lined up at first. Both teams shook hands. The kids picked up their gloves and hurried to the shade of a water oak outside the dugout. A plump woman with wisps of grey in her brown hair wheeled an ice chest full of juice boxes and Cokes to the waiting crowd. Behind her stood a Sugar Land clone, some trophy wife with short shorts and big boobs, who handed out packs of Oreos. Apparently another Little League rule was that each player must experience a post-game sugar high.

"Great game, kids," Coach Bob said to a round of parental applause. "Everybody ready for our team party? Let's do our cheer one more time."

The players circled Coach Bob, stacked hands with their teammates, and chanted, "One-two-three. Yankee Pride!"

It was all I could do to not roll my eyes.

The last kid to exit the dugout was my son, a freckled-face boy with blonde hair that curled under his cap. Kellen flung a red Louisville Slugger bag across his shoulder and slumped under its weight. No wonder. It was stuffed with two bats, including the blue and silver twenty-seven-inch Easton with a negative-eleven drop that had set us back more than a hundred bucks last Christmas. The bag also contained his fielding glove, batting gloves that were merely decorative, and a helmet with protective faceguard.

He lifted the snack bag to his face and extracted a cookie, anteater-like, with his tongue. "Did you shee me hit, Dad? Did you shee me shcore?"

"Don't stuff your mouth. And yes, I saw your hits and scores. Good job, buddy."

I lied because I understood the cardinal rule of baseball parenting: you always saw your son hit the ball, make the catch, or score the run. At least that's what you told him.

"I slid twice!" Kellen beamed.

"Proud of you, son." I patted him on the head and brushed blades of grass from his shoulders.

Kellen may have enjoyed his first year of baseball, but he was no ballplayer, as his athletic genes had passed maternally. My kid had a rag arm, average glove, and weak stick.

Ever since the ultrasound revealed a penis, I had expected my son to follow in my footsteps. He was destined to become a star athlete like his old man, Jack "The Cannon" Kennedy, the golden boy with the ninety-plus heater, the most heavily recruited high school pitcher in Texas.

I wanted another *Cannon*, but I got a cap gun. Of course I loved my son, but I accepted the common truth: boys disappoint their fathers.

Just ask my dad.

"Come on," I said. "Let's find your mom. We have a team party to get to."

"Yes!" he said, punctuating the exclamation with his fist.

Melanie stood at the end of the cyclone fence dugout, dressed in a pale-yellow *Baseball Mom* t-shirt, folding a string of pennants. She broke into a huge smile when she saw us. "Super game," she said, opening her arms.

Kellen dashed into her hug and accepted a peck on the top of his head. "I scored two runs."

"That's great! Would you put these pennants in that box? I want to talk to your dad."

"Sorry about having to go to work." I kissed her forehead. "And for yelling during the game. This Little League stuff just drives me crazy."

She rolled her eyes. "Kellen won't play again until next year, so I guess I don't have to worry about you acting like a lunatic for a while."

I brushed my hand against her cheek. "I really am sorry. Promise I'll get home early so we can spend some time together."

"I'll cook something nice for dinner. Grill some steaks. Have a little . . . dessert." She leaned closer and whispered, "I miss being with you."

"Me too."

She responded by nestling her head on my shoulder and lightly kissing my neck. With a sigh, she said, "I guess we oughta get going. Walk me to our car?"

Then she slipped her hand into the gnarled fingers of my right hand. A stab of pain radiated from my pinky, through my wrist, and up my forearm; I reflexively yanked it back.

"Sorry," she said. "Didn't mean to hurt you. Is it worse than usual?"

I flexed my wrist and wiggled my fingers, trying to shake off the pain. For twenty years, I'd lived with that injury. Sometimes it hurt more than others.

"Don't worry about it," I told her, and grasped her other hand with my left. I gave it a brief squeeze, then laced my fingers in hers. Then we walked hand-in-hand through the Little League complex—I felt like the luckiest guy there.

As we made our way to the parking lot, we passed a diamond filled with players a year older than Kellen. A steel-blue pitching machine stood on the mound. "Kel, that's where you'll play next year."

"I know. It's gonna be awesome!"

A ball flew from the machine and whizzed past the batter for a strike. Next year the pitches would be tougher. No more easy lobs from the coach. Despite his bravado, Kellen didn't know the challenges that lay ahead. Of course, neither did I.

"We need to swing by the house," Melanie said when we reached the car. "We're bringing baked beans to the party."

"And I need to pick up the Lexus. Scott's expecting me around three."

Melanie sighed. "Don't remind me."

"I'll be home this evening. We can celebrate later. I promise."

∞

After a not-so-quick turnaround at the house, with Melanie loading team trophies into her Camry and me securing my cargo—a crock pot on the front seat and Kellen in back—we zoomed along the Sugar Land boulevards, well past fashionably late for the party. The sugary-sweet aroma of baked beans that wafted from the passenger seat made me wish I'd brought a spoon. The Texas staple, its recipe perfected by my mother and duplicated by Melanie, always reminded me of simpler times: family reunions, Lutheran barbecues, and Sunday dinners at the farm.

I sped under a canopy of native pecans and perfectly spaced live oaks, leaving luxury sedans and monster SUVs in my dust. Melanie trailed behind, and we chatted on our cell phones.

"I know we're already late," she said, "but I need to stop at the pharmacy. Won't take long."

"The two of us will go ahead without you." I looked into the rearview mirror and blew her a kiss, then accelerated to fifty. Then fifty-five. Melanie matched my pace.

I gestured toward the backseat. "Hey, buddy, I want to hear more about your game."

Before he could respond, an explosion sounded from behind, snapping my eyes instinctively to the mirror. The nose of Melanie's car pointed down and to its left, like a racehorse crippled on its foreleg. A blowout.

Her car veered hard to its left, struck the curb of the median, flew airborne, then slammed into a hundred-year-old pecan tree. The sound was sickening.

I jammed my brakes into the floorboard. Kellen screamed, and the crock pot shattered against the dash. My car swerved and screeched to a stop in the middle of the road.

"Are you hurt?" I yelled, taking no time to listen for an answer. Kellen was crying in the backseat but in one piece, fastened securely in his seatbelt. "Don't get out of this car, you understand me? Stay here!"

I stumbled from the door, got caught in the dangling seatbelt, and fell to my knees on the pavement. Then I ran the hundred yards to what was no longer a car.

The Camry's right-front tire spun freely two feet in the air. Plumes of smoke rose from the engine. The pecan appeared to be growing through the driver-side hood; the front grill had melted around the ancient tree.

Melanie was barely visible through the shattered driver-side window. She lay motionless in her seat, belt fastened, head slumped to the right. The deflated air bag hung flaccid out of the steering column.

"Oh my God." I banged on the window. "Melanie! It's me, honey." When she didn't respond, my knees buckled. "Oh God. Please, God." Then I began yanking wildly on the door.

A woman rushed up. "I called 911. Is she conscious? Breathing?"

I had no answers. All I knew was that my beautiful wife was unresponsive, trapped behind a twisted metal door that refused to yield.

A man in a t-shirt began tugging on the passenger-side door. With a jolt and a groan, the Camry's door gave way—an automotive death rattle—and the man peered into the wreckage.

"Don't touch her!" I yelled.

I ran to the open door and crawled inside. My fingers trembled as they found the soft skin of her face. I just wanted her to open her eyes, tell me she wasn't hurt.

Then my fingers slid to her neck. I couldn't find a pulse.

The firefighters arrived first. A paramedic with tattooed, muscular arms examined Melanie. "Just the driver," he called to his partner. "Female. Thirty-something." Looking around, he continued, "Advise PD. We need traffic control, or we're gonna have another wreck. We've got cars parked all over the street."

Oh God. Kellen.

I turned to the woman who had placed the 911 call and pleaded, "Ma'am, you gotta help me. That lady's my wife—"

"Sweet Jesus." She staggered slightly.

"And my son's in that white car. Please get him out of the street, but don't bring him here. I can't let him see this."

"Anyone I should call?"

My mind sputtered, and I found it difficult to focus.

"Any family?" she repeated.

"My sister. She's local. Kellen knows her number."

The woman darted away and I turned back to the firefighters. "Don't give up on her. LifeFlight her to the hospital. Anything. Please."

The younger paramedic was an albino with wispy, colorless hair. He placed his hand on my shoulder. "We're doing everything we can."

"I'm her husband." The word felt heavy.

"Oh, no. Sir, please sit down. Let me examine you."

"I'm okay. I wasn't in the car." I moaned, wishing it had been me instead of Melanie.

The paramedic sat me down, took my vitals, and told me to control my breathing. At some point he wrapped a blanket around my shoulders.

I have no idea how much time passed. Red and blue lights from emergency vehicles flashed around me. Uniformed police officers lit traffic flares and conducted measurements of tire markings. My pants pocket vibrated and I fished out my cell phone. I recognized the number immediately—Leah was my older sister, my only sibling.

"Jack!" she shrieked. "Some lady called and said there's been an accident . . . and that she has Kellen . . . and that Melanie might be . . . I'm driving your way right now. Tell me what happened."

I don't know what I told her. My world had just crumpled around a tree.

❧

The next day, still feeling shell-shocked, I returned to the scene of the accident and inspected the tree that took Melanie's life. The thick pecan stood straight, as it had for years, long before Sugar Land invaded the forest with master plans, but now it bore a new wound. The impact had left a three-foot scar in its bark.

I stood in stunned silence for minutes. Eventually I walked to my Lexus in the nearby parking lot. When I opened its door, a horrible odor struck me. Baked beans had splattered and caked on the dash and in the footwell. The hot Gulf Coast sun had turned my symbol of success and wealth into a compost bin.

I'd never forget that rotting stench of death.

Chapter 2

Lord, help me get through this day. Not that I expected much from the man upstairs. If God wasn't the architect of Melanie's death, He had surely allowed the devastation to happen.

After pulling on dark trousers and buttoning my white dress shirt, I stepped to my sister's bedroom dresser to knot my tie. I once took pride in how young I looked, but the puffy, dull eyes and blank expression on the face in the mirror were unfamiliar. The sad stranger stared back, and I noticed his collar was stained crimson. A drop of blood had seeped from a nick under my chin and wended its way around my Adam's apple before settling on the starched fabric.

"Dammit," I said. This was no way to dress for a funeral. I peeled off the dress shirt and blotted the stain with a handkerchief, which only made matters worse. The blotch spread to quarter-sized. "No!" I yelled.

Leah rushed into the tiny bedroom that I'd used for the past three days. "What's wrong, Jack?"

I showed her the bloodstain. "I can't wear this to the service."

"It'll be okay. Did you bring another shirt?"

"Only this one." I remembered yesterday's painful trip home to select the clothes that Kellen and I would wear at church. Leah and my mom had flanked my movements, afraid I might shatter like a fragile vase. I'd chosen the black suit I'd worn to the company Christmas party two years ago, a fancy shindig held downtown where Melanie and I had danced until the band stopped playing.

"Don't panic," Leah said. "We'll fix it." She inspected the shirt, then moved to the closet to rummage through the hangers. "Nothing in here. Maybe Dad brought an extra." She dashed away.

If only we were at my house. There were at least a dozen freshly pressed shirts hanging in the closet. Staying with Leah and her family, although comforting in some ways, was rapidly proving unworkable.

Leah returned with a replacement. "Here. Try this."

After wiping my neck, I pulled on the shirt. Decent fit. Clean at least. The tie wouldn't cooperate, though, even after several attempts.

"Hold still." Leah wrapped my tie into a half-Windsor, tugged the knot tight, and slid it to my neck, pausing to smooth the collar. For the past few days, my big sister had been my rock. Immediately after the accident, she took charge, whisking Kellen and me to her house and single-handedly serving as chef, chauffeur, and nursemaid.

Leah Drane, four years my senior, didn't own fancy clothes. She wore a plain, black dress which would suffice for the funeral. Her mousy hair grew down to mid-back and hadn't seen a stylist's scissors in years. Two decades of marriage to a lump of humanity named Richard Drane had lined her face with worry, and her waist and hips ran together.

I turned toward the window when I heard a car back out of the driveway. "Mom and Dad are going with Richard and the kids to church," she explained.

"No. Kellen should be with me." With Melanie gone, I wanted my son more than ever.

"I told them we'd be right there. You ready?"

Is a man ever ready to bury his wife? I closed my eyes and the accident played out once again, a cruel rerun with random show times. The loud boom. Mangled metal. Frantic fear giving way to cold numbness. I took a sharp breath and slowly exhaled. "Let's get this over with."

Leah swung her car into the parking lot of Merciful Savior Lutheran, the same Sugar Land church where Kellen had been baptized. We entered through a set of heavy oak doors. A knot of mourners parted as we passed.

Pastor Steve greeted me with a tight smile and perfunctory hug. He stood a head shorter than me, and I couldn't help eying his receding hairline, poorly camouflaged by a comb-over. "Kellen's in my office with your mother," Pastor Steve said, answering my unasked question. He gestured toward the far hall. "If you need anything . . ."

I turned to Leah. "Find your family. We'll join you inside."

Getting to Pastor Steve's office required walking through the church's narthex and navigating a multitude of people, all dressed in their black uniforms of sorrow. As I rounded the corner, the crowded room buzzed with the murmur of whispered conversations. Above the muffled voices, I heard, "Beth told me they were racing at, like, sixty miles an hour."

I froze. Did people blame me? Melanie? It was an accident, for God's sake. I turned away, not wanting to face the attention. The accusation.

Before I could retreat, a woman called my name. The room hushed and I felt the stares. Patsy-somebody, one of Melanie's fellow Sunday School teachers, embraced me in a warm hug, her cheek damp against mine. "I'm so sorry," she said in a shaky voice. "Melanie was wonderful. Great with kids."

"Thanks for coming," I replied automatically, my mind reeling. The room slowly spun around me as others stepped forward.

By the time I reached Pastor Steve's office, a dozen mourners had consoled me, their faces blending together. "Thank you for coming," was all I could say, although I wanted to scream at everyone to leave me alone. When I opened the door, I heard soft music emanating from a radio on Pastor Steve's desk. The piano notes—almost a lullaby—washed over the room like gentle ocean waves. My mother sat on a loveseat, cradling Kellen's head in her lap. He lay in a fetal position, and for a moment I thought my second grader was sucking his thumb.

I knelt at the sofa and stroked his hair. "I'm here, Kel. You doing okay?"

He didn't reply, but I could see his body tremble. I turned to my mom. "How long has he been like this?"

"Since we got in the car. Says he doesn't want to be here."

"Everyone's looking at me," Kellen whispered.

I stood, then lifted Kellen underneath his arms and wrapped him a bear hug. He threw his arms around my neck. "We'll get through this together," I told him.

Kellen clung tightly to me as I carried him into the church. I stepped to the open casket where Melanie lay and brushed the back of my hand across her cheek. For years, this simple caress had preceded kisses, apologies, and lovemaking, but this time her flesh was unresponsive. "I love you, Mel," I whispered, my voice breaking. "I'm gonna miss you."

I lowered Kellen and asked, "Do you want to tell Mommy anything?"

He shook his head, his eyes squeezed tight. I paused for another look at Melanie, then turned and moved into our designated place in the front pew. Leah and her family sat to my left; to my right, beside the aisle, Kellen sat with his face in his hands.

"My tummy hurts, Dad."

I leaned over and patted him on the shoulder, then cast my gaze toward the sea of somber faces in the congregation. More than three hundred people jammed the sanctuary, and scores more spilled into the narthex. Who were all these people? Besides my immediate family and a handful of friends and colleagues, I recognized no one. Did Melanie know them from church? Kellen's private school? She had obviously endeared herself to many. Had I missed so much of her life?

Somber organ music filled the room. My eyes welled up. My breathing quickened. I wasn't sure how long I could keep it together. And Pastor Steve hadn't even welcomed the congregation yet.

My mother and father stood at the end of the pew, waiting for Leah's family to clear some room. Mom looked frailer than I'd ever seen her. Dad supported her with his arm. He could have passed for an undertaker, a tall, stoic man in a dark suit. Except for the quarter-sized splotch of blood on his collar.

Kellen tapped my thigh. "I don't feel good."

"Need to go to the bathroom?" Kellen's bladder conveniently shriveled on Sunday mornings. Whenever Pastor Steve delivered one of his feel-good sermons, the kind based on the prophet Oprah, Kellen often asked to slip out.

"Maybe," he said.

"Can you hold it, buddy?"

He shifted in obvious discomfort. A teddy bear, received from a kind police officer less than a week ago, lay between us. I picked it up and bounced its fuzzy legs on Kellen's lap, then lifted the bear to his chest. He clutched Mister Copper and snuggled deep into my side.

The only funeral I'd ever attended was that of my grandfather, Paw-Paw, back when I was sixteen. On his seventy-first birthday, lightning struck him while he tended to a pregnant cow in the middle of a rainstorm. All in all, it wasn't a bad way to meet your Maker. At Paw-Paw's funeral, I pretended his death didn't affect me.

Two decades later, I couldn't pretend this pain away. Melanie's body lay in a mahogany casket fifteen feet in front of me. My peripheral vision shrank and my senses dulled, as I disappeared into the zone known only by those who mourn a loved one. Pastor Steve's sermon didn't register. The congregation sang *The Old Rugged Cross*, Melanie's favorite hymn, and a woman across the aisle wailed.

"I gotta go to the bathroom," Kellen said urgently.

"Not now." I was barely hanging on myself, my breath shallow and skin clammy.

"Please, Dad. I don't like seeing Mommy in that box."

A gasp caught in my throat, and I realized we'd been sharing the same terrible thought. Kellen buried his head in my chest, and I held him close—I could feel his shaking arms and rapidly beating heart. I turned to Leah. "Could you take him to the restroom?"

She placed her hand on mine. "Be right back."

They shuffled out of the pew and stood in the middle aisle facing the congregation. Everyone's eyes fixed on Kellen. The boy who lost his mommy.

He turned around as if to escape. An odd look crossed his face. His hands covered his stomach and he leaned closer, as if to tell me something. Then with a shudder, he began to vomit.

Chapter 3

My sister raised two kids—three if you counted her husband. Leah and Richard shared a modest house in the oldest section of Sugar Land, in a development that blue-collar families called home. Their neighborhood looked nothing like Sugar Meadow, the swanky master-planned community where we lived: the land of perfect houses, perfect landscaping, and perfect schools.

On Friday evening, I stood in Leah's cramped kitchen, grasping for normalcy. The pizza guy had just left after exchanging three pepperoni and sausage pizzas for twenty-five bucks. I set paper plates on a table which bore a thin, jagged crack in its glass top, while Leah poured root beer into plastic cups emblazoned with our names in black Sharpie.

"You ordered too much pizza," she said, shoving the stacked boxes to the edge of the counter, where they hung precariously, a jutted elbow away from being knocked to the floor.

I shrugged and said, "Leftovers, then." I didn't tell her that pizza reminded me of Melanie, how we had once shared a gooey, meaty pizza on the last night of our honeymoon and how we used to celebrate date nights by holding hands along our local hiking trail, watching the sun set, and then visiting our favorite pizza joint to split a meal and talk about our future. I moved to the refrigerator, where I located a shaker of Parmesan cheese, then spied what was left of a twelve-pack of Budweiser. For a moment I considered having a liquid dinner. "Where's Richard?" I asked.

Leah flattened her lips into a tight smile. "He goes out on Fridays."

"Oh. What's he up to?"

She inhaled and held the breath. Her head bobbed as she searched for the words. "It's Friday. He's . . . out."

Two boys stampeded into the kitchen. Trevor was a year older than Kellen, with dark hair and an olive complexion. He looked more like his father than his mother, with teeth that would make some orthodontist a wealthy man. "I want the cheese pizza!" Trevor announced.

"Me, too," Kellen said. He flipped open the first two pizza boxes and scrunched his nose in disgust. After lifting the third lid, Kellen threw up his hands. "No cheese?"

"Sorry, guys," I said. "I ordered all the pizzas the same. Just pick off what you don't want."

"We always order one cheese and one veggie," Trevor said. "Marissa's gonna be mad."

As if on cue, my fifteen-year-old niece entered the room. With curly, bright-red locks and a face of freckles, she looked like the Wendy's girl on a bad hair day. "Why am I gonna be mad?"

Trevor pointed to the pizza boxes. "Uncle Jack didn't order a veggie."

Marissa rolled her eyes. "Well, I'm not eating anything with meat. Someone get me a frickin' yogurt and a frickin' spoon."

"Cut it out," Leah said, "Your princess act is getting old. And give your uncle a break, for God's sake."

I watched as the boys played musical chairs, attempting to pick the best spot to eat pizza and watch television. Marissa parked herself at the end of the table, her back turned, and spooned blueberry yogurt into her mouth. Leah tried to clear room for the pizza boxes. An arrangement of white tulips and peach roses, a remnant from the funeral a week ago, rested in the center of the table. She picked up the basket; bits of dry petals fell like snowflakes onto the glass surface.

"That's too bad," Leah said. "Those were pretty flowers."

"They needed water," Kellen said matter-of-factly.

He was right, of course. The cut flowers had thirsted since we'd moved in. Leah had been too busy helping others to notice. She shook the basket over a trash can, creating a small pastel cloud, then shrugged her shoulders and tossed the whole thing into the garbage. Another needless death.

Eating dinner in silence, I thought about Melanie. I remembered her infectious laugh, so often accompanied by a cute hiccup, and her boundless energy when she breezed into a room. My eyes drifted toward the living room, where I half-expected her to appear in the doorway. All I saw was the pile of dead flowers in the trash.

I considered how Kellen and I would get on with our lives. Would we too eventually dry up and crumble like petals of a neglected flower? I couldn't allow that to happen. "Leah," I began. "You've been great. Opened your house, took us in."

"That's what family's for."

"Yeah. I guess I take family for granted sometimes. Look, Kellen and I should move back home. He needs to play with his friends and get back in his own room." I picked up a napkin and blew my nose.

"You know you're welcome to stay."

"I know. But we have to get on with our lives. Whatever that means. Right, Kellen?"

Kellen didn't reply but nibbled at his pizza. He seemed

disappointed—or maybe resigned to his fate, as if he'd just heard the governor wasn't going to grant a reprieve.

When dinner was over, I returned to the guest room, knowing this would be my last night on an uncomfortable mattress in an unfamiliar bed. Sleep would come easier in my own bed, I told myself.

The following morning, a little before noon, Kellen and I loaded our belongings into my car, which still reeked of rotting beans. The same auto shop that had hauled away the pieces of Melanie's Camry had promised to restore my Lexus to its original condition. They steam cleaned the carpets and upholstery, disinfected the interior, and pronounced it good as new. But the putrid odor of baked beans remained.

I accelerated out of Leah's unassuming neighborhood and crossed the Brazos River, where its bridge afforded a panoramic view of the distant skyline. The surrounding flat land, once only good for farming sugarcane and cotton, had become some of the most highly valued property near Houston, with master-planned communities housing the rich and very-rich. I took a deep breath and drove. Home.

I wanted a return to normal. Carl Gates, the balding, big-eared man in my front yard was light-years from normal. He stood dripping wet, the result of washing a twenty-five-foot ski boat in his driveway. He wore blue jean cutoffs and no shoes. His t-shirt read *Starfleet Academy* and, on its back, *Trek Unity - 1998 Convention.*

Captain Carl, as I'd nicknamed him privately, fancied himself like his TV hero, Captain Jean-Luc Picard. His wife Beth was equally weird. When the last Star Trek movie premiered, they showed up wearing full Starfleet uniforms.

"Glad you're home," he said, shuffling his feet nervously. "We picked up your newspapers."

"Thanks." We stared at each other, and a clumsy pause grew into an awkward silence. "Your boat's looking good," I continued, communicating in the manner that people from my suburban galaxy were accustomed, superficial and judgmental at the same time.

"Just getting it ready. Tomorrow we're going water skiing."

His Boston accent made it sound more like *wottuh skane*, and I envisioned Captain Carl at the wheel of his boat, zinc oxide on his nose, yelling "Maximum warp!" as he pulled his twin boys across the lake.

"Hey, look," he said. "I know you're just now getting back. But . . . uh . . . we'd like to have you guys over for dinner tonight."

Dinner with Trekkies was the last thing I needed. "Sorry, I planned on a quiet evening."

"I'll grill some steaks. You don't need to worry about cooking." He twisted his sponge, wringing out suds that rolled down his forearms to his elbows, then dripped onto his toes. He attempted an assuring smile.

"We're good," I said.

"Come on over about five-thirty."

I shook my head. "No, Carl. Really. I've got a lot to do." I retreated to my open car and lifted three bags from the trunk.

The Captain followed. "Just trying to help."

"You want to help? " I said, my voice rising. But then I caught myself. I knew what he was trying to do. Everyone—me included—wanted life to be normal again. But *normal* didn't exist anymore. A random tree took care of that. "Appreciate it, Carl. But you need to give me some space."

"I just . . . Well, Beth and I are really sorry about Melanie." He placed a wet hand on my shoulder. "If you change your mind about dinner . . ."

Two boys ran across the yard, firing water guns at each other. A stream splattered against the hood of my car. "Over here, guys," Captain Carl shouted, clearly grateful for the distraction. "Look who's home." The boys ignored him until he growled, "Patrick! Stewart!"

Identical twins appeared instantly at his side. They were short and wiry, with dark tans that resulted from long hours of playing outside. I couldn't tell them apart. Patrick and Stewart were born a couple months after Kellen, but they acted years younger. They were hyperactive, hypersensitive, and perpetually medicated.

"Can Kellen play?" the boys asked simultaneously. "Please?"

I considered everything that could be accomplished while Kellen played with his friends. Put away our stuff. Organize the house. I needed to contact Scott as well—he probably wondered when I'd return to work. "Kellen's inside. Tell him I said it's okay."

Back inside my kitchen, I realized the house hadn't registered any change during our absence. The air conditioning blasted cold; video games cluttered the carpet. I dropped the unopened mail onto the table and collated the envelopes. Five sympathy cards had accumulated during the past several days, one from my aunt and uncle in San Antonio, another from Scott at work—definitely needed to call him—and three from out of state. I built another stack for envelopes containing bills. Melanie's latest issue of *Cosmopolitan* claimed there were twelve ways to increase your bust size. I set it aside, then realized it would forever remain unread. I muttered, "Sorry, babe," and tossed the magazine in the trash with the rest of the junk mail.

A long envelope from the county coroner almost suffered the

same fate. As it hung from my fingertips over the trash can, the return address finally registered: Fort Bend County Medical Examiner's Office. They'd promised to send a report once they'd completed all the tests. Bracing myself, I opened the letter.

The medical examiner reported matters scientifically, which made sense, but I still found it difficult to see my soul mate described as a "normally developed, well-nourished Caucasian female measuring 68 inches in length, weighing 132 pounds, and appearing generally consistent with the stated age of thirty-six years." The report summary identified the cause of death as basilar skull fracture. Massive trauma. Crushed left pelvis. Broken right femur. The force of the collision had caused a tear of the aorta, which would have likely proven fatal had she not broken her neck.

At least she died instantly. No sign of drugs or alcohol in her system, which was all the insurance company and police cared about.

The medical examiner noted a final observation, clinical and straightforward. I had to read it twice before it registered. The female subject carried a nonviable fetus of six weeks.

My fingers went numb. I dropped the report to the floor. Then my knees buckled and I dropped to the floor, too.

Pregnant.

I buried my head in my hands and wept, then collapsed into sobs. Why would God kill a person who did so much good in the world, along with the innocent baby growing inside her? She— they—were gone, and I felt a deep ache in my own torn heart.

Then I cried for Kellen. No mom. No brother or sister. He'd just be stuck with me.

Chapter 4

The doors of an elevator opened, and I stepped into a cavernous room, which my sleeping mind registered as the centerpiece of the Gemini Devices office building. Brown, dying ferns, some that looked like fox tails and others with tiny, teardrop-shaped leaves, covered the sloping walls. A marble fountain gurgled dark, thick blood.

I searched for a door among the mirrored walls. Confusion and fear enveloped me. Where was Melanie? She needed to help clean the car.

In my reflection, I spied a monkey perched on my shoulder. He wore a baseball cap and pointed accusingly at me. He rolled back his head and laughed. The laughs turned to loud screeching. The mirrored walls shattered around me, showering glass at my feet.

I woke with a start. The screams came from inside the house, upstairs, in Kellen's room. I bolted from my bed and scaled the staircase two steps at a time. Throwing open the door, I saw bizarre shapes race along the walls and quickly realized the shadows were caused by a striped nightlight just inside the doorway.

Kellen sat in the far corner of the room, his arms wrapped tightly around his knees. He rocked forward and back.

My stomach lurched. "What happened? Are you hurt?"

He answered with a plaintive wail, and I wasn't sure he even realized I was in the room. Through the odd streaks of light, I saw a pile of books scattered around him. Tufts of white foam littered the carpet. A cold, black eye stared up from the dark mound at Kellen's feet. It was the dismembered body of a teddy bear—Mister Copper.

"Kellen!"

He blindly threw a book toward me, and it struck the nightlight to my left, shattering the bulb like the mirrors of my nightmare. Kellen's bedroom flooded with the black, moonless sky.

I clambered along the carpet to his barely discernible form. "Kel, it's Dad. I'm here."

We sat side by side, shaking like campers lost in the snow. After a while Kellen said, "I had a nightmare."

"Me, too."

"Mom left me all alone at the zoo. She went to buy popcorn, but she didn't come back. All the cages opened—"

"It's just a dream—"

"And the giraffes and the bears chased me." He wept softly, the image obviously still fresh in his memory.

I knew he didn't realize his teddy bear lay in pieces, destroyed in his panic. "It was just a bad dream. I'll tuck you back in."

"I don't want to go to sleep. I hate bad dreams!"

We hugged again in the pitch-black bedroom. His hair smelled like Melanie's. "Come with me," I said.

By the time we reached the kitchen, I had turned on every light in the house. I poured Cocoa Puffs into a bowl and placed it on the table in front of Kellen. I watched him eat, first tentatively then ferociously.

"Feeling any better?" I asked when he finished his cereal.

"Ready to go back to bed?"

He covered his ears and shook his head, then darted into the living room. I followed.

An hour later, the television glowed softly. Kellen's head lay in my lap, his tired eyes watching Woody and Buzz Lightyear. We'd viewed the movie numerous times, and I wasn't paying any attention. Images of an inconsolable Kellen filled my mind. I stroked his hair. About two-thirty, he finally fell asleep, his rhythmic breathing and gentle snores slowly calming me, and I didn't see the end of the movie either.

The next morning I called Leah. "He just lost it last night," I said, kneading my unshaven face. "Really scared me."

"I'm worried about both of you. Maybe you should come back and stay with us."

"No. This is where we need to be." I looked around Kellen's bedroom. In the late-morning light, his room appeared as if it had been ransacked by burglars. "I'm just not sure how to help him. I understand what he's going through, you know? But it's like he's pulling away. You've seen him. He won't talk to me."

"You both need to see a therapist. I'm sure Dr. Mike can help." For the past few months, Leah had bragged on her psychologist, how smart he was, how helpful he was. According to Leah, he specialized in family counseling.

A shrink didn't seem like the answer, but I was at a loss for how to help Kellen. I picked up the furry remains of Mister Copper and tossed him in the trash. "Okay, give me this guy's number."

She recited Dr. Mike's phone number, then said, "We missed you at church today."

"That's not a priority," I snapped. I wasn't a fan of Pastor Steve or of his church. Leah and her family attended faithfully, and she was the grand poobah of the Altar Guild. Melanie used to drag me there on Sunday mornings, knowing full well I didn't want to go.

I wasn't a heathen—I was a bona-fide Lutheran with full credentials: baptized as an infant in my folks' rural church, confirmed at age thirteen, and married by a minister who traced his roots back to Martin Luther's hometown. But by the time I entered high school, I realized many at church didn't practice their faith. A bunch of hypocrites is what they were, praising and confessing God on Sunday morning, drinking and cussing the rest of the week.

God wasn't any better. The biggest hypocrite in the world preached love and salvation, but when the chips were down, He let Melanie die. Killed her.

⚬❦⚬

Standing in front of the Gemini Devices elevator, I turned my head to observe the atrium, its cream walls whitened by overhead skylights. Three ceramic containers cradled lush ivy plants and ferns. The bright, expansive atrium looked nothing like the grotesque room of my nightmare. Relieved, I stepped into the elevator and pressed the button for the third floor.

Scott Anderson sat at his computer, a phone pressed to his ear, a power-red tie knotted crisply at his collar. His suit jacket hung from a coat rack next to his desk. A good-looking Californian with a perfect tan, manicured nails, and an eye for the ladies, Scott was my best friend.

"That's not gonna be a problem, Dr. Miller," he assured the caller in his most soothing voice. "I can change your order. We're always willing to help out our better clients." He had barely cradled the phone when he said, "What a dumbass."

"Bad news?"

"Any other kind these days? Good to see, buddy. How are you holding up?"

I shrugged. "About like you'd expect. Let me check my email, and then you can update me on these contracts."

I spent the rest of the morning trying to restore order. Selling cardiac devices to Houston's flourishing medical community was my job, my career, my identity. Months before Kellen was born, I had bluffed my way through an interview and joined Gemini Devices as a medical equipment salesman. My only sales experience had been behind the counter at Zimmerscheidt's Tractor Supply, and my medical expertise was limited to a biology course that I had attended half-drunk in college.

In the two and a half weeks I'd been absent, everything had gone wrong. Summer was usually a decent time of year to work with hospitals—no one seems to take vacations—but my biggest client was balking on its order for our new line of surgical technology, which placed my lucrative commission at risk. Two hospitals had seriously reduced their capital programs due to budget cuts, which meant they needed to "talk to me."

Lunch didn't happen until after one o'clock, par for the course at Gemini. Normal routine was in by seven and out by seven, although sometimes I didn't arrive home until after ten o'clock, when Kellen and Melanie would already be asleep. I didn't like it, but that's what it took.

Turning off the light above my cubicle a little after six o'clock, I told Scott, "I'm headed out. Gotta pick up Kellen at my sister's."

I found my newly purchased Hyundai Sonata in the parking garage, slipped in, and turned the key. Nothing happened. "Come on, you stupid car," I muttered, then cranked the engine again. I wanted to hear its four cylinders roar to life, but the only noise it made was a rapid clicking. "I can't handle this today," I told the car. I continued turning the key.

When the clicking stopped, I realized I'd run the battery down. I dug out my cell phone and called Scott. "Hey, help a buddy out. You got cables?"

By the time Scott jumped the Sonata's battery and I hit the Houston freeway system, traffic had backed up farther than I'd ever seen. The giddy reporter on the all-talk AM station announced that the commute from downtown to Sugar Land was running well over an hour, thanks to an overturned eighteen-wheeler at the beltway. I topped an overpass and saw the grim news for myself, nothing but miles of brake lights—six lanes wide. The dull ache behind my eyes swelled to a full-blown migraine.

I switched the radio an oldies-rock station, and strains of Gerry Rafferty's *Baker Street* filled the car. If I was going to deal with all the yahoos on the freeway, at least I had the songs of my youth to accompany me. When the song ended, its guitar solo fading away, the Sonata's air conditioning suddenly squealed loud and long. Hot air poured from the vents. I pounded the dashboard.

By the time I reached Sugar Land, it was almost eight o'clock and I was dripping with sweat. Leah met me at the car. "I thought you were gonna eat with us."

"Car trouble. Then horrible traffic. I tried calling your cell."

She shrugged. "I think my phone's in Richard's car. Never mind. You missed dinner." Her stern look melted to one of pity. "There's leftover meatloaf in the fridge. I don't know when Richard's coming home, so you go ahead and eat."

As I gulped down my dinner, Leah loaded the dishwasher. She wiped down the countertop with a damp dishtowel that matched the color of the daisies in her wallpaper. "Jack, have you talked with Dr. Mike?"

I grimaced. "Not yet."

"When? You told me Kellen needs help. Want me to call?"

I shook my head, then squeezed ketchup across the meatloaf and shoveled a forkful in my mouth, not wanting to engage Leah in some big discussion.

She stood with hands on hips, clutching the yellow towel at her side, then waved it at me like a football referee about to call a penalty. "And what are you going to do with Kellen once school starts? I'll be back at work."

"We'll manage."

"Come on, Jack. Kellen's just drifting along, and you don't even notice. Step up and handle this."

"I don't want to talk about it."

"Dammit, Jack—"

"Leave me alone." I pushed away from the table. "Look, I'm not Richard. I'll be around for my kid."

She winced. I'd crossed the line. Leah spiked the towel to the floor—unsportsmanlike conduct, fifteen yards. "Kellen's back there watching TV. I'll get him."

"I'm sorry," I called as she left the room, but the harm had already been done.

Kellen trudged in wearing one of his cousin's t-shirts. His blond hair looked as if it had been sheared with hedge clippers. "Hey Dad, can I sleep over?"

"No, buddy. You've spent a long day over here already."

Kellen walked to the refrigerator and grabbed a handful of grapes. "Aren't I coming over here again tomorrow?"

"That's not the point. What's with the haircut?"

"Aunt Leah said I looked like a girl." He popped three grapes into his mouth. "I want to spend the night."

"Maybe another time. Let's go. Tell everyone goodbye."

Night was finally falling as we reached the car, but the

temperature still hovered in the nineties. Heat lightning flashed inside dark clouds to the north.

Kellen stood at the car's rear door. "Why were you and Aunt Leah arguing?"

"We weren't arguing. It was a discussion."

"About me?"

"About what's gonna happen when school starts." I offered a reassuring smile. "Remember, you and I need to be a team. It's just the two of us now."

"I can count," he snapped, flashing a too-familiar look of disapproval. I'd received that glare before, many times from my father but never from my kid.

"Shut your mouth," I said. "Get in the car."

Kellen gave a noncommittal shrug and crawled in the rear passenger seat. We didn't talk during the ride home. Even the sweltering heat, aggravated by the broken air conditioning, couldn't thaw the divide between us.

Chapter 5

With a dramatic wave, Dr. Michael Carpenter ushered Kellen and me into his elegant office. Perhaps my expectations were skewed by a half-decade of watching TV's Bob Newhart treat crazies in his minimally furnished room, so finding gold-lined drapes and an ornate cherry desk in a therapist's office was certainly a surprise. A whiskey-colored leather sofa sat across from a matching chair which reminded me of a throne. Basketball trophies and other memorabilia dotted built-in oak shelves.

"Glad you've come," said the towering man with jet black hair, slicked back with a heavy dose of gel. He looked like Pat Riley, the long-time basketball coach. "I'm Dr. Mike. Have a seat."

Kellen and I quietly slipped onto the leather couch. Dr. Mike folded his six-and-a-half-foot frame into his throne. "Sorry about your loss. How long has it been?"

I didn't need to consult the calendar to know that Kellen and I had endured sixty-two days of holding our collective breath. Bad days. Wretched, miserable days. No good days. "Two months," I said. "It was early June."

He steepled his fingers at the tip of his nose, then inspected our faces. "How can I help?"

Kellen didn't say a word. In fact, he hadn't spoken since he'd climbed into the car. He shrank deep into the sofa and picked at a frayed hole in his t-shirt.

"My sister recommended you. We're going through this whole grieving process. Kellen's been waking up with terrible nightmares."

Dr. Mike focused on Kellen and flashed an *I'm-your-buddy* smile. "Hey, young man, been having trouble sleeping?"

When Kellen didn't respond, I slid closer and nudged him. "Dr. Mike just wants to talk. Tell him about your bad dreams. That's why we came here."

"I didn't want to come here." Kellen pushed me away. He picked up a box of tissues from the end table and cocked it behind his ear as if to hurl it at me. He hesitated, glowered at me, then placed the box in his lap. Slowly and methodically, he extracted a tissue and laid it across his leg. Then he repeated the process with another tissue. Then another.

I turned to Dr. Mike. "This stuff drives me up the wall."

He waved me off. "Kellen, just do what makes you comfortable. We'll talk when you're ready. What about you, Jack? Tell me what's going on."

I shook my head. "Let's worry about him. I'm fine."

Dr. Mike nodded thoughtfully and scribbled in a leatherbound notebook. Then he tapped his pen on the page. "So you're not having trouble sleeping or coping with things?"

I shifted uncomfortably on the sofa and stared back at him. When I noticed him lean closer, like a mugger reaching for my wallet, I raised my hands palms-up. "Just wait a minute—"

"Oh my, what's wrong with your hand?"

I immediately dropped my hands back into my lap. The swollen knuckles and misaligned bones of my last two fingers always seemed to spark curiosity—even revulsion—in strangers, so I covered up my bad hand with the good one.

"Were you injured in the accident?"

"No. And you don't need to concern yourself with that. Look, Dr. Carpenter—"

"Call me Dr. Mike." He wasn't looking me in the face anymore; he seemed more interested in my screwed-up hand.

"I just want you to know that I'm real . . . positive on the whole therapy deal. Getting back on track and everything." I nodded optimistically and forced a smile. "Definitely committed to . . . talking and . . . being positive."

"You didn't answer my question. Not feeling lonely or devastated? No feelings of anger or abandonment?"

"I try to downplay all the negative stuff."

"Because you're trying to be positive," Dr Mike suggested.

I realized I wasn't going to have much luck keeping this guy at arm's length. "Look, Kellen and I are going through the worst thing anyone can imagine. My wife's gone, and, hell yes, I'm upset. But I'm coping." I looked over and saw that Kellen's legs were covered in white tissue from his hips to his knees. His left arm lay in his lap, and he'd already begun mummifying it. Jabbing my thumb toward Kellen, I said, "I can't get inside his head."

"I have an idea." Dr. Mike stood and crossed to his desk, where he opened several large drawers. He scratched his chin. "Hang on. I know it's around here." He turned and bent low to inspect the contents of a long credenza behind his desk, and then rose holding a regulation-size red, white, and blue basketball. "Found it."

Dr. Mike dribbled the basketball on the carpet as he returned to his throne. He began spinning the ball on his index finger, and Kellen perked up.

"Ever hear of the Harlem Globetrotters?" Dr. Mike continued to spin the basketball on his finger, slapping the side to maintain momentum, then transferred the ball to his other hand. "Those guys are amazing."

Kellen sat transfixed, mouth agape.

Dr. Mike flipped up the ball and caught it with both hands. "Did you know I played against those guys? I was team captain for the Washington Generals seven years ago." He fired an imaginary chest pass to Kellen, whose face had spread into a wide grin, then handed the ball to me.

"Whenever you want to hear about my old days pounding the hardwood with the Globetrotters, you just let me know." Kellen nodded, hypnotized, and with a flourish Dr. Mike extracted a large sketchbook and a handful of markers from the drawer of a side table. "I need some cool art for my office. You an artist?"

Kellen shrugged.

"Draw anything you like while we talk. Deal?"

I looked at the basketball in my hands. I'd never met anyone who played professional sports. I inspected the ball for any Harlem Globetrotter autographs—I grew up watching Meadowlark Lemon and Curly Neal on *ABC's Wide World of Sports*—but this ball was nothing special, just a simple basketball that he could have bought at an exhibition game. My instinct told me that the slick Dr. Mike was a bald-faced liar.

As Kellen began drawing in the sketchbook, Dr. Mike turned to me. "Play therapy," he explained. "Kids love art, writing, drama. Jack, tell me about your life now. Your daily routine. That sort of thing."

"I don't see how this can help."

"Humor me."

I dropped my voice into a flat, disinterested monotone. "I'm back at work. Kellen stays with his aunt during the day. Plays with his cousins. It works for us."

"I see. What do you and Kellen do to-geth-er?" he asked,

dramatically emphasizing each syllable. "There's bound to be something you two have in common. Typical father-son things. Do you fish? Play soccer? Collect coins?"

"I play baseball with my dad sometimes." Kellen's voice registered barely above a whisper.

Dr. Mike clapped. "I kinda thought you might be an athlete, Kellen. So you like throwing the ol' baseball around with Dad?"

Kellen met my eyes. I realized he felt the same as I did about playing catch. Neither of us enjoyed it, and we only participated because of Melanie's coercion. When we did play, the experience fell far short of *Field of Dreams*—the best baseball movie ever— which showed how a father-son relationship strengthens through the quasi-spiritual tradition of tossing the ball around . . . unless I missed the part where they yelled at each other.

"He's still young. Hasn't learned to play yet."

"You should teach him. You look like a baseball guy."

I was a baseball guy. My life used to revolve around the game. I played every year of Little League, including the Junior and Senior programs, until I turned fifteen, and then almost all of high school. Although my father forced me to work in the hay fields, I made time to pitch next to the barn. To encourage me, my dad hung an old tire from a branch so I could practice. When that became too easy, he propped up a metal wheelbarrow against the barbed-wire fence. Dad painted red circles in the wheelbarrow's concave well to represent strike zone targets. High and tight. Low and away. Right down Broadway.

I pitched into that wheelbarrow for years, often accompanied by my father's criticism. When my control was good, a loud clang announced each strike to the cows. Wild pitches were silent; they passed through the fence and into the pasture, occasionally rolling through a pile of manure before coming to a stop. I'm not sure what I learned from the hours of practice, other than not to lick my fingers between pitches.

Dr. Mike interrupted my thoughts. "Jack, you should take Kellen to a baseball game." He sat back and gave a self-satisfying nod, as if he'd just cured cancer.

I placed the basketball on the coffee table and frowned at him. "Isn't our time about over?"

He consulted a wall clock. "No, we're good. By the way, at our next session, I want both of you to tell me what you're doing to develop common interests."

I had no desire for a return visit with this manipulative charlatan. "I'll have to look at our schedule," I said blandly. "School starts next week."

"Perfect time to establish a routine."

I ignored him and began to collect the tissues Kellen had strewn about. I was tired of arguing with this guy.

Kellen tugged on Dr. Mike's sleeve. "Will you tell me about those Globestrutters now? Here's that art. Thank you for the markers."

"And thank you for the picture. It's very colorful." Dr. Mike picked up his basketball and carefully laid Kellen's picture open on the coffee table.

In the drawing, a tall stick-man flanked the left side of a boxy house, complete with smoke curling from a chimney and a yard of bright pink flowers. The man held a basketball and wore Dr. Mike's toothy smile. On the other side of the house stood two stick figures with stern faces, each mouth replaced with a horizontal slash. And floating above the house was a figure with yellow hair, a radiant smile, and a pair of wings.

I stifled a gasp. My eyes whipped to Kellen, who stood moon-eyed in response to a spinning basketball being placed on his index finger.

Dr. Mike whistled the jazzy *Sweet Georgia Brown* while grinning at Kellen, then cocked his head toward me. He mouthed the word *Normal.*

I looked back at the sketch, its awful truth revealed in washable marker, then offered Dr. Mike a grudging nod. I'd take normal.

❧

Ever since the morning appointment with Dr. Mike, Kellen had been upbeat and accommodating, so I decided to treat him to an evening at Sugar Land's favorite family friendly hangout. I pushed open the door to Miss Skeet's, and Kellen squeezed by to hurry inside.

With large-screen TVs and NFL cheerleader posters adorning the walls, the restaurant had always been a fine place to kill an evening. Melanie had enjoyed the variety of its menu, because she could order a salad while Kellen and I ate something cheese-covered or deep-fried. But I knew the real reason we usually ended up at Miss Skeet's: the bank of arcade games in the rear of the restaurant. Kellen loved video games.

"Can I have some quarters?" He extended an open hand. "I want to play Hoop Fever."

I gave him three dollar bills. "I'll get us some burgers. And I want to talk about Dr. Mike over dinner." Kellen's drawing had been nagging at me all afternoon—I'd been half-expecting him to pepper me with questions about heaven and angels, but I felt unprepared to help him. "You doing okay?"

Kellen wrinkled his face, confused by my question, and then smiled broadly. "I got three dollars. I'm excellent!"

I joined a queue of customers to place our order, pausing to allow a white-haired couple to pass ahead of me. They wore identical red plaid shirts and blue jeans, and they held hands as if they were teenagers. They reminded me of my parents, country folk with liver spots, except I heard these two discussing plans that included honky-tonk dancing at The Swinging Door, something my father wouldn't be caught dead doing.

A baby cried behind me, and I turned to see a young mom cooing to her infant as her husband rifled through a diaper bag. Just as the baby's cries began to turn into frantic wails, the man located a pacifier and quickly slipped it into the baby's mouth. He stood behind his wife, one hand on her waist and the other caressing his baby's bald head, when he noticed my gaze. "The magic binkie," he explained.

"You seem to know what you're doing."

The baby spit out its pacifier, which tumbled down swaddled legs, off mom's chest, and toward the floor. The man's free hand shot out. He plucked the binkie clean out of mid-air and popped it back into his baby's mouth. Then he flashed me a proud smile. "Comes with being a dad. You know how it is."

"Yeah," I said, not believing it. I'd been a father for seven-plus years and still felt clueless. Melanie, on the other hand, had been comfortable with motherhood from the moment a nurse laid Kellen in her arms. Now I found myself stuck in the icon of suburbia, the neighborhood burger joint, surrounded by happy kids and happy parents—happy families. And I was completely alone.

I reached into a metal washtub packed with ice and twenty-plus brands of beer and pulled out a longneck. I opened the bottle and swallowed, not bothering to enjoy the taste.

After ordering, I scanned the crowded restaurant for a place to sit. Seeing the restaurant's party room, which was crawling with uniformed soccer players, I was reminded of the Yankees' team meeting we'd held there back in February. That was the night Kellen's baseball coaches had preached their *every-kid-is-a-winner* philosophy. The night when Kellen hammered down so many hot dogs and bottles of root beer that he'd developed an upset stomach. The night after Melanie's miscarriage. I took another swig of beer.

Near a flashy jukebox in the far corner, a woman with brown hair stood, picked up her purse, and walked away. I quickly snagged the table.

Moments later, an indignant female voice said, "Excuse me. I was sitting here."

I looked up to see the same brunette who had just vacated the table. "I thought you left."

She stared at me, hands on hips. "Only for a minute. I took some money to my son. He's addicted to video games."

"Mine, too." I leaned back and stretched my arms, thinking how the woman looked vaguely familiar.

"Do you mind?" she asked, motioning toward the table.

"Right. Sorry." I rose and surveyed the room—not an empty table in sight. I didn't feel like chasing a place to sit. Maybe I'd just have them sack up our food to go.

The overhead speaker boomed, "Order for Stacy is ready."

"That's me." She started toward the counter, then turned. Her face softened. "Will you watch my table? You wouldn't believe the people around here who'd steal someone's place."

I grinned. "Sure. I'll keep out the riff-raff."

She returned with her food, and then asked me to wait a moment longer while she fetched her son. I'd seen this Stacy before. Met her, in fact. But before I could place her, she reappeared from the arcade. Two boys trailed her. The first kid was tall and heavy-set, wore glasses, and swung his arms with an exaggerated motion. Kellen trotted alongside.

"Hey, Dad," Kellen said. "Can I have more money?"

"Already spent those three bucks?"

"I'm really good at Hoop Fever."

I dug into my pocket. "One more dollar. We're eating soon."

The teenager's voice crackled overhead, "We have an order for Kennedy. Kennedy, your order is ready."

I took back the dollar. "I'll get our trays. Find us a table."

She pointed at Kellen and then to me. "Oh, my goodness! You must be Melanie's husband. Sit with us."

"That's nice of you . . . Stacy?"

"That's right."

Now I remembered who she was. Melanie had often talked about her friend Stacy. They had worked together on projects for Kellen's class. Stacy had organized the Christmas party and had come dressed as an elf. When her husband dumped her for a Florida bimbo a couple years ago, she hired a ruthless divorce attorney and took her ex-husband for most of what he had. According to Melanie, he had a lot.

"Stacy Flint. We met at the ceremony in May."

That's where I'd seen her—Kellen's graduation. Melanie had convinced me to take the morning off and watch second graders parade across the stage to receive their diplomas. I'd noticed the brunette who shifted easily through the room, managing a long-lens camera, snapping pictures of students. After the ceremony Melanie had introduced her.

"I remember. You took all the photos."

"More than three hundred. Thank God for digital cameras."

During dinner, I got a chance to meet Stacy's son Mitchell, who seemed like a polite kid, always careful to say "Yes, sir" and "No, sir". He and Kellen had shared the same teacher in second grade, but they weren't close buddies.

"Can't believe school starts next week," Stacy said when the boys left for their post-dinner video game fix. "I guess you're in a carpool already."

"Haven't thought about it."

"Maybe we can team up. I can probably take the kids three days a week. If you can drive the other mornings, it'd really help."

We hammered out the logistics over my third beer and spent another half-hour talking about life in Sugar Land. It was easy to see why Melanie and Stacy had hit it off.

"How's Kellen doing?" she asked. "You know, since his mom . . ." Her cheeks turned a deep pink, and she covered her eyes. "Oh God, I'm sorry."

A series of images shotgunned through my brain: Melanie pushing Kellen on a swing set, Melanie doing a drunken limbo on a Cancun beach, Melanie lying motionless in her casket. "Don't worry about it," I said and drained my beer. My misty eyes drifted to the jukebox, absentmindedly scanning song titles as impressions of Melanie invaded my thoughts. I pushed my chair back from the table. "It's getting late."

I searched the arcade for Kellen and found him shooting miniature basketballs. "Time to go, Kel."

When we reached our car and clambered inside, I paused a moment before starting the engine. I turned to Kellen and searched for the right words. Where to start? Analyzing his drawing? Explaining eternal life? Discussing our future?

Kellen buckled his seatbelt and said, "Thanks, Dad."

"For what?"

"For today. Going to see Dr. Mike. He's cool. And for all that money at Miss Skeet's. I got top score on Hoop Fever."

I was speechless. I couldn't remember the last time Kellen thanked me. Maybe I was finally doing something right.

Or maybe it was like my dad said when I landed that job with Gemini Devices—even a blind mouse occasionally finds the cheese.

Chapter 6

To calculate how long a Yankee transplant has lived in Texas, see when he complains about the heat. When Captain Carl and his weird family moved here from Boston five years ago, he griped about the hot weather before Memorial Day arrived. Captain Carl's a wuss. Miserable doesn't kick in until the Fourth of July. That's when weather shifts to hell-hot and rain disappears for three months. Lakes turn into ponds. Seatbelt buckles turn into branding irons. Neighbors turn into hermits, cowering in air-conditioned homes until October, when a random cold front eventually finds its way south.

My hometown of Giddings is a German community equidistant between Houston, Austin, and San Antonio. Instead of "mom and apple pie", people live by the credo "God, hard work, and barbecue." My dad and I re-roofed the tin barn during the summer before high school, and I've never complained about the heat since.

"I can't wait to see Grandma and Grandpa," Kellen said from the back seat.

That made one of us. Ever since my mom extended the invitation, I had dreaded making this trip. Going back home always reminded me of the old arguments with Dad. "It's gonna be a short visit," I said. "Don't start begging them to entertain you. You're a big kid now."

He didn't answer.

"You hear me?"

"Yes, sir."

Driving to my parents' house was like watching Disney's *Carousel of Progress* as it rotated in the opposite direction. An hour out of Sugar Land, where expensive cars and upscale shopping were *de rigueur*, I navigated a two-lane asphalt road through Bellville, passing the Dairy Queen and a Wal-Mart. All vestiges of civilization disappeared during the last half of the trip, replaced with cows. Lots of cows.

Just after we crossed a bridge over Rabb's Creek, a billboard proclaimed *Welcome to Giddings—Home of the Buffaloes*; in its shadow was my old high school. A bronze bison stood guard near the football stadium, the place where Coach Richter once told me I didn't hit hard enough to merit playing first string. When we cleared a small grove of live oaks, I felt my chest tighten as the baseball field came into view. The place where I once dominated central Texas baseball. Where I whupped the sorry ass of my nemesis. Where I proved Coach Richter wrong about my toughness.

"We're almost there!" Kellen announced. "That's your old school."

"Yep."

"They called you the Canyon."

"The Cannon," I said, immediately regretting the correction.

"Yeah, my dad was the Cannon."

✆

My mom, all five-foot-one of her, stepped onto the porch and waved. She wore a long cotton skirt and a plain blouse. Not her church clothes—she and my father had surely come back from Sunday service at least an hour ago. Besides, she was wearing sneakers. We'd caught Grace Kennedy in the middle of preparing lunch.

"Saw your car come up the road," she said with a gentle drawl as we climbed the rickety porch stairs. She wrapped Kellen against her petite frame. "Go inside, and I'll slice some fresh bread. There's tea in the icebox if you're thirsty."

"Thanks, Mom."

"Jack, I'm so glad y'all came."

She held open the screen door, and Kellen and I entered. A thick layer of humidity hung in the room. My parents' only air conditioning was a window unit in their bedroom, on the opposite side of the house. I broke into a sweat every time I visited.

Mom led us to a small room off the kitchen, marginally cooled by a noisy oscillating fan and furnished with an inadequate table, two recliners, and an ancient nineteen-inch television with rabbit ears. A rickety bookcase held photos of their three grandchildren, plus a set of encyclopedias that must have been forty years old. The breeze from the fan knocked off only a few degrees from the summer heat. It wasn't that my parents didn't have money to install central air. Change just came slowly to a Kennedy home.

"I swanee, you get bigger every time I see you," she told Kellen, setting a plate of homemade bread and pickles and a jar of dewberry jelly on the table. Returning to the kitchen, she donned her apron—an excellent sign. My mom was the finest cook in Lee County, and she had the ribbons to prove it. Her apple streusel coffee cake had won awards at the Ledbetter Picnic for the past fifteen years.

"Where's Grandpa?" Kellen asked between bites of his jelly sandwich.

My mother didn't answer. She stood over an iron skillet, turning golden-brown pieces of fried chicken.

"Where's Grandpa?" Kellen repeated.

I whispered, "Grandma doesn't hear too good." I secretly hoped my father had been called away to some out-of-state convention for retired farmers, but I knew he was probably in a back room or in the barn, too busy to acknowledge our presence. "Mom," I said in a louder voice, "Where's Dad?"

"Pulling some family's car out of the ditch."

"An accident?"

"Nah, they just tried to turn around and drove off the road. Mud ain't too kind to those SUVs, especially if they ain't four-wheel-drive. They'd been stuck for over an hour before your father and me got home from church. He should be back here shortly."

Sure enough, my father showed up just as I delivered a plate of fried chicken to the table. The screen door to the back porch squeaked, followed by a series of slams. He wasn't mad, or so I hoped. Their screen doors always made a loud racket. Rusty springs caused the noise, and I had once offered to replace them, but my father refused. He told me that when he flung open a screen door, he wanted to hear the satisfying thwacks against the jamb, the rattle as the door settled closed. My parents didn't mind the noise as much as they did the flies.

"Grandpa!" Kellen exclaimed and ran to hug my father, who managed a thin smile before disappearing into the bedroom.

We tap-danced around the kitchen pretending to finish last-minute lunch preparations. Then my father finally reappeared, wearing a white t-shirt that made his deep tan more noticeable. Years of hard manual labor had kept him robust. Except for the occasional bout of cellulitis, a byproduct of driving a tractor for long hours during growing season, he presented a picture of good health.

He shook my misshapen hand with a bone-crushing grip, either unaware or unconcerned of the pain he inflicted. "Good to see you, boy." His voice was as firm as his handshake.

I never knew what to say to him. He intimidated the hell out of me. "Mom says you were helping some family with their car."

"City folks," he huffed. My father didn't tolerate anyone with callus-free hands or pasty skin, like the weekend landowners and wannabe-farmers from Houston. I think he secretly despised me for moving to suburbia. Dad was a man of the earth, with a strong work ethic hardwired into his DNA. He branded and vaccinated his own cattle. Hunted and butchered wild animals. A redneck to be sure, but absent any trace of ignorance or bigotry.

But if you weren't up to snuff, or if you let him down—the biggest mistake I ever made as a teenager—my father wouldn't respect you. That was the harshest punishment Frank Kennedy could dole out, far worse than whippings delivered with a yaupon branch.

We took our seats as Mom delivered dishes of noodles and fresh peas to the table. She scurried to retrieve fresh butter and the salt and pepper shakers. We recited the obligatory table prayer. The rituals hadn't changed since I was a kid. Our meal proceeded in traditional silence, due in part to our reserved Germanic culture, but mostly to the fact that our mouths never stayed empty long enough to hold a conversation.

"I've missed your cooking, Mom," I said with a sigh.

Kellen was working on his third piece of chicken and second helping of noodles. He grunted, concurring with my sentiment.

"Save room for dessert," she said. "Dewberry cobbler and ice cream."

"Astros are playing," Dad said as my mom retreated to wash dishes and Kellen rushed outside to explore the farm. He reached to the top shelf of the bookcase and clicked on a Seventies-era radio, which served double-duty as a makeshift bookend for Mom's recipes. The booming, nasal voice of Milo Hamilton crackled to life. Milo had been the voice of the Astros for fifteen years and calling play-by-play for more than fifty.

"I didn't come here to listen to a baseball game," I said, then realized how whiny I sounded.

Dad rolled his eyes. "Then go somewhere else. Help your mom or play with your son. Or stay here with me. I don't care."

I hated how my dad always told me what to do and how he acted like I was a complete failure. It had been twenty years since the Tate Gillum fiasco, but I could still hear my father's admonitions—grow up, be a man. Bucking my father's authority hadn't worked as a teenager, and I knew it wouldn't work now. So I settled into the recliner and flipped open a *Texas Longhorn Trails* magazine. "Who are the 'Stros playing?"

Dad turned up the volume and Milo briefed us on the game. "Astros lead 1-0, thanks to an opposite-field shot by Bagwell in the home first. And Piazza will lead things off here for the Mets in the top of the second."

I hated Mike Piazza, their cocky, right-handed catcher. Strong arm, great stick. The Johnny Bench of this generation. And I'm sure I'd have been his biggest fan if he was an Astro, but he wasn't.

"Reynolds sets . . . and the pitch . . . smash line drive into left-center. Looks like trouble. Berkman dives . . . He caught it! Holy Toledo, diving catch by Lance Berkman to prevent extra bases!

"And Piazza slams his helmet and starts jawing at the second base umpire. He's complaining that Berkman trapped the ball.

He's pointing at the ground . . . Replay in the booth says the ump called it right. Piazza's still pleading his case."

Dad clapped and cheered. "Get back to the dugout, you moron!"

As I listened to the game, memories flooded back. When I was a kid, the whole family used to tune in faithfully to major league baseball on the radio. We listened to Gene Elston and Loel Passe broadcast Astros games, and I always stayed up until the game was over or eleven o'clock, whichever came first. Loel Passe was a folksy, unabashed homer who told cornball jokes and said things like "He breezed him one more time" and "Now you chunkin' in there!" He would've been laughed out of the game these days.

Dad fell asleep around the fourth inning and woke with a muffled snort when Milo went nuts over an inning-ending double play in the seventh. "How are they doing?" he asked groggily.

"Astros are still up four to one. Piazza just hit into a double play with bases loaded. Milo said he thought ol' Pizza-Face was gonna cry."

"What a baby. What's up with Kellen and your mom?"

"Sorting through a jar of coins in the other room. Kellen thinks he's a collector now. He's hunting old pennies."

"Well, this is the place to look. Everything around here is old."

When the game finally ended, with the Astros hanging on to win by one measly run, Kellen wiped purple dewberry stains from his lips and asked, "Can we go fishing now?"

"Man, it's too hot to fish," I said.

Mom piled dessert plates on the kitchen table. "Frank, take Jack and Kellen down to the creek. Show them that snakeskin you found. They're only staying for a couple more hours. Spend some time with them." For an instant, I heard Melanie's voice in my mom's words.

When I stepped onto the front porch alongside my dad, I could see Kellen had already dashed ahead and was tiptoeing across a pile of railroad ties next to the chicken pen. He hopped onto a metal gate and held on as it lazily swung closed. Then he bounced off, inspected the pipes of a cattle guard, and ran back toward us. He was like a dog cut loose from his leash.

"Let me show you where I was throwing rocks!" Kellen said.

"You better not be throwing things at the cows," I said.

"I'm not. Over here!"

We walked toward the barn I once helped build. Propped under a cedar tree was the rusted-out shell of an old wheelbarrow. It was falling apart, with a gaping, football-sized hole in its middle. I could still make out the flakes of red paint that used to mark my pitching targets.

"Watch me, Dad!" Kellen threw a rock at the wheelbarrow. The metal clanged and produced a puff of rust. Years of abuse had taken their toll.

"You know," my father began, "Your daddy used to pitch into that wheelbarrow."

"Really?" Kellen's eyes widened.

"Yep. From the time he was in Little League until . . ." His voice faded away.

Just say it, Dad. Until I was a senior in high school. Until I pissed my life away. Say it, old man. I didn't understand why he hadn't thrown the wheelbarrow away. We'd spent all that time out here pitching together. And then everything fell apart.

Chapter 7

Two days later, I padded upstairs to Kellen's bedroom. "Wake up. Don't want to be late on the first day of school."

"I don't want to go," the voice under the covers replied.

"Hurry up and get dressed. I'll make breakfast."

When I was a kid, my mom always prepared a hearty breakfast: fresh eggs, thick-sliced bacon, toast, and home-canned jellies. She also observed an annual tradition. On the first day of school, in addition to her usual fare, Mom baked homemade biscuits, served them with a tasty, artery-clogging gravy, and whipped up a platter of buttermilk pancakes.

One look in my refrigerator reminded me that I wasn't my mom—or Melanie. No eggs, no bacon. I opened the half-gallon of milk, its expiration date listed as a week ago, and gave it a test sniff. Instantly I gagged at its sour fumes, so I poured the chunky milk down the sink.

"What's for breakfast?" Kellen asked as he entered the kitchen. He wore a t-shirt that barely covered the waistline of his shorts. Ragged sneakers adorned his feet.

"Those clothes are worn out. Find a nice shirt."

"This is nice."

"That shirt's too small. Wear something else." I opened a

bread bag and extracted two stale slices. I popped them in the toaster.

Kellen returned a minute later wearing a different wrinkled t-shirt. "Where's my new backpack?"

A hollow formed in my stomach. I could almost see the Post-it note that I'd written and attached to my computer monitor: *Buy backpack and school supplies.* I'd completely forgotten. "Gonna buy it at lunch," I fibbed. "You won't need everything today, anyway."

Kellen slumped into a chair. "Mommy would make sure I was ready."

I ignored his comment and slathered peanut butter across the two slices of toast. "Here's your breakfast. Eat up."

Kellen laid his head on the kitchen table. "I'm not hungry. And I'm not going to school."

"We're not having this conversation."

"I'm not going to school," he repeated. His cheek remained pressed on the table, as if he'd fallen asleep mid-bite. His eyes scrunched closed. "All the kids are gonna ask me about Mommy."

I sat next to him and threw my arm around his shoulder. "It's okay to be nervous, but don't worry about your friends. I bet they'll be extra nice to you."

He exhaled deeply. "I just want to be like other kids. Kids with a family."

I lifted his chin with my hand. "You have a family. You have me."

"Yeah. But you don't do mommy things."

He was right. *Mommy things* regularly fell through the crack in our house, which meant school supplies were forgotten, home-cooked meals were never considered, and dirty clothes were washed on a just-in-time basis. No matter how much I tried, the house was a total wreck. To top it off, I wasn't all touchy-feely like Melanie.

"Let's make a deal," I said. "I'll try harder on the mommy things, but I need you to be more responsible." I checked my watch. "Let's go. Carpool time."

"My backpack?"

"Just use last year's."

If we drove straight to the Flint home, we'd have to pass by the scene of Melanie's accident, but I refused to put Kellen through that agony every day. The alternative route took me away from Sugar Land's wide boulevards and onto a meandering cobblestone road through a swanky neighborhood.

As I turned into the subdivision, Kellen said, "Is that a house?"

"Looks like a castle, doesn't it?" I glanced at the obnoxious turrets on the three-story home. It was the kind of over-the-top house that had always chapped my butt. And the one next door, with seven white pillars spaced evenly across its exterior, looked like some rich plantation owner had relocated from Mississippi. The street was lined with custom homes, some brick, others stone or stucco, each one decked out with enough luxury appointments and expensive landscaping to validate the owner's self-importance. But for all their differences, houses were painfully the same in Sugar Land. Stepford Land.

I had hated the dirt and plainness of my childhood home, and that's why Melanie and I moved to the big city after we married. The suburbs offered stable property values, highly regarded schools, greenbelts, and in the case of the master-planned community of Sugar Meadow, a certain cachet. Life in Sugar Land was everything we'd hoped for, the modern-day equivalent of the white picket fence.

However, my disenchantment grew as I realized the most

commonly shared value among the citizens was conformity. Keep your lawn manicured. Dress nice when you go to the mall. Don't rock the boat.

I pulled to the curb outside a massive Victorian-style house and saw Mitchell bouncing behind the glass of a bay window. He dashed out the front door, a backpack slung across his shoulder, and raced to our car.

He opened the rear door. "Hey, Mr. Kennedy. Hey, Kellen."

Stacy called out, "Your lunch!"

I turned my head to see her standing in the doorway. She wore an emerald blouse with a black slitted skirt that revealed a little too much thigh, and I half-wondered what kind of job she held.

Stacy walked to the passenger side and handed Mitchell his lunch bag through the lowered window. Her right hand waved tickets. "I come bearing gifts. You have plans for Sunday?"

"Nothing I can think of." Kellen and I didn't plan weekends or evenings anymore. We were lucky to survive one day at a time.

"My boss gave me two tickets for the Astros. I forgot that Mitchell and I are going to Brenham to see my folks. If you want them, they're all yours."

I thought of Dr. Mike's admonition to take Kellen to a ballgame. But if I did, Dr. Mike's inflated ego would be vindicated. On the other hand, my birthday was Saturday, and I hadn't been to Enron Field since it opened. "Appreciate the thought, but—"

"I don't want to give them back to my boss. Please, they're great seats." She leaned through the open window and handed me the tickets. I caught a glimpse of cleavage and quickly readjusted my eyes to her face. She smiled, and I wasn't sure if I detected a hint of mischief. Then she waved, spun on open-toed sandals, and headed back toward the house.

"So, Mitchell," I said as we drove away, "you seen the Astros at the new ballpark?"

"Yes, sir. My Grampy took me twice. We tried to catch homeruns during batting practice."

"That sounds fun. Whatcha think, Kellen?"

He didn't respond, so I looked in the rear-view mirror. He was staring out the window. "Kellen?"

"I guess so."

I lifted the slice of uneaten peanut-butter-on-toast from the passenger seat. "Need to finish your breakfast." Hearing no reply, I said, "Mitchell, how about you? Breakfast of champions."

"Can't. I'm allergic to peanuts."

I shrugged and bit into the toast. With my mouth full of peanut butter, I said, "Your grandparents live in Brenham? I grew up a half-hour west of there."

"We go see them every few weeks. Grampy takes me fishing at Lake Somerville. He's gonna let me shoot his twenty-two this weekend. I'm his hunting buddy."

It sounded like his grandfather was trying to fill the void left by the father's absence; Mitchell would be the better for it. I wondered whether Kellen would share a similar fortune.

Just as we reached the school parking lot, Kellen piped up. "Dad, where's my lunch?"

He wasn't going to like the answer.

❧

In Sugar Land, students stagger under the weight of ridiculously high expectations. Children from Garrison Keillor's Lake Wobegon may all be above average, but the kids in our community are bred to be successful in everything. School administrators label kindergartners as *gifted and talented*. Parents hire tutors for math, band, and traveling soccer teams. High schoolers suffer from ulcers and register high suicide rates, but the survivors can beat the crap out of any wimpy, only-above-average Lake Wobegon kid. And that's just in Sugar Land's public schools.

Bright Minds Academy, Kellen's private school, steps it up a notch. When I stepped through their front door, I half-expected to find students already studying for the SAT.

I trailed Kellen and Mitchell as they headed toward the classrooms, then stopped when a gravelly voice called, "Mister, come back here." The voice came from a woman who was the spitting image of my mean fourth-grade teacher, Mrs. Kochersperger, a stout German woman who shared the same poufy grey hair and the same stern face.

"I'm just walking my son to class."

"Our policy for opening day is to eliminate teary goodbyes and to get kids studying right away. We don't mind parents being involved—in fact, we encourage it. Like during lunch or special projects. Just not today." She crossed her arms and made it clear she'd been in the school Gestapo for years.

"I understand you've got rules." I looked back to the hallway, where Kellen and Mitchell had disappeared.

The woman waved at a group of kids shoving each other at the water cooler. "Get to class," she commanded. She turned to me, folding her arms on top of an old computer monitor, and leaned close. "We held orientation for parents and teachers last week. You know the ropes. You've already signed all the paperwork."

"I don't know what you're talking about. I haven't seen any paperwork."

She gave an exasperated sigh. "What's your child's name?" She began tapping on a computer keyboard.

"Kellen Kennedy."

She stopped typing and looked up. "Now I understand." She extended her hand. "I'm Dorothy Battle, Kellen's principal. Your son's teacher is Ms. Blankenship. She's new here. Room nineteen down that hall. She has a folder of papers for you." She lowered her voice to a whisper. "If there's anything we can do . . ."

That phrase had been uttered so many times to me that I responded out of habit. "Appreciate your help." Remembering Kellen's concern about being probed with questions, I said, "Please don't say anything to my son."

"Don't worry. We want him to feel safe."

"That's what I wanted to hear." I bid goodbye with a casual salute and turned toward the hall.

I hadn't made it more than three steps when Ms. Battle's voice rang in my ears. "Mr. Kennedy," she said sternly. "We have rules." She pointed to a spiral bound book. "Sign in."

As much as the principal reminded me of Mrs. Kochersperger, Kellen's teacher reminded me of Wilma Flintstone. Tall and thin, wearing a pearl necklace that looked like white marbles strung together, Ms. Blankenship wore her orange-red hair in a bun— the only thing missing was a dinosaur bone. She stood next to Kellen's desk, patting him on the shoulder, and then her eyes caught mine. "Can I help you?"

"I'm Kellen's dad."

"Oh, yes. I have some stuff for you." She moved to a cabinet next to her desk and began flipping through file folders.

I knelt in front of Kellen. "You doing okay?"

"Yeah," he answered, but his voice was subdued, his body rigid.

"I see Mitchell's in your class. That's pretty cool."

Suddenly my cell phone rang, its rock'n'roll ringtone blaring in the quiet classroom. I shielded the mouthpiece with my good hand and whispered, "Scott, I told you I had this school thing.

No, I didn't forget the conference call." I looked around and noticed all the kids watching me—everyone except Kellen. Ms. Blankenship stood cross-armed and she didn't look happy. "Gotta go." I flipped the phone closed. "Sorry about that."

The teacher handed me a manila envelope with Kellen's name printed in large letters. "You need to sign these tonight."

"I can do that."

"We're about to start class. Can I talk to you a second before you leave?"

"Yeah. I wanted to talk to you, too." Turning to Kellen, I said, "Pick you up this afternoon. Remember, we've got that Astros game this weekend." I hoped the ballgame reminder would perk him up, but he ignored me. I waved, then made my way to the door.

Ms. Blankenship followed. "Kellen doesn't have any school supplies. Is there a problem?"

"Sorry, I kinda forgot."

"Mr. Kennedy, students need to be prepared to learn. And parents have to help facilitate this. I put another school supply list into his envelope."

"Don't worry about Kellen."

"I'm a teacher. I worry about everyone."

She ushered me into the hallway and closed the door behind me so fast that I didn't get a chance to tell her about Kellen's concerns and my hopes for him making friends. I was about to turn the handle on his classroom door when I felt a tap on my shoulder.

"If you're a parent, it's time to leave." The woman wore a name tag that read *Aide* and pushed a wheeled cart.

"I have to ask the teacher a question."

She was unmoved. "You can leave her a note at the front desk."

"You don't understand."

She placed her hand on the door, blocking me from opening it. "I understand it's the first day of school and you already miss your child."

I shook my head, wondering why I shelled out tuition for a private school that sequestered students in sterile classrooms and made parents feel like lepers. "I just need one minute. That's it."

The school bell sounded and I jumped. A gravelly voice said, "Welcome, you bright minds! It's going to be a wonderful year. Everyone please stand for the Pledge of Allegiance."

The lady stepped aside, and I peered into the classroom through the door's narrow window. Children stood, hand over heart, as they recited the pledge to a small American flag. Kellen participated, but his eyes darted nervously around the room. I hoped that he'd see me, that he'd know I was there for him. But he didn't. He finished the pledge and dropped into his seat.

I watched Ms. Blankenship gesture toward the wall. A familiar rush of panic swelled as I read her message on the dry-erase board. Underneath her printed name, she had written their assignment: *Journal Time—What was the most interesting thing that happened to you this summer?*

Chapter 8

By Saturday, I was at my wit's end. The first few days of school had been terrible, fighting Kellen every morning to get ready, always showing up late for work, never being able to catch up on the *mommy things*.

Then Kellen set fire to the kitchen.

I had woken early, mindful about turning another year older. Birthdays in our home had always been observed with traditions ranging from goofy to sensual. Remembering the celebratory lovemaking from prior birthdays, I rolled over to Melanie's side of the bed. It was cold.

I clutched her pillow, but it was a poor substitute. So I padded to the dresser and retrieved one of her best little nightgowns, a peach camisole that I had given her as an anniversary gift. I wrapped the camisole around the pillow and spooned against it, keenly feeling her presence through the lingering scent of her perfume and in the texture of charmeuse silk, which was slowly turning damp from my tears.

Loud beeps from the smoke alarm pierced the silence.

I dashed from the bedroom and into the kitchen. Flames were shooting up from a frying pan and licking up the wall. I pushed a kitchen chair away from the front of the stove. "Holy shit!"

At the sink I filled a copper pot with water. A vague

recollection of a company safety seminar came into focus. *Never use water on a grease fire.* I dropped the pot into the sink.

The smoke was ink-black now, rolling up the wall and around the vent hood, circling the ceiling like a storm cloud. I coughed, then covered my mouth with the back of my hand. With my other hand, I turned off the heat.

From the living room I heard Kellen scream, "It's all on fire!" He was cowering behind the sofa.

"Go outside where it's safe! Grab my cell phone. Call 911."

I rushed to the oven, where I had heated a pizza the night before and had left a baking sheet on the top rack. I pulled out the baking sheet, ran it to the stove, and slammed it over the frying pan. Instantly the flames snuffed out.

Smoke hung thick in the room. Coughing, I opened all the windows and raced out the front door. Kellen stood on the lawn in a pair of Spiderman pajamas.

"I called 911," he said. "I'm sorry—"

"Are you okay? Did you get burned?" I hacked up charcoal-colored sputum and spat it into the grass.

"I'm sorry," he repeated. "I wanted to cook you breakfast in bed, like Mommy used to do on your birthday."

I was barely listening to him now, frantic to make sure he was still in one piece. I patted down his arms and legs. In my imagination, I could see Kellen standing over the stove as fire exploded from the frying pan and covered him in burning grease. I shook away the mental image, believing instead what I could see for myself—Kellen was unhurt.

Then I grabbed him by both shoulders and shook him. "Are you out of your damn mind?"

The fire truck left thirty minutes after it arrived. Kellen left shortly thereafter, once I called Leah to break the news and to beg her to take him off my hands for a while.

For three hours, I wiped down the kitchen walls and cabinets. The intense heat had ruined the stove and warped the metal vent hood. The tile backsplash, a colorful mural of vegetables and flowers and bread loaves that Melanie had hand-painted, was charred and covered with a layer of soot.

I kept seeing Kellen's face, how terrified he was and, later, how sorry he was. And that made me feel worse.

This was all my fault. I should have prevented the fire, but I had been holed up in my bedroom, unaware he was even awake. The whole house could have burned down. He could have died.

What kind of father was I?

❦

My dearest Melanie:

I can't keep doing this, pretending it's somehow God's plan for you to be in heaven. That's just not true. I wish you could see us now, recognize how everything's falling apart.

Kellen worries me. He's so much your son, and I know how heartbroken he is. He's had so many bad dreams that I'm afraid for him. And this fire—he may have caused it, but I'm the one to blame.

I know I'm not the best person to raise him. Please don't hate me for feeling that way. Kellen deserves someone better than me. Someone that can keep him safe and love him. Someone that knows what they're doing. He should be with Leah and her family.

My life doesn't mean anything without you here. I will always love you.

—Jack

The pen fell from my trembling hand, clacked against the granite countertop, and rolled to a stop against a tiny prescription bottle.

I placed Melanie's note next to the instructions I'd written out for Leah, then ran my fingers over an envelope containing a letter to Kellen. Hooked on the doorknob was the nightgown I'd held so tight. I gathered it in my hands and pulled it to my face, inhaling the memories.

I twisted off the childproof cap and shook a pill into my palm. Then another. Then six.

Take for pain, as needed.

I was in a lot of pain.

⚬⚬⚬

I emptied the prescription bottle and stared at the mound of pills in my hand. Just swallow them down. Chase them with alcohol. Get it over with.

Kellen banged on the bathroom door. "Dad, you there?"

I didn't reply.

"Aunt Leah dropped me off."

"Go away."

"I'm really sorry about everything. Can you forgive me?"

His words were a duplicate of mine, the last lines in my goodbye letter to him. I considered the pills. We all needed forgiveness, some more than others.

Then I realized that no matter how much pain I was in, I couldn't let Kellen find me like that, dead on the bathroom floor. And although it might be the easy way out, I couldn't leave him an orphan.

Ever since Melanie died, I had thought Kellen deserved someone better than me. But maybe what he needed was *me*. Maybe I just needed to be *someone better*.

I flushed away the pills, then opened the door. Kellen

sheepishly walked toward me. I wrapped him in a big hug and inhaled his fragrance, silently promising myself I'd never again think of suicide as an option.

"I know I blew it," he said.

"Hey, we all blow it sometimes."

"Well, I just came to tell you happy birthday."

"Speaking of birthdays . . ."

"Yeah?"

"Next year, I just want cereal."

Chapter 9

I stood in the kitchen and pitched a burned toaster into a thirty-gallon trash can. The hum of the dishwasher, now on its third load, competed with the whir of an oscillating fan that was failing to clear the room of its smoky smell. The morning sun peeked over the back fence and flooded through the kitchen window; I checked the clock and realized I'd been up for a couple of hours.

Hadn't been any use lying in bed anyway, staring at the ceiling and trying to figure out how to make sense of everything. Nothing had made sense in almost three months.

The sound of footsteps thudded through the ceiling and then, moments later, down the stairs. Kellen raced into the room. "When are we leaving for the Astros game?"

"It's only seven o'clock. Game's at one. Go back to bed."

"I'm not sleepy. Can I have some breakfast?"

I swept my arms toward the disaster that had been our kitchen. "Help me for fifteen minutes. Then I'll get us some breakfast."

A half-hour later, I carried freshly baked kolaches and a flimsy cup of steaming coffee out of the local donut shop. Kellen was inside, supposedly going to the restroom, but I suspected he was on a reconnaissance mission for video games. I located a wooden bench next to a palm tree, ate my kolache, and waited for Kellen.

Assorted customers passed through the donut shop's entrance, and I watched them absentmindedly: Cub Scouts in full uniform, an old man shuffling along with a walker, four guys decked out in almost-identical golf shirts. I looked out over the parking lot and saw a blonde woman walking by herself, her back to me.

She looked just like Melanie. She had the same color hair, the same style clothes, the same confident walk. Bewildered, I stood to get a better view.

But she was gone, having disappeared between two SUVs. I blinked to clear my vision, not sure if I had imagined her. Had imagined Melanie. Then I sat back down on the bench, sadder now, and put my head in my hands.

Kellen appeared at my side. "You sick?"

"I'm fine," I said and took a sip of coffee.

He grabbed a kolache from the bag. "The Astros are gonna be so much fun!" He flopped onto the bench, rattling the wooden slats. The bench shook and hot coffee spilled down my shirt and onto my shorts.

"Damn it, Kellen!" I tore to my feet and ripped off my shirt. "Why do you ruin everything?"

Minutes later, my car lurched to a stop in our driveway. I got out, then slammed the door shut with a satisfying thud. "Go watch TV or something."

Kellen scurried away. I started toward the house, then stopped. That was the last place I wanted to be. I needed to get away from Kellen and the charred kitchen—from the feelings of inadequacy, loneliness, and guilt.

I marched to the side door of the garage. The door was stuck, so I knocked it open with a hard punch of my open hand. A sharp pain tore through my right wrist as I aggravated the old injury, a broken hand from a long-ago sucker punch thrown in anger. Some wounds never completely heal.

Fluorescent lights buzzed as I flipped the switch, then flickered briefly before illuminating the garage. Three dozen boxes were stacked across the far wall—Melanie had run into one of the stacks when she rushed home from a Christmas shopping trip, so those boxes leaned to the right and, even nine months later, seemed to be in danger of falling. A garden rake lay like an alligator, teeth bared, on the concrete floor. Rat droppings dotted the shelves.

I shook my head at the chaos. "Where do I start?" I asked the empty garage.

I moved to my workbench and collected a hammer, three screwdrivers, and a bag of Allen wrenches, and hung them up on the pegboard. Then I picked up a spray can of silver paint and turned toward the cabinet where I stored pesticides and hazardous chemicals. A bag on the floor caught my foot—the paint can flew from my hand and bounced across the concrete. "I hate this house," I said, looking down to the red bag that had tripped me.

A memory of Kellen and his red bat bag zoomed into focus. Slung over his shoulder. Tossed into a car trunk. The love of my life had died when she slammed into a tree, but the bat bag had survived.

Kellen had been looking for it ever since we received the Astros tickets. He held this fantasy that he was going to catch a home run or a foul ball and then get the player's autograph. I unzipped the bag and reached inside for Kellen's glove. When I pulled it out, something dark fell to the floor.

I knew what it was immediately—a navy New York Yankees towel. Melanie had bought it for Kellen back when his season started. She had told him it was a lucky towel, something he could rub on his bat for a hit or wipe on his face to get rid of nerves. I knelt to pick it up, trying to stem tears that blurred my vision.

Minutes passed. The tears eventually stopped, and I wiped my face with the towel. Slumped against the workbench, I began to dwell on the same thoughts I'd had yesterday, the ones that had driven me to the brink of my sanity. I was tired of being a full-time parent, tired of not knowing what to do, tired of being sad all the time. I was tired of feeling like I was the one to blame.

And that pissed me off. Kellen knew how to push my buttons—from griping about doing chores, to dousing me with coffee, to setting the kitchen on fire—but he wasn't the one who'd put me in this position. Melanie had ruined our plans for a long and happy marriage, had left me to raise a son I hardly knew or understood. She had it easy, playing a harp in the clouds or walking like a ghost in the parking lot. Screw her.

I threw the bat bag in the corner and stomped out of the garage. When I found Kellen, he was plugged in to a Disney cartoon.

"You still mad?" he asked.

"Not at you." I tossed him the baseball glove. "Let's go catch us a home run."

❧

I still remember my first game in the Astrodome—just me and my dad—back when I was a kid. To a ten year old, everything seemed enormous: the field of bright-green Astroturf, the curving roof, and the lighted scoreboard wrapped around the outfield wall.

Dad tried to explain the phenomenon of the famous *exploding scoreboard*, but I couldn't fully appreciate its impact until Doug

Rader, the "Red Rooster", slammed a homer, and then the scoreboard erupted in rich, animated celebration. Red, white, and blue lights flashed as a smoke-snorting longhorn and a lassoing cowboy made their colorful appearance. In my imagination, Jesus would return to earth accompanied by a similar production.

Now Houston had constructed a real baseball park, Enron Field, in the heart of downtown. The civic-minded folks at the energy giant had ponied up money for the naming rights, which meant Houston and Enron would be forever linked, like Chicago and Wrigley, like St. Louis and Busch. Our city was just busting its buttons.

We arrived at Enron Field forty-five minutes before first pitch. I flashed our tickets to a stoop-backed old man wearing a red Astros cap. Kellen and I stepped through the turnstile and onto the main concourse. Whereas the Astrodome's halls were dark and foreboding, lending it the nickname *Astrotomb*, this new park was open and bright. I oohed at the sight of natural grass.

Over the past two days, I'd considered skipping the game altogether. But one look at Kellen told me I'd made the right call. He wore a grin that I fully understood. There's nothing like the anticipation of seeing, or playing, a baseball game.

We found our seats about twenty rows back on field level, halfway between home plate and first base. They were occupied by a young couple decked out in matching Lance Berkman jerseys. I re-read my ticket, then tapped the guy on the shoulder. "You're in our seats."

He dug his own ticket out of his pocket and inspected it. "Oh, we're two rows down. Just take ours."

I looked to the empty seats below us. On one side, a woman wrestled with a squirming toddler. One the other, an obese man wrestled with a bowl of nachos. "I'd rather stick with what the tickets say. Sorry."

The man rolled his eyes. He nudged his girlfriend. "Loser wants us to move."

I crossed my arms and waited for the couple, who took their sweet time vacating our seats. If Kellen hadn't been with me, I would have probably called the man an asshole. Instead, Kellen and I sat down, and I began pointing out some of the park's highlights: the glass and steel retractable roof, the high-resolution video screen, and the distinctive hill and flagpole in center field. I looked toward the dugout, hoping to glimpse a player, but noticed instead the Berkman fan two rows down. *Jerkman* was staring back at me. He slowly extended his middle finger.

The gesture sparked a memory, and I thought again about that last game in high school. The day my life's plans took a detour. I looked to Kellen, who had drawn his baseball glove to his head. He was chewing on the end of a lace.

"Take that out of your mouth."

He spat out the strip of leather, then dropped his eyes to the floor. His face had the same look of worry as it did on the first day of school. "My throat's sore. Can I have a Coke?"

"You're at a ballgame. You're supposed to drink beer." Kellen didn't appreciate the joke and gave me one of his *what-kind-of-dad-are-you* looks. I shrugged.

We managed to haul two foot-long hot dogs, a bag of peanuts, two soft pretzels, a large Coke, and a Budweiser back to our seats. Kellen held his pretzel in the pocket of his glove, taking an occasional nibble between sips of his drink. I balanced a hot dog and pretzel on my lap and swigged my beer.

Some teenager sang the national anthem, the Astros hit the field, and before I knew it, the first inning was over. Fans crowded the aisle, and I considered bouncing a peanut off Jerkman's head.

Kellen tapped my arm. "See him?"

"See who?"

"Pastor Steve. He's coming this way."

Oh joy. And he was walking with a guy from the congregation who I recognized as part-time usher, full-time blowhard.

"Jack!" Pastor Steve leaned across an empty seat to give me a limp handshake. "Miss you guys."

"Yeah, well." It had been three months since Kellen and I had attended church, and I didn't have any plans to return.

Pastor Steve motioned to the man next to him. "Anthony, do you know Jack? He's the guy I mentioned to you. He sells medical equipment."

Anthony snapped his fingers, then pointed at me. "Oh yeah. I've wanted to contact you. Church wants to buy one of them heart defibrillators."

"I mostly work with hospitals—"

"I'm on the committee. I'll give you a call. Hey, where's your wife?"

My jaw clenched. "It's just me and Kellen now."

"Separated, huh? That's too bad."

Pastor Steve grabbed Anthony's arm and pulled him away, apologizing profusely to us as he left. Kellen looked stunned, as if he'd been beaned by a fastball.

"Ignore that guy," I said.

Kellen's face was pained. "I need to go the bathroom."

And I needed another beer.

❧

By the fourth inning, I was holding onto the arms of my seat to keep the ballpark from spinning. My tongue felt thick. The game was still scoreless, and I was tired of watching guys hit soft grounders and lazy fly balls for outs.

The Astros leadoff batter, right fielder Moises Alou, grounded the first pitch into the hole between short and third. The shortstop backhanded the ball and whipped it across the diamond. It was a bang-bang play at first, but Alou beat the throw by a half-step. The umpire raised his fist and ruled an out.

"Come on, Blue!" I yelled. "That was a horrible call!" I swatted my hand dismissively. "Get a new umpire. This guy sucks!"

Jerkman turned his head and shot me a disapproving look, then had the nerve to shush me. I ignored him and let out a long, satisfying boo. When the next batter followed with a monster solo home run, the crowd roared in appreciation, but I was still mad at the previous call. "That should have been two freaking runs! You know it. Yeah, you screwed up. Moron!"

"Dad, can we go somewhere quiet?"

"This isn't a library. You're supposed to cheer and yell. Act like you want to be here."

Kellen clammed up the rest of the inning, even as the Astros hit back-to-back doubles and scored again. Between innings, he asked for another drink.

"You turning into a camel?" I asked.

"My throat hurts. It's like someone twisted my neck around, and I can't swallow. Like I have a tennis ball stuck in my throat."

"You probably ate too much. Let's walk around. Maybe that'll help."

We circled the concourse and paused to watch the game from behind the Crawford Boxes in left field. I bought him another soft drink. "Any better?"

"A little. Maybe." He massaged his throat again.

I hoped he wasn't coming down with a cold.

By the eighth inning, the Astros had scored four runs, matching my total beers for the game. In a complete surprise, our wacky Dominican pitcher had given up only one run, a towering homer over the Crawford Boxes.

"We already know the Astros are gonna win," Kellen said in a whiny voice. "Can we just go?"

"Don't be like your mother. She always had to leave early to beat traffic."

He shrank into his seat and didn't say much the rest of the game. The Astros pulled out the victory by a score of five to three, and management treated the crowd to celebratory fireworks.

We joined the crush of people exiting the park. It seemed that everyone had waited for the final out—the concourse was congested with rowdy fans. A lady tripped and fell, screamed, and then cackled with drunken glee. Kellen clutched my hand.

"It won't be as crowded once we get outside," I explained.

When we reached the Houston sunshine, Kellen let go of me, staggered, and fell back against the brick wall. A look of panic washed over his face.

"What's wrong?" I asked.

"Don't know," he responded in gulps. "Can't . . . breathe."

Chapter 10

Kellen slumped to the ground, his arms steadying him from keeling over. He was puffing as if he'd just finished a hard sprint. His eyes were closed and a sheen of perspiration glistened on his forehead.

I dropped to my knees next to him. "Relax," I said, placing my hand lightly on his trembling chest.

"Dad," he pleaded.

This flipped some sort of parental switch, and a powerful shot of adrenalin hit my system. With a swift move, I scooped him up in my arms. "Hang on, Kel."

A memory flashed of him as a baby, the day he took his first steps and tripped face-first into the sharp edge of a coffee table, when I held him against my chest as Melanie tried to stanch his bleeding mouth. It had taken the two of us to soothe Kellen back then . . . and to keep each other from freaking out.

The doors we had just exited were still jammed with fans headed out of the ballpark. Over their heads, I spied a Houston police officer standing at the curb. "Make room!" I yelled and carried Kellen through the crowd. Within seconds I reached the officer.

"What's going on?" he asked, giving us the once-over.

"My son can't breathe." The horrible truth hit me hard again.

"He can't breathe."

"Lay him down. Prop his head up. What's his name?"

"Kellen." I laid him face-up on the sidewalk and placed his head in my lap. His breaths were rapid and shallow.

The officer knelt, his right hand resting instinctively on a shiny black holster. "Kellen, I need you to take deep breaths."

"Through your nose," I said, acting on instinct. "Breathe from your tummy."

It seemed an eternity, but in reality less than a minute passed before I sensed a change in Kellen. His breathing fell into a slow rhythm. The muscles of his arms and shoulders relaxed; he felt heavier. When his eyes blinked open, I held his face in my hands. "Talk to me, Kel."

He shifted in my lap, then rose to a sitting position. "What happened? My throat just closed up. Like something was pressing on my chest."

"Take him to First Aid," the officer said. He cocked his head and sniffed the air. "Sir, how much have you had to drink?"

The question came across as an accusation, and I knew I didn't want to go down this road. I already regretted the beers I'd drunk, which had probably clouded my judgment and kept me from noticing Kellen's problem in the first place. "I'm totally sober," I lied. "Where's First Aid?"

"Behind section one-fifty. Unless you want me to call the paramedics."

I didn't know what to do—go to First Aid, call 911, or rush Kellen straight to a hospital. It was the same decision Melanie and I had faced years ago, when Kellen bled all over us after his tumble. I had been ready to whisk him to the ER, but Melanie had urged patience. "Faces bleed," she explained. "Let's wait 'til it stops, and then we can see how bad it is."

Kellen took the hand of the officer and stood, inhaled deeply, and gave me a reassuring nod. His voice was clear and steady. "I want to go home."

Melanie's long-ago words repeated in my mind: *Wait 'til it stops. Then see how bad it is.* Whatever storm had struck Kellen had subsided. I thanked the officer for his help and was grateful when he didn't follow up on my sobriety. Then I led Kellen to our car, my eyes fixed on him for any changes.

My mind clicked off the hospitals we'd pass on the way home. If necessary, we'd divert to an emergency room.

I was on the cell phone before we entered the highway. "Pick up, pick up," I told the ringing phone.

The answering service operator took my number and within minutes Kellen's pediatrician returned the call. He was a doddering old man who dealt in snot and vomit, but Melanie had always liked him. I hadn't seen him enough to form an opinion. He had me relay Kellen's symptoms and current condition.

"Should I go to the ER?" I asked.

"It's up to you Mr. Kennedy. From what I understand—and mind you, I haven't examined your son—it sounds like a transient episode. If you go to the hospital, know that you're going to have to wait, maybe a long time, because he's not in any distress right now."

"What if I take him home and watch him? We only live two minutes from a hospital."

"Like I said, it's your decision. That's not a bad option, though." Before hanging up, he reassured me I could call back with any questions and recommended I follow up with a specialist.

I relayed the news to Kellen, who seemed satisfied with the remote diagnosis. I spent the rest of the drive thinking about what had happened at the ballpark and what the pediatrician had advised. After calling Scott, our company expert on pulmonary equipment, to solicit his opinion on a qualified ear-nose-and-throat doctor, I felt better. I had a plan.

I tucked Kellen into bed at nine o'clock after reading him a story, then slowly smoothed his hair until he fell asleep. For the rest of the night, I sat next to his bed listening to his light snores and reading some of Melanie's old parenting magazines. I know I stayed awake until four o'clock, but eventually exhaustion grabbed me and I fell asleep against the wall.

Dr. Timothy Boyd's office was located in Sugar Land, inside a sprawling one-story professional building immediately next door to St. Mary's Catholic Hospital. Thick-trunked ornamental pears and the occasional crape myrtle lined the path where Kellen and I walked. A mottled duck crossed in front of us and waddled into a nearby pond.

"What does Otto-Larry-Googly mean?" Kellen asked, pointing at the name engraved on the glass door.

"Otolaryngology," I said, chuckling. "He's a doctor who treats your ears, nose, and throat."

"Oh. That's a long name." He pulled open the door. "Do you think he'd mind if I called him Dr. Otto?"

I was still grinning when we reached the receptionist. "We have an appointment with Dr. Boyd," I told her.

She crinkled her face. "Dr. Boyd isn't in today."

"But I called."

"He slipped in the shower this morning. Broke both wrists. I can reschedule you for another doctor. We have openings next week."

"No, please. I've been up all night." I leaned close so Kellen wouldn't hear me. "He really needs to see a doctor today."

The phone rang and she answered, "Fort Bend Otolaryngology. Can you hold?" She pressed a button to send the caller into limbo, then told me, "If you can wait, I'll try to fit you in with Dr. Lincoln."

I considered how drunk and stupid I'd been, how I'd let Kellen down. If something happened to him before he saw a doctor, I could never forgive myself. I nodded reluctantly. "We'll wait."

Two hours later, I was tired of waiting. My stomach was growling, my bladder was full, and I was tired of seeing patients ushered in who I knew arrived after us. I mumbled expletives under my breath.

"I don't need a doctor," Kellen insisted.

"Look, we've spent our entire morning here already. You're gonna see the frickin' doctor." I marched to the receptionist's window, rapped my knuckles on the frosted glass, and waited. And waited.

"Kellen Kennedy?" said a young male nurse, opening the side door. He stood more than six feet tall, with long, brown hair and a gold stud earring in his left lobe.

The receptionist finally opened her window. I held up my hand. "Never mind."

We followed the nurse into a cramped examination room. A poster of the human ear was affixed to the wall, and two plastic models, one of the nose and another of the throat and larynx, sat on a shelf above the sink.

The earring-clad nurse, who fit in better at an arcade than at a doctor's office, slipped a pulse oximeter on Kellen's forefinger and wrapped a cuff around his upper arm. "Just gonna check your oxygen and blood pressure. If it looks good, you're cleared to be an astronaut." He winked at Kellen and pressed a button on the machine.

The pressure cuff ballooned around Kellen's arm, and I saw his eyes grow huge. "You gotta be able to handle the G-forces of liftoff, man," the nurse said. When the cuff deflated, he noted the readings. "You're definitely astronaut material." He turned to me. "What brings you guys in?"

"Kellen couldn't breathe yesterday."

He flipped open the chart. "Start from the beginning."

I gave him the basics but didn't feel the need to go into every detail, because I'd have to repeat the story to the doctor anyway.

When the nurse left, Kellen said, "He looked like a pirate, didn't he, Dad?"

"Maybe this is a pirate's office. Maybe the doctor has a patch on his eye and a parrot on his shoulder."

Kellen covered his left eye with his hand and giggled. The laughter was like a tonic for me.

A few minutes later, a woman in a white coat entered the examination room. She didn't have a patch, a parrot, or even a wooden leg. She was in her early thirties and reminded me of that famous actress with the last name Hepburn. Not the old, wrinkly woman who won all those Academy Awards, but the young, pretty brunette with the short hair.

Flashing a warm smile, she said, "Hi, I'm Dr. Lincoln."

Scott had told me that Dr. Boyd's practice included two other old guys and a woman that was maybe the smartest and friendliest of the bunch. He hadn't mentioned anything about how attractive she was.

"Sorry you had to wait," she said. "It's been a crazy day." She read the nurse's report, pushed back several strands of hair from her eyes, and said. "So, Kellen, what's going on with you?"

"My throat's been hurting. Sometimes it feels too small, and I can't swallow."

"He said it's like a tennis ball stuck in his throat. And

yesterday we were leaving a ballgame when he had trouble breathing." I relayed the details of Kellen's attack, how it came on strong and then, just as quickly, disappeared.

She listened to everything and jotted down some notes on his chart. "Well, let's take a look. Hop up on that table, Kel."

I did a double take—no one called Kellen by that nickname except me. Even his mom had always insisted on using his full name.

Dr. Lincoln wielded an otoscope and carefully examined his ears. "There's some light scarring on his eardrums. Nothing to worry about."

I mumbled, "That's good," and fidgeted in my chair. I pulled at my collar as a prickly warmth rushed up my neck. Discussing Kellen's ear problems with Melanie had always devolved into arguments, with me as the bad guy, and I didn't want to revisit the subject.

After inspecting Kellen's nose and mouth, the doctor slipped her stethoscope under his shirt. She finished listening to his breath sounds, then asked him a series of questions. Have you been coughing or wheezing? Do you have problems breathing after playing hard? Have you had a cold recently? Kellen considered each question and answered with a maturity that surprised me.

When she completed her examination, she patted Kellen on the knee. "You're gonna be fine."

"What's wrong with him?"

"Well, he doesn't have an ear infection, his throat looks okay, and his lungs are clear."

"That's . . . good?"

"Oh, definitely. You said he's never been diagnosed with asthma. Any other medical history?"

"I'm thinking." Coordinating doctor appointments had always

fallen to Melanie. I racked my brain for anything dealing with Kellen, but all I could come up with were a couple of annual visits I'd made to his pediatrician. Melanie had handled all the fun stuff: the puking and diarrhea, the colic, the ear infections.

The door opened and the nurse peeked in. "Hey, buddy," he said to Kellen. "Doc give you the all-clear to go to Mars?" He motioned to Dr. Lincoln. "They need you in room one."

"Excuse me."

Kellen gestured to the door after she left. "See, Dad? Told you I was okay."

"I'm sure you are. But that's why we came to see the doctor."

"I like her," Kellen declared. "She's nice. And pretty."

I found myself staring at the door, waiting for her to return. Kellen was right—she *was* pretty. But did she know what was wrong with him?

While I thought about everything, Kellen waved his arms and pretended to float weightless around the room. If only I'd paid more attention to his health, maybe I'd have a better idea of what we were facing. At least I'd done the right thing by taking him to a specialist, even if she wasn't the one Scott had recommended.

Dr. Lincoln came back in and apologized for the delay. Then she said, "Kellen, you're good to go."

"Hold on," I said. "You're sending us home?"

"Kellen seems healthy. He could have an over-reactive airway. Let's just watch things. I can send you home with a rescue inhaler—"

"So he has asthma."

"That's not what I said. We can follow up with more testing if the symptoms occur again."

"But . . ." No way was I going to leave her office without getting to the bottom of things. "I need some answers."

She wrote some notes on his chart, then closed it. "I'm sure yesterday was very scary, Mr. Kennedy. But all signs point to a one-time occurrence. His oxygen level is fine, he doesn't have wheezing or stridor—"

"But he couldn't breathe!" I didn't understand why she wouldn't listen.

"Dad, she said I'm okay. Can we just go home? I'm tired."

"See? Maybe that's another symptom."

She gave a wan smile. "Let's do this. If anything changes, bring him back. We can do a chest x-ray and pulmonary function testing. We can check him for allergies as well." I started to interrupt, but she held up her hand. "Give him warm fluids and keep his stress level low."

"What do you mean, stress?" I could almost feel my temples pulse as the blood began to rise.

"Sometimes anxiety can trigger things like this. Kellen, do you get nervous in tight spaces?"

He shrugged. "I don't think so—"

"He's not claustrophobic," I said through gritted teeth.

The doctor moved toward the door. "I'll get that inhaler and have the nurse explain how to use it."

I intercepted her before she left. "Look, maybe he is okay," I whispered. "But what if you're wrong? Doctor, please tell me. Is there anything I need to worry about?"

Her eyes darted to Kellen and back to me. "We'll know more once we run some tests."

Chapter 11

The next morning I dragged into the office a half-hour later than normal, thanks to a protracted discussion with the school nurse. Scott met me at my desk. "How's Kellen doing?"

"He's fine. I think." I set down my briefcase and extracted my notebook computer. "At least that's what the doctor says. She didn't think it was serious."

"She?"

"Dr. Boyd's out of commission. Broke his wrists or something."

Scott pulled up a chair and scooted next to my desk. "So you saw Dr. Sweetbottom?" he said, practically drooling on himself.

"You're an idiot, you know that? I went to the doctor to get Kellen checked out. I wasn't looking to get laid." A computer cable caught on something at the bottom of my briefcase, so I gave it a yank, and an entanglement of wires and papers dropped on my desk, then pitched onto the floor.

"Sounds like she had an effect on you."

"Oh, shut up."

An hour later, as I was poring over Internet articles on breathing disorders, Scott showed up at my desk. "Did you hear the news?"

"What are you talking about?"

"Corporate is beating the drums about our numbers again. I think they're serious this time. Deb said Mr. Swokowsi dropped a couple f-bombs in the teleconference. And he made a not-so-veiled threat about layoffs."

I should have been concerned, I guess, but I had more important things on my mind. "Whatever happens, happens," I told him.

He rolled his eyes. "Glad you can be so cavalier about layoffs, Jack. It's only our effing career." He thought for a couple of seconds, then said, "Sorry, man. I know you're stressed about Kellen."

I nodded. I didn't tell Scott I'd been pondering one worrisome thought for the past forty-two hours: *Something's definitely wrong.* I didn't tell him I'd second-guessed my every action—and inaction—since Kellen collapsed. And I didn't tell him I'd managed only ten hours of sleep over the past three nights. Because Scott wouldn't understand. He didn't have kids.

"Tell me what you know about Dr. Lincoln," I said.

"Only what I've heard. She's single, super cute—"

"Medically. Does she know what she's talking about?"

For once, he dropped the frat boy attitude. "Renee Lincoln," he said, casting his eyes to the ceiling as if attempting to access the part of his brain not dedicated to T&A. "I hear she's smart. She wouldn't be with Dr. Boyd's practice if he didn't believe in her, that's for sure. And she's supposed to have a good bedside manner."

"Can't say I got off on the right foot with her," I said, remembering how we butted heads about Kellen's diagnosis. "But she really connected with Kellen. I need to know whether she can help him."

"She's your best shot at getting things back to normal."

Over a late lunch, I nibbled at a grilled chicken salad as I considered the doctor's diagnosis. She hadn't thought it was asthma, maybe just a reaction to stress. I pulled out a pen and began jotting down potential stressors. *Mom's death*—I underlined it twice. *Fire.* Either of those would be enough to trigger an episode. But there was something unique about last Sunday, I just knew it. I wrote *Coffee spill*, then added *Astros game??*.

Kellen had always enjoyed going to ballgames; in fact, Sunday's game was more like real baseball than we'd ever seen at the Dome. Enron Field was like a Little League park on steroids. I dwelled on that thought for a few seconds, rolling it around in my mind like a loose shoe in a dryer. Maybe watching the Astros reminded Kellen of Little League. Oh no—maybe he made a mental leap to thinking about the day of his last ballgame.

That long day had been seared into my consciousness, and I could remember every detail. That morning in our bedroom, fooling around with Melanie, being interrupted by Kellen. At the ballpark, smelling cut grass and bubble gum, hearing the sounds of boys being boys. Then the horrible rest of the day, helplessly trying to free her, realizing the worst after overhearing the paramedics' conversation. Telling my son that his mommy had died.

The day of his last Little League game, full of joy—then in an instant, full of grief. A question popped into my head. Did he somehow blame himself for his mom's death? And did the Astros game bring it all back?

⁂

At seven o'clock, with the afternoon sun still beating down, I rang the bell at Stacy and Mitchell's house. No one answered, and I heard shouts from the backyard, so I followed the driveway past a red sports car to investigate. Through a high iron fence, I watched Kellen leap from the pool's edge, arms outstretched, as he attempted to catch a tennis ball. His hands clapped together over his head, coming up empty as Mitchell's throw sailed high. When Kellen surfaced from the pool, he tiptoed to an azalea bush and retrieved the ball.

"Having fun?" I asked, jiggling the gate latch in a vain attempt to open it.

"Hey, Jack," a female voice called, and a hand waved from behind the elevated spa near the center of the pool. "Hang on, I'll help you. It's tricky."

Stacy stood and came toward me. She wore a bikini top, striped in aqua and deep blue, and matching boy shorts. Her body revealed the results of an intense exercise regimen—her legs were muscular yet shapely, her abs flat and hard. I hadn't seen that much skin in a long time.

"The boys have been swimming for almost two hours," she explained, turning the gate's safety latch. "Figured I'd work on my tan, too. Would you like something to drink?"

"No, thanks." I wanted to get Kellen home and discuss what was bothering him. "Ready to go, Kel?"

"Ah Dad, can I stay longer? I don't have any homework."

"No problem for me if the boys want to keep swimming," Stacy offered.

It took serious concentration not to stare at her breasts, barely covered by the blue material. Even as I focused on her face, they loomed in my peripheral vision. "Appreciate the invite, but we gotta pass."

"Come on," she said. "If you don't have any plans, hang around a while."

I looked at Kellen, who appeared happy and relaxed, and figured another hour wouldn't kill us. We certainly didn't have anything else on our agenda. Plus, it was hard to turn down a woman in a bikini. "Okay," I said. "At least let me spring for pizza."

Stacy retreated inside to place the order. She returned wearing a white, sleeveless t-shirt over her suit top and holding a Corona in each hand. "Hola, Señor," she said with a cheesy Mexican accent. She tipped a bottle toward me. "Cerveza?"

"Gracias."

Dusk settled, the temperature cooled slightly, and reflections of pool light danced on the side of the house. Kellen and Mitchell sat at the edge of the pool, legs dangling in the water, and chomped on cheese pizza. Stacy and I sat in teak chairs and discussed how the boys were faring in school.

Two beers later, Stacy's playfulness may not have been conscious, but it did have an effect. I no longer averted my eyes. We chit-chatted about her pool service and the new Sugar Meadow Mall, and my gaze drifted to her chest.

"What are you doing, Dad?" Kellen called.

My eyes darted to the cabana roof. I felt my face flush with embarrassment. A memory emerged of my father asking a similar question, "What are you reading there, boy?" as I tried to quickly stuff a *Playboy* under my pillow.

"Dad?" Kellen said.

"I was . . . uh . . ."

"Are you doing anything? I'm thirsty."

I stammered a response and caught sight of Stacy guffawing in her chair. "Hush," I said, laughing.

Stacy's cell phone rang, and I took the opportunity to duck inside the house. Stepping into the half-bath off the kitchen, I smelled the pleasant fragrance from a potpourri basket. It reminded me of how Melanie used to mix her own combination of dried rose petals, cinnamon sticks, and jasmine oil.

Suddenly I felt guilty. I'd never cheated on Melanie in our entire marriage—was never even tempted—but it seemed that somehow I was dishonoring our vows. Maybe Kellen saw me ogling Stacy; that wasn't fair to him either.

When I returned to the patio, I found Stacy frantically pacing, phone to her ear, her mouth pulled tight. "Dad, please call me when the neurologist comes in."

I listened to her end of the conversation, able to glean basic facts. Her mother had fallen at home and apparently suffered a small stroke. No one was sure if the fall precipitated the stroke, or vice versa.

"Your mom gonna be okay?" I whispered.

Stacy covered the mouthpiece. "Not sure." She frowned, then waggled her wrist to indicate her mom's condition was so-so.

"We're gonna leave," I said. "Need me to watch Mitchell?"

She shook her head, then turned her back and continued speaking with her father. And just like that, with the sharp reality of a single phone call, the spell of the pool, the cervezas, and the bikini was broken. Stacy transformed from flirty hardbody back into Mitchell's mom.

She was a divorced single parent with a sick mother.

I was a widower.

Driving home in the dimly lit car, with Kellen safely secured in the backseat, I broached the subject I feared discussing. "I set up another appointment for you. That's the follow-up visit we talked about with the doctor yesterday. They're gonna run some tests."

"What do you think's wrong with me?" His voice quavered slightly, at a frequency detectable only by a parent.

"Nothing you should worry about," I said, gripping the wheel so tightly that I could feel my fingers start to cramp. The doctor had guessed it might be stress-related, psychosomatic, which meant Kellen didn't need any unnecessary anxiety. I steadied my voice. "You could be allergic to things in the air, like dust or pollen. Could be asthma."

Kellen perked up. "A kid in Ms. Lathrop's class has asthma. He carries around an inhaler. Like what the doctor gave me."

"She also said you might be worried too much. What do you think? Maybe remembering your mom makes you nervous—"

"I'm not nervous about Mommy," he replied. In the mirror, I saw Kellen turn his face to the window and look into the night. After a moment he whispered, "I don't even think about her anymore."

No one, especially a kid, should have to relive such a traumatic death, so I understood Kellen not dwelling on the accident. He'd probably blocked it out.

Yet I knew what Kellen meant. He hadn't pushed the accident from his mind; he was forgetting *her*.

I never imagined that I could forget my wife, the woman I'd shared everything with, but she was receding, mostly in small ways. A restaurant hostess might ask how many were in our party and I'd automatically reply "Two," with no thought we were actually "Three minus one." When Kellen's teacher wanted to set up a conference, it no longer occurred to me that Melanie could go instead.

Obviously I hadn't purged my mind and soul of Melanie—I'm sure Kellen hadn't either—but I feared she would inevitably blur in our memory.

A few weeks ago, I had dreamed the three of us were standing at the edge of the Grand Canyon. Kellen and I climbed down to a rocky spot where Melanie could snap our picture from above, from a shade tree where she sat wearing her *Baseball Mom* t-shirt.

A loud noise sounded, boulders crashed around me, and our observation point gave way. Kellen and I plummeted down the canyon. My hands scrambled for a handhold, while he clutched at my jeans. His grip on my leg was excruciating, and I yelled at him to let go of me. Looking up, I saw Melanie drifting away; her face had disappeared behind the trunk of the tree. My own scream woke me from the nightmare, and I spent two restless hours in the dark, praying for dawn to break.

I wanted to reassure Kellen that time was the great healer, that his stress would diminish but the memory of his mom would not. But I wasn't sure I believed it myself.

Chapter 12

When I dropped off Kellen the next morning, Stacy greeted us at the door wearing a fleece bathrobe and slippers. Her brown hair was a mess, frizzy and misshapen. "Long night," she said as Kellen hurried inside.

"How's your mom?"

"Stable. They're thinking TIA. You know, mini-stroke."

Stacy's eyes, which had been sly and flirtatious last night, were absent of makeup and wrinkled at the corners. I recognized the look, had seen it in my own mirror. She'd been through the wringer too, struggling to keep her marriage intact, then raising Mitchell without his father. Now her mom was sick. I'd been a single dad for only three months and was totally overwhelmed.

She pulled at the blue cotton nightgown peeking out of her robe. "Aren't you going to the Dads and Donuts breakfast?"

"Can't today." I had no intention of repeating last year's experience, where I showed up at the school's donut breakfast without an umbrella, got drenched as I crossed the parking lot, and then had to choke down some stale donuts without coffee. "Besides, Kellen and I like to do our own father-son kolache thing."

"Jack, you gotta make time for this. It's a big deal."

"You going?"

"I'm a mom. Can't upset the whole testosterone vibe." She offered a wan smile. "Seriously, you need to be there."

I thought of Kellen arriving at school, only to find himself alone in the cafeteria. "Where's your dad?" the kids would ask, just like the *what-happened-to-your-mom* questions he'd been so afraid of. There was no way I could do that to him.

❧

"I want you to meet all my friends," Kellen said as we passed a thirty-foot-wide poster that read *Bright Minds - Bright Future*, its letters formed with painted handprints.

"It's just breakfast, Kellen. Not a party."

"I know."

"Is there someone in particular you want me to meet? It's a girl, isn't it?" I teased.

As expected, Kellen looked horrified. "A girl? No way, Dad. Girls are like the worst."

We entered the school commons through a set of French doors and found a crowd teeming with middle-aged men and young kids in tow.

"Derek!" Kellen hollered.

A black kid wearing a Rockets jersey looked up and waved. He sat at a table across from what must have been his father, a muscular African-American with a shaved head. Kellen ran over and gabbled something at his friend, then sprinted back to me. "Derek said we can sit with them."

"I don't know your friend," I whispered.

"That's Derek."

"Maybe we can find someone we both know." I eyed the room for a familiar face as we joined the line for donuts.

A man shouldered me as he walked by, then stopped. "Get

your food and then come join us." When I saw who it was, my stomach tightened. The only thing worse than sitting alone or with a stranger was sitting with my odd neighbors, Captain Carl and the twins. Just then, Patrick and Stewart buzzed past, each waving a glazed donut.

"Rats," I said, faking my disappointment. "Someone's already saved us a spot. We'll have to catch you later." I watched where Captain Carl landed and made a mental note to avoid that side of the room.

I got us each a donut, feeling sorry for the teachers who'd inherit a classroom of kids jacked up on sugar. At the beverage table, Kellen grabbed a plastic bottle of orange juice from an Igloo cooler. I filled my Styrofoam cup at a coffee urn. Ever since the first time I drank coffee in a freezing duck blind at age fifteen, my morning seemed incomplete without caffeine.

Kellen led us to Derek's table, plopped down next to his friend, and immediately began eating. I sat across from them, with the boy's dad to my left. Within seconds, each kid had crammed the donut into his mouth like a participant in a food-eating contest. Sugar crystals covered their lips.

Kellen managed to avoid choking and said, "Can I get another one?"

"Wipe your mouth first. And just one more." I figured if Kellen was determined to be the fastest eater in the room, I might get out of here sooner. I didn't have a problem with that.

The boys hurried to join the line, and I looked to my left. "You must be Derek's dad. I'm Jack."

The man ignored me. My first thought was that he'd been distracted, maybe seen someone he knew, but I realized he was simply looking around the room. I tried again. "Hi, I'm Jack Kennedy. Are you Derek's father?"

He stood and stretched, lazily scanned the cafeteria, then

returned to his seat. It was the classic suburban technique of dishing out the silent treatment for people you didn't want to associate with. So I returned the favor.

After a bit, the boys returned with huge grins and strawberry-iced donuts. Kellen sat down and promptly dropped his. The donut fell on the table, then bounced into his lap, where he trapped it against his t-shirt. He lifted the smashed donut triumphantly. "I caught it!"

"What does your shirt look like?" I asked, not wanting to know the bad news.

Kellen shrugged. He stood and looked down at the white shirt which read *SMLL—Real Baseball*. Below the image of a batter, Kellen's belly button was surrounded by a giant, pink circle.

"Smooth move, son. When you're done, go to the restroom and clean up."

Derek looked at his father and said, "Dad, this is Kellen. He's my friend from Ms. Blankenship's class."

"Hello, Kellen. At least you saved your donut." The man spoke with a conspicuous nasal accent.

"And this is Kellen's dad," Derek continued, pointing to me.

Derek's father turned and stuck out his hand. "Nice to meet you. I'm Pete Leathers." It sounded closer to "Nite to meed you. I'm Pede Ledderz," and it was obvious the guy had a speech impediment.

In my book, that didn't excuse his prior behavior. It aggravated me that he pretended to act friendly with the kids around, but he wasn't going to make me look bad.

I halfheartedly shook his hand—I really hated shaking hands with strangers—but didn't meet his eyes. "Jack Kennedy."

"Excuse me. I didn't see what you said." He pointed to his ear. "I'm deaf."

"He reads lips, though." Derek said.

Suddenly I felt like an idiot, a judgmental idiot. "Sorry. I didn't know. Jack Kennedy."

"Don't sweat it. Call me Pete."

His accent was more familiar now. He sounded like the deaf actress Marlee Matlin, but he was easier to follow. He could have passed for a guy with a bad cold.

Kellen and I switched seats so Pete could see my face. I didn't know what to say to the guy, but I wasn't such a dolt as to ask him about his hearing. Instead, I broke out the old standby. "What do you do?"

His face brightened. "You heard of Texas Sports University?"

"Yeah. The new gym?"

"It's more than that. Batting cages, complete workout area, rock wall, video games, the whole enchilada. I'm the manager." He enthusiastically rattled on about the business and how his wife and Derek had joined him in Sugar Land. They'd moved from Knoxville the same weekend Melanie had passed.

The deafness impacted his speech, but I didn't have any problems understanding him, and became accustomed to it rather quickly. I was curious about how long Pete had been deaf, what caused it, and why he and Derek didn't use sign language, but he'd probably heard those questions many times before.

"I'm hoping to get Derek involved in local sports. What do you know about them?"

"Not much. It's soccer season."

Pete pointed at Kellen. "Your son plays Little League. Nice shirt."

Kellen had received his *SMLL—Real Baseball* t-shirt as a token from last year's baseball program. For their big fundraiser, the league had signed up local advertising sponsors, distributed a free shirt to every player and coach, and sold the rest to parents for twenty bucks apiece. Unfortunately the league hadn't realized the mischievousness of kids. When one boy took a Sharpie and reformed the message of his shirt, half the kids followed suit, resulting in a new fashion craze: a shirt that read *SMeLLy—Real Baseball*. Kellen's shirt bore the original message and a circle of pink icing.

"Sugar Meadow Little League," I said. "They have five or six fields near old Sugar Land. It's a good setup."

"You coach?"

"No way. You'd have to be crazy to get roped into that."

"I don't know—might be fun." He pulled a pen and a spiral pad from his pocket. "How would I get Derek signed up?

I had no idea how Melanie registered Kellen, maybe at school or maybe on the Internet. My theory was that suburban moms communicated telepathically, ensuring kids never missed an activity. I wanted Pete to find another topic.

"Just need their phone number or the website," he said.

"I'm not up on all the details. Sorry." I hoped he wouldn't ask for directions to the fields, since I'd only been twice and Melanie had driven both times.

He nodded. "I know where you're coming from. My wife just points me where to go every day. Give me your wife's number, and I'll have Vanessa call her."

I'd been asked about Melanie before, and it was never easy to answer the questions. I picked up my empty Styrofoam cup and tapped it on the table. "I'm sure the league puts up signs."

"I just don't want to miss registration. Vanessa would kill me. Better to dump the responsibility back on her. Your wife have a cell phone?"

Looking down, I mumbled, "Actually, she passed away—"

"Excuse me. I can't see your mouth."

I gathered myself, then just laid it out. "My wife died."

Now Pete was the one looking uncomfortable. "Man, I'm

sorry."

The awkward pause was broken by several loud tones, noises I noticed but Pete did not. The gravelly voice of Ms. Battle came over the loudspeaker. "We want to thank all our dads for visiting today. That was our first bell. Time for students to go to class."

I pointed to the ceiling and then at my watch. Pete nodded. We looked at the boys, who were playing and oblivious to our conversation. Kellen stacked three empty orange juice bottles on the table as if they were bowling pins, and Derek slid a half-donut toward them, knocking two of them over.

Pete rolled his eyes and lightly smacked his forehead. "Come on guys, throw this stuff away. Time for school."

When we stood, I noticed Kellen's pink stain again. "Clean your shirt," I said. He wiped his shirt with a napkin and made it worse. "No, go to the bathroom and use water." This kind of stuff gave me headaches.

As we left with the other fathers, Pete and I walked side by side through the commons and into the lobby. I quickly shuffled ahead and turned around so he could read my lips.

"Good to meet you, Pete."

Chapter 13

O f all the dumb suggestions cast my way, "Get him a dog" ranked right up there with "Take him to Hawaii." I could understand the appeal of an island escape—that was Scott's idea—just get on a plane and fly the hell out of this crazy situation. But adopting a pet, a thought originally floated by Leah in private and later by Captain Carl within earshot of Kellen, was singularly idiotic.

Kellen had glommed onto the idea and had been pestering me about it for days. He didn't let up, even as we waited in Dr. Lincoln's office.

"How about a wiener dog?" he asked. He lay on his side on the examination table, his head propped in his right hand, a pleading grin spread across his face.

"Already told you. We don't need the hassle."

"It's not a hassle. I'll feed it every morning and when I get home from school."

"Yeah, right. And guess who'll be stuck taking care of it when the doctor says you're allergic?"

"Derek's family has a schnauzer. He says they're good for allergies."

"We're not getting a dog."

Kellen shrugged and rolled onto his back. He cocked his

fingers into make-believe pistols and fired at imaginary targets on the ceiling. "I don't want a sheltie, though. You gotta brush it a lot. That's what Derek says. He thinks we should get a wiener dog."

I snapped my fingers. "Drop it."

The verbal sparring had left me with a headache, as if a belt were being constricted around my skull. And with each new dog reference, Kellen tightened the belt another notch. I turned away, wishing that thoughts of a new puppy would vanish from his mind.

Kellen scooted off the table and pushed a chair against the sink. He stood on tiptoes, reaching for something.

"What are you doing?" I asked.

"Just wanted to look at the crocodile."

"The what? Sit down."

I heard two small raps on the door, then Dr. Lincoln entered. She wheeled in a device that looked like a garden hose spray nozzle, connected to a notebook computer by a long cable. "Didn't keep you waiting too long, I hope."

I had steeled myself for today's appointment, had half-expected them to say we were wasting everyone's time, but she flashed a disarming smile and I instantly felt reassured. *You did the right thing, bringing your son back to the doctor.*

"So, Kel," she said, uncoiling the cable. "How are you feeling?"

"Good. Well, I do get a little squeezy."

"You mean, queasy?" I said. "Like when your tummy hurts?"

"No, there's times I feel all squeezy, sort of like something's squeezing me and won't let go."

"Kel," I said, "why didn't you tell me?"

"It usually happens at night before I go to sleep. Then I forget."

Dr. Lincoln took this as her cue to perform a thorough examination of Kellen. When she was done, she looked at me and gave a small shake of her head. *Nothing.*

I nodded back, still worried about Kellen, but relieved she was trying to get to the bottom of things.

"We're going to figure out this little mystery," she said, reading my mind. "That's why I brought in this cool computer."

"What is that?" Kellen asked.

She pressed the power button on the device. "This is a spirometer."

"No. Up there. The crocodile."

I looked to where he pointed. On the shelves above the sink, above the latex gloves and tongue depressors, above the giant model of a human ear, an odd, two-foot plastic reptile surveyed the room.

"Oh, that," she said, smiling warmly. "It's an American alligator." She plucked it from the top shelf and handed it to Kellen. "You can hold it. I don't mind."

Kellen turned the green and yellow toy over in his hands, examining it from all angles. He wiggled the plastic tail. He fingered the plastic teeth. And he reminded me of when I was a student, how I loved science and math, how I dreamed of becoming a doctor.

I looked back to her. She was watching Kellen with a huge, satisfied grin, the same kind Melanie used to flash when he passed a major milestone such as completing a puzzle or tying his shoes. Then Dr. Lincoln turned her attention back to the machine. Her eyebrows furrowed in concentration as she initialized the system, then relaxed again when she looked at Kellen.

She passed him the spirometer tube. "Okay, put this in your mouth. I want you to take a big breath and then blow out as hard as you can." She clicked a few items on the computer screen and pointed to Kellen. He inhaled deeply and blew into the tube, causing the spirograph on the computer monitor to spike upward, as if he were trying to ring the bell at a *Test Your Strength* carnival booth.

"See that?" she said, turning the screen so I could read it. "His pulmonary function readings are already in the normal range."

"I don't understand."

"He doesn't have asthma."

I guess I should have welcomed the news, but instead I felt a prickling uneasiness. A part of me felt disappointed that he didn't have asthma. At least asthma was straightforward, common and treatable. At least we would have known what we were dealing with.

"Now what?" I said.

"Intradermal skin testing. If he's got an allergy, we should see it."

Kellen coughed, and we both looked over at him. He was sitting on the examination table, waving the alligator like it was an airplane. Suddenly I remembered all the coughing that had racked me after the fire.

"Wait. What about smoke? We had this kitchen fire back . . . uh . . . it was the day before this happened."

"A fire?"

"There was a lot of smoke. I don't know how much he breathed."

"Smoke inhalation. That might explain things." She produced an otoscope, attached a disposable speculum, then patted Kellen's leg. "Let's take a closer look. Open your mouth, Kel."

As the doctor inspected his throat and nostrils, the feeling of overwhelming guilt returned. I imagined Kellen lying on the kitchen floor, smoke filling the room and his lungs, his life slipping away while I lay in bed.

She slid the scope back into her coat pocket. "There's no swelling or burns in his nostrils. No soot. If he was exposed, it was very minor."

"That's good."

"I do want to get a chest x-ray. Kids have sensitive lungs. Even minimal exposure can trigger shortness of breath." She tousled Kellen's hair. "Shouldn't be any long-term damage, though. Kel seems like a tough little guy."

Kellen peered into the gaping jaws of the toy gator. "Did you have alligators where you grew up?"

"Oh yeah, millions. I lived in Florida, near the Everglades. Ever seen an alligator, Kellen?"

"At the zoo."

"You should go to Brazos Bend. It's a state park only thirty minutes from here. You'd like it—lots of alligators. I volunteer there most weekends, unless I'm on call. Have your mom and dad take you."

I saw Kellen wince at the reference to his mom. Then it passed. He reminded me of my father and his arthritic knees, how Dad would tough out the occasional jolt of pain and then act as if nothing had happened.

Kellen flipped the alligator over and slowly rubbed its yellow, ribbed belly. "Did you have one as a pet?"

I could see where Kellen was heading; a random thought of *wiener gator* flashed in my mind.

He tugged her white coat. "Did you have a pet?" he repeated.

But she stood there mute, a pained expression on her face. "I'm . . ." She swallowed hard and said, "I lost my dog yesterday. She died." Dr. Lincoln's eyes misted over. "Sorry, I've been fine all day."

Kellen's face was somber, earnest. He handed her the alligator.

"I'm sorry about your loss," I told her, reaching out reflexively to touch her hand. Her skin was warm and soft. She responded by lightly touching my arm, and I felt an unfamiliar tingle of energy pass between us.

"Does your family have a dog?" she asked. "Because you gotta be careful. My Molly got run over by a car."

I looked to Kellen. His face paled; his lips drew tight. I could see the grief washing over him, could feel it pulsing in my own body. Uh-oh. "Doctor—"

"Everything happened so fast," she said. The toy alligator fell from her hands. "This car came out of nowhere. I couldn't do a thing to save her."

Kellen doubled over and clutched his throat. Then he flung back his head and gasped for air. I heard wheezing, as if he were choking on a bone.

I rushed toward him. "Kel!"

She whirled around, did a double take, then seized the stethoscope from her shoulders.

"His mom died three months ago in a car accident."

"Oh, no." She slid the stethoscope under his shirt. "Breathe, Kellen. In. Now out." Turning to me, she said in a hushed voice, "I think we found the problem."

Chapter 14

"Sir, is there a problem?" The police officer standing outside my car didn't act concerned; he was just reciting his speech like an experienced telemarketer. He was one of Sugar Land's motorcycle cops, the guys whose job seemed to consist of nothing but aiming radar guns and scribbling on ticket pads. "Did you know you just ran a stop sign?"

"Back there? I stopped."

"Uh-huh. Well, I saw otherwise. You rolled right through it."

Of course I'd run the four-way stop sign. It was the most ridiculous traffic control device in the neighborhood. Everyone rolled through that intersection. I took a deep breath. "Officer, I really believe I stopped back there. But I would appreciate it if you gave me a warning."

"License and insurance, please."

I fished out my license and an expired certificate of liability insurance. The cop took them and went back to his motorcycle.

"Are you in trouble?" Kellen asked from the back seat.

"No, I'm not in trouble." I looked through my driver-side mirror and could see the cop talking into the radio affixed to his shoulder.

"Are you going to get rested?"

"What?"

"Is he gonna rest you? Charlie's uncle got rested one time. The policeman said he was driving wild and constipated."

"You mean driving while—never mind. Just hush. I need to concentrate."

The cop reappeared at my window and handed me a small clipboard. "Sign this."

I looked at the ticket. "Are you joking? You pegged me for running the stop sign and for no insurance? And what do you mean, no seatbelt? I always wear my seatbelt."

"You're not wearing one now."

"I *always* wear my seatbelt. I just unbuckled it out of habit after I put the car in park."

"Uh-huh. Well, we have seatbelt laws for a reason. Seatbelts save lives."

I could see Melanie unconscious behind her steering wheel, the air bag deployed, the shoulder belt secured across her chest. I remembered the paramedics having to cut the belt to free her.

Seatbelts save lives. What a crock of shit.

❧

The door opened and Dr. Mike waved us in. He wore a polo shirt tucked into faded jeans and sported a hideous black eye. The bruising ringed his left eye like an oversized monocle. The white of his eyeball was tinged red.

"Whoa! What happened?" Kellen asked.

Dr. Mike ran a finger along his eyebrow. "Got elbowed in the face at a basketball game. Looks pretty nasty, huh?"

"It looks cool!"

Dr. Mike chuckled. "You're the first person to tell me that. Thanks, buddy. How are you doing?"

"My dad got a ticket."

"Totally bogus," I said. "The cop was ridiculous."

Dr. Mike gave me a sidelong look. "Today I want to do something different. Kellen, I'm going to take you to the activity room for a few minutes. You can play while I talk with your dad. Then you and I can talk. And then maybe all three of us."

He led Kellen away. I thought briefly about sitting in Dr. Mike's favorite chair; instead, I wandered around his office. The guy was certainly a piece of work. On one wall hung his two diplomas and every certificate he'd ever earned—I wouldn't have been surprised to see an award for his fourth-grade spelling bee. Built-in shelves displayed his book collection, but seemed more geared to highlighting his trophies, bobbleheads, and framed photos. I took a closer look. There were photos of him smiling with politicians such as Congressman Tom DeLay and Houston's mayor, with local news media, and with Houston's pro athletes.

On the credenza behind his desk, a framed eight-by-ten caught my eye. In the photo, Dr. Mike wore an ugly green basketball jersey. He stood between two black guys taller than him and wearing matching stars-and-stripes uniforms. My mouth fell open. Dr. Mike had told Kellen the truth—he *had* played against the Harlem Globetrotters.

"Kellen's all set," Dr Mike said as he entered. "Let's you and me have a talk."

"I don't get why he's not here."

"This way you can get things off your chest without having to worry about what Kellen hears. And vice versa. Take a seat."

Resigning myself to the leather couch, I told Dr. Mike about how Kellen had seized up at the doctor's office, how we now knew all his breathing problems were stress-related. "I'll be honest," I said. "I think he's losing it."

"What do think you should do, Jack?"

"What should *I* do? You're supposed to be the expert. Get him in here and fix him."

Dr. Mike didn't say anything. He just wrote in his notebook. "You mentioned a fire."

I scoffed. "Don't get me started. A few weeks back, Kellen thought he could cook breakfast, and he practically burned down the kitchen."

"Where were you?"

"Does it matter?"

"You tell me."

I wasn't going to share the details of that terrible day: clutching Melanie's nightgown, fighting the flames, contemplating the pills. "The fire was just a crazy accident."

He considered my response. "You sound irritated."

I shifted uncomfortably on the couch, then pulled a throw pillow from behind my back. I tossed it onto the floor. "Want to know why I'm irritated? Because you think therapy's all about you. Look at your office. Aren't therapists supposed to be some sort of anonymous friend? This whole place screams, 'Look at me! I'm a genius. I'm popular.'"

"Sorry you feel that way, Jack."

"Oh, don't act all high and mighty. Like you're the smartest guy in the room. Get Kellen back in here."

"If that's what you want. First, could you tell me about Melanie? How things were before she died?" He sat back, legs uncrossed, the fancy notebook closed on his lap.

"I'm not talking, man." I looked past him toward the bookcase and began counting bobbleheads. Then I eyed the clock. Five minutes should be enough, I thought. Enough time for Kellen to believe Dr. Mike and I had held a meaningful conversation.

"I'm sensing that you don't want to be here."

"Really? What was your first clue?"

Dr. Mike stopped talking and absentmindedly groomed his hair. He pressed his index finger against his cheek, just below his black eye, as if he were testing the freshness of a tomato. The only perceptible sound in the room was the hum of a printer alongside his desk.

For a long minute, he let the silence settle like a thick fog. I listened for any sounds of Kellen in the other room, but couldn't hear anything. So I began cracking the knuckles of my left hand, first folding the fingers inward, then twisting the fingers side-to-side. Melanie used to hate that habit, and I figured Dr. Mike might be similarly annoyed.

He was a statue.

I rolled my neck, popping the joints as loudly as I could. Then I moved to the wrists—if necessary, I was capable of producing sickening noises from my ankles and knees as well. The left wrist cooperated quickly, a double-pop. But when I twisted my right wrist, pain shot up to my elbow.

In that instant, I was transported back to the Giddings baseball field, to the day of my last baseball game. Tate Gillum was on the mound. He was the little prick from our rival high school who cost me my shot at college and, probably, the pros. He froze me on a 1-2 curveball when I had the chance to drive in a run. The strikeout hadn't bothered me as much as the jerk pumping his fist and pointing at me as he left the field. He wanted me to know that he'd beaten me, that he was better than me.

Dr. Mike was exactly like Tate Gillum. He sat there perched on his chair with that condescending attitude. Then it dawned on me—I'm paying this guy to sit on his ass.

"Let's stop this charade," I said. "Kellen's the one with problems. You're wasting your time talking with me."

"Is that what we're doing? You think it's a waste of time to talk about Melanie?"

Something snapped inside me. "Look, it doesn't matter how much we talk about her. I could sit here for hours and tell you how wonderful she was as a wife and mother. And you still wouldn't know her. I mean, *know* her."

Dr. Mike folded his hands loosely in his lap and nodded.

"Did you know she was a teacher? Taught fifth grade until Kellen was born. Then taught him how to read by age four. Worked with illiterate inmates down at the prison, too. Wanna know why? Said she wanted to leave a legacy of learning. Believe that crap?

"You think you'll know her if I tell you all her little details? Let's see . . . She was orphaned in college . . . Her favorite color was lavender . . . She loved crappy eighties music like Air Supply and Lene Lovich . . . I once saw her shoplift a Bible—how's that for irony?

"Is this helping you any, Dr. Mike?" I sneered.

He didn't respond.

"Maybe you want details of our sex life? Is that what gets you off?

"Or maybe you get off on hearing how she died. You want me to tell you how she rammed her fucking car into a tree and broke her fucking neck? How she left me with this crazy shithouse of a life . . . Is that you want?"

I wagged my finger at him. "You don't know what it's like to lose someone like Melanie. Thinking about her every day and getting this terrible pain in your gut. Praying you could have just one normal day again. Wishing you had swallowed those pills so you could be with—"

I couldn't believe what I just said.

Chapter 15

During the remainder of the session with Dr. Mike, and for two days afterward, I felt like I was drifting through an out-of-body experience. It's hard to imagine I could have told a total stranger about my feelings of loneliness and despair. But I had.

I'd smoothed the ugliest details, of course, presenting Dr. Mike with a sanitized version of events. In my account, the pills had been Tylenol and not prescription painkillers; they had been safely sealed under a foil wrapper instead of heaped in my hand. And I hadn't written a letter to my dead wife.

When Dr. Mike brought Kellen back into the room, he never mentioned our discussion. For that, I was grateful. My mind was spinning the entire time—that whole conversation with Kellen was a blur—something about the importance of grief uniting us instead of dividing us. The main thing I remembered was Dr. Mike's suggestion that Kellen and I develop common interests and to spend more time outdoors.

❧

I drove through the entrance of Brazos Bend State Park,

passing a massive live oak filled with wisps of bluish-grey Spanish moss. Long, thick branches hung low like a grandfather's open arms, inviting us in, but the buzzard perched on the top branch suggested a less friendly welcome. I could have sworn the bird looked right at me, then flapped its wings and rose into the sky.

It was as if I'd stepped into some old movie about prehistoric Earth. The two-lane road cut a swath through forest overgrown with yaupon, past swampy bottomland that mankind had no desire to explore. Wood signs flashed by: *Do Not Feed or Approach Alligators* and *Poisonous Snakes Exist in This Park*. I would have turned the car around, except Leah and her family were waiting for us.

When we pulled into the nature center parking lot, Kellen pointed and said, "There's Trevor and Marissa."

"Remember what we talked about with Dr. Mike. I know your cousins are here, but I want us to spend time together."

"That's why I brought my baseball glove."

Lord, give me strength. I would walk every mile of trail in this park with Kellen, would examine every tree, every vine, every interesting bug. But I didn't want to play baseball with him.

Leah met me as I stepped out of the car. She kissed my cheek. "I'm really glad we could do this family picnic together. Isn't it a beautiful day?"

A breeze gusted, causing tall oaks and nut-laden pecan trees to sway. I looked up to the cloudless sky . . . and saw two buzzards circling.

Leah adjusted a hip pack around her waist. "Everyone ready to see some alligators?"

"No, Mom," Trevor said. "I want to show Kellen the snake first. The ranger man's letting it wind around his arm." And with that, the boys raced inside the A-frame building.

Leah and Marissa stepped away to the restroom, and I found

myself face-to-face with Richard. He leaned against a live oak that must have been fifteen feet in circumference, the sole of his right shoe resting on the bark, a burning cigarette at his side.

"How's things?" I asked.

Richard shrugged and grunted. He lifted his foot from the tree and extinguished what was left of the cigarette into the heel of his boot. Then he discarded the butt onto the ground.

I'd never liked my brother-in-law. He was selfish and lazy, had been that way for the nineteen years he'd been married to Leah. And I hated the way he yelled at her—not that Melanie and I didn't argue, but we were never as condescending or disrespectful as he was to my sister. The bottom line was that Richard wasn't the man I would have chosen for Leah. Sadly, I believed she had reached the same conclusion.

I moved away and sat under the canopy of a water oak. As I settled onto the cool, shaded grass, I tried to wrap my head around the previous session with Dr. Mike. Once I had let slip the information about half-considering suicide, he harangued me for the longest time. How long had I felt like this? What will I do when I feel the same way in the future? Then Dr. Mike fetched Kellen, and we spent a long time discussing *The Future*. "You should never forget the past," Dr. Mike told us, "but you guys will only heal by working together and looking ahead." Easy for him to say.

"Who's ready for a picnic?" Leah called as everyone exited the nature center. She gave me a long look which made me self-conscious about having sat under a tree instead of looking at the snake. Then as we walked back to our cars, she pulled me aside. "Jack, can you at least pretend to enjoy your son's company?"

"I wasn't doing anything different than your husband."

"Give me a break." She leaned closer. "I expect more from you."

We found an empty table at the picnic area. The kids carried grocery bags of snacks and supplies, and Richard wheeled an ice chest to the spot.

"Boys," Leah said, "I know you're hungry, but first we're gonna work up our appetites with a hike around the lake. You can have a fried apple pie and a juice box to take with you, and I'll pack a couple of bottled waters. Marissa, you coming?"

"You know I hate this place."

"You don't like anything we do as a family."

"That's because it's a stupid family."

"Watch your mouth. Stay here and sulk for all I care." Leah sighed.

"I'll start the grill while you four take your walk," Richard announced. It was the longest sentence he had uttered so far, but I knew he wasn't being noble. Hiking with his wife and kids would be way too much effort for Richard, and I was confident he'd just lie around in our absence, doing nothing constructive while the charcoal turned to embers without his assistance.

Leah ignored him, filled her backpack with granola bars and bottled water, and strode away from the picnic table. I followed her to a narrow gravel path.

"I wish people would learn that life is for living," she muttered.

"Where did you say that lake was?" I asked, trying to lighten her mood.

She looped a pair of binoculars around her neck. "Right there, on the other side of those tall reeds."

"I don't see anything."

"Keep walking."

The four of us hiked a few hundred yards before we came upon a stretch of water fifty feet across. A white bird with a curved, orange beak stood in the water and probed for food.

Kellen tapped my arm. "Look, it's got a crooked beak."

"That's an ibis," Leah explained. "We're gonna see a lot of birds along the trail."

"Where's the lake?" I asked again, refusing to believe this could be a forty-five minute hike.

She swept her arms in front of her. "Just past those trees. Most of it we can't see, but we'll still be able to see a lot of birds and animals up close. Look in the water and near the shore—you may see a gator's head."

Trevor whispered something to Kellen, then said, "We want to go look for alligators." Leah nodded, and they darted ahead.

"Stay on the trail, you two!" I called. "Be careful."

Leah and I walked in silence for several minutes before she said, "I'm worried about you and Kellen."

"We're fine."

"I don't think so."

"I used to say we had our bad days and our worse days. Now we're having good days and bad days. That's an improvement."

"You two still seeing Dr. Mike?"

"Yeah. I just don't want to talk about it."

She let the matter drop, but slung her arm around my shoulder like she used to do when we walked to school together. We continued walking like that, big sister and little brother, until we stopped at a wooden pier that jutted over the lake. We leaned over the railing and startled three turtles that had been sunning themselves on a log.

A shriek pierced the afternoon quiet. I knew immediately that it came from Kellen. I took off running.

Another loud shout sounded from the trail ahead. Fifty yards in the distance, Kellen stood on a fallen log and pointed toward the lake.

"What's wrong, Kellen?" I asked, gulping breaths as I sprinted toward him.

"It's an alligator, Dad. It's huge!"

He pointed across the water to a greyish-black, seven-foot reptile, which lay motionless on the ground on the far bank some forty feet away. Its long snout was covered with twigs and leaves as if intentionally camouflaged.

"You're screaming because you saw an alligator? Don't ever scare me like that! I thought you were hurt." My heart wouldn't stop pounding.

"Isn't he awesome? I can't wait to tell everyone at school."

Great idea. And make sure to tell them you sound like a little girl when you get excited.

Within five minutes, we encountered a half-dozen more alligators, including two juveniles resting near the shoreline and a menacing adult floating some thirty feet out, with only its nostrils and the top of its head protruding from the water. I could see Kellen's eyes light up with each sighting, and he made sure to flash me the running count—we were up to seven fingers.

A slow-moving crowd of people walked ahead of us along the trail. As we approached, I noticed they were accompanied by a park ranger. She wore a khaki shirt and a green baseball cap with an official-looking patch above the bill.

"That's a yellow-crowned night heron," she told the group, extending her walking stick toward the opposite shore, where a slate-grey bird stood at the water's edge. The bird was streaked white across its face and several long, light-colored plumes grew out the back of its dark head as if it were some sort of aquatic porcupine. "He's one of my favorites. The feathers on his head look like a crown."

She turned and I could clearly see her face. I recognized her right away—Dr. Renee Lincoln.

I'm not sure why, but I stopped dead in my tracks. Kellen, who'd been flanking me the past few minutes, ran into my hip and fell onto the ground. "Ow, Dad. What did you do that for?"

I leaned over and whispered, "Sorry about that, buddy. And use your inside voice."

"But we're outside, Dad," he said, his voice louder than before.

I peeked over to where the doctor—the park ranger—stood. It didn't make any sense, but I didn't want her to see us.

"There are more than two hundred species of birds in the park," she said, seemingly unaware of our presence. "Many of them stop here during their migration to and from Central America and the tropics." She turned in our direction. "Can you folks hear me back there?"

Startled, I dropped to a knee behind the crowd and found myself face-to-face with Kellen. He gave me a *what-are-you-doing-down-here* look, so I untied—then re-tied—his shoelaces. "You're all good now," I told him, patting him on the shoulders, and he gawked back at me like I was crazy.

"Dad!" Kellen yelled and pulled at my arm. "Look who's here. It's my doctor. Hey, Dad!"

I swallowed hard and forced a smile. As I slowly stood, Kellen frantically waved his arms. "Doctor! It's me, Kellen. I've already seen seven alligators!"

Her face registered confusion and then, a moment later, comprehension. Her mouth turned up in a crooked smile.

"There's another gator up here," shouted a kid carrying a fishing pole. "He's swimming!"

That news caused a minor commotion and everyone surged forward, including Kellen, Trevor, and Leah. I suddenly found myself alone with Dr. Lincoln. "Hello," I said awkwardly.

"You guys made it out here. I'm glad. How's Kellen?"

"Um . . . good. He's seeing a therapist."

"Excellent."

A warm rush filled my cheeks. "Thanks for all your help, Dr. Lincoln."

"Please. I'm not on call today. My name's Renee. Sorry, I forgot yours."

"Jack," I replied tentatively, as if I was unsure of my own name. "But I'm confused. You're a park ranger?"

Renee glanced at her group, which was moving farther away. "Gotta go," she said. "Come on." She touched my shoulder, slightly nudging me, and I felt a wave of energy pulse through my body. Just like in her office. She strolled away and I couldn't help but follow. Because something about seeing her made me feel, well . . . squeezy.

I watched her glide through the crowd and step up on an old stump. "Cool alligator, huh? For those of you just joining our hike, my name's Renee, and I'm one of the weekend volunteers here at Brazos Bend. We lead hikes, fill the water jugs on the trail, and run the nature center."

"Why doesn't he swim underwater?" asked the boy with the fishing pole.

"Because alligators are reptiles, and reptiles have lungs. He has to stay above the surface to breathe."

I couldn't wrap my head around why I felt so weird. Maybe it was seeing Renee—Dr. Lincoln, I told myself—someplace other than her office.

We stayed with Renee's group for another ten minutes as she pointed out various birds, turtles, and trees. I liked how animated she became while answering questions, her little hand gestures as she talked, the way her eyes danced.

"Enjoy the rest of your day," Renee told us, stopping next to a wooden stand with a red sign that read *Water*. "If you want details about the park's volunteer program, check the nature center."

"Dad, is the hike over?"

"I guess so. Leah, how long before we reach our picnic table?"

"Maybe ten, fifteen minutes. Why?"

"Nothing. Y'all go ahead. I'll catch up."

The water station was nothing more than an elevated plywood enclosure that housed two large jugs. I pulled a paper cup from a dispenser and pressed the button. Several drops trickled out of the spigot. Then nothing.

"If you can wait," Renee said, "cold water's on the way."

I nodded, then crumpled the paper cup and tossed it into the trash can. Maybe spending a couple minutes talking with her would make me feel less weird. "I wanted to thank you for that toy alligator you gave Kellen."

"That's the least I could do. He was so distraught. I . . . I didn't know about your wife."

"Of course you didn't," I said, motioning dismissively with my hand. "Not the first time for us, I can assure you."

Renee looked at my mangled hand but didn't say anything. Finally, she told me, "I'm glad you brought Kellen here. The park is so relaxing. Should be good for him."

She was right—Kellen seemed more relaxed than he'd been in a long time. The park was starting to have the same effect on me. "I'd never really known about Brazos Bend," I said. "So quiet and peaceful. Not like Houston, or even Sugar Land."

"That's why I like it here. You mind if we sit for a minute? I've been going all day."

I followed her to a wooden bench at the lake's edge. Although hardwood trees heavily shaded this part of the trail, a single shaft of sunlight pierced through the canopy of branches and leaves, illuminating the lone bench. I could feel the warm sunshine on my back almost immediately.

Renee took off her ballcap, wiped her brow with a bandana she'd pulled from her pants pocket, and then swept her hair back behind the ears. "Sometimes I come out here at dusk," she said. "You think it's peaceful now? Wait 'til the sun goes down and no one's on the trail."

"I wouldn't come out here at night." I thought of the lonely nights I'd spent inside my own home. Even with the safety provided by brick and stone, nighttime was never peaceful.

"You worry too much." She rolled her eyes—they were brown and black-flecked, like the shells of ripe pecans—and shook her head. "The more you know about something, the less scary it is."

"I'll keep that in mind."

"Nature, for example. You ever do any birding?"

"Not really." My birding prowess was limited to three easily identified species: the cardinal, the blue jay, and the bald eagle. "But I do like birds."

"Just keep your eyes open and pay attention to the details. You can learn all sorts of things." She pulled on her cap then raised a pair of binoculars that hung around her shoulders. "You see that flock of about a dozen birds in the water?"

"Uh-huh." I wasn't looking at the birds but at Renee. Beneath her chestnut hair, I could see a red mark on the back of her neck. A hickey.

I couldn't believe it. A hickey. On such a nice lady like her.

"They have long red bills and pink legs. And they have a white circle around each eye. See it?"

I turned away, embarrassed at what I'd noticed on her neck.

"Here. Try these." She handed me the binoculars.

The hickey was so obvious now; I couldn't help but stare. It was dark red and shaped like the state of California. But the more

I looked at it, the more it reminded me of the dark salmon patches on Kellen's forehead when he was born. *Angel kisses*, Melanie had called them—they'd disappeared after his first birthday. I took another look at Renee and realized the red splotch on her neck was just a birthmark. I felt like an idiot.

"Jack?"

"Uh . . . yeah?"

"You zoned out on me. Am I boring you with my description of Black-bellied Whistling ducks?"

I shook my head to clear it. *Pay attention to the details, Jack. Learn something.* "Boring?" I said. "Not at all. Wait, you didn't just call those Black-bellied Whistling ducks, did you?"

"Yep."

"You're messing with me, right?" I said with a smile. "That's not a real bird. Just like on the hike, what'd you call that? Yellow herring crown?"

"Yellow-crowned night heron." She pointed at the water. "Okay, so there's our Black-bellied Whistling ducks. And over there, I see a snowy egret and some anhinga and a grebe—"

"You're making up all these names," I said, laughing. "They sound ridiculous!"

She smiled impishly. "It's actually a Pied-bill grebe." Her smile widened. "Okay, you're right, they sound ridiculous."

We stayed on the bench and Renee continued to chatter about her love of the outdoors. I was really enjoying myself—sitting on the bench with her, talking with her, making up bird names with her. I couldn't remember the last time I'd felt so comfortable talking with someone.

"Hey, Jack," she said, peering into the moss at the edge of the lake. "Can you help? Someone's dropped a plastic bottle into the water. It's right there, underneath the pier."

"A gator's not gonna get me, right?" I said, smiling broadly. I knelt down at the shore and reached for the bottle, but it was too far away. I braced myself with my right hand on the pier and leaned farther over the water. I was able to grab the bottle, but when I pushed off the wood, a protruding nail snagged the underside of my wrist. I jerked back and yelped.

"You're bleeding," Renee said.

"It's nothing."

"No, you're hurt." She led me to the water station and produced a first aid kit, then sat me down. "Let me see your hand."

I reluctantly showed it to her. A four-inch scratch ran from the middle of my palm to just past my wrist. On my screwed-up hand, of course.

Renee cleaned the wound with an antiseptic wipe, applied an antibiotic ointment, and taped it down with gauze. "You need to get a tetanus shot if you're not up to date." Then she ran her fingers along the back of my hand toward the old injury. "What happened?"

"Long time ago," I said, trying to pull my hand away. "I don't like to talk about it."

As she gently examined my gnarled fingers, I found myself remembering the day I'd hurt them. The old baseball field, Tate Gillum, the fight—the images were as fresh as the day it all happened. No one knew the whole story, not even Melanie.

Just then, a dust-covered utility vehicle pulled up, driven by an old lady wearing one of those volunteer ballcaps. Two big orange Igloo jugs stood in the bed of the vehicle. "They need someone to lead the Creekfield hike," the old lady called to Renee. "You available?"

"Sure. Give me a minute to change out the water jugs." Renee moved to the water station box, turned a key in the lock, and opened the hasp. I noticed she wore no ring on her left hand, although I'm not sure why I even looked for one. She pulled the two empty jugs from the box and placed them next to the idling utility vehicle.

"Let me help," I said, reaching into the bed of the vehicle to grab a replacement jug.

"No, I got it."

"They're too heavy."

She seized my arm. "I move these by myself all the time. Let me do it."

Ignoring her, I yanked on the side handles of the water jug. I raised the cooler out of the bed and, as if to prove how strong I was, lifted it higher so my elbows locked. In weightlifting, it's called the clean and jerk.

"Not like that," she said. "Be careful!"

Standing there with fifty pounds above my head, I felt my arms tremble. I wished I'd paid attention to the cooler before lifting it, how heavy it was, how loosely its plastic lid fit on top. When I turned, the lid dislodged and knocked me on the head. Startled, I lost my grip.

And six gallons of ice-cold water spilled over Renee.

Chapter 16

When I was in fourth grade, my best friend Larry Wayne Tucker tossed me into a pond during Christmas break. We were goofing around at his family's farm, throwing rocks across the water, trying to reach the far shore. Out of nowhere—or maybe it had something to do with me calling him a sissy—Larry Wayne shoved me. I flew off the end of the dock and into the frigid pond.

The instant Renee was drenched by ice water, she had the same reaction I had thirty years ago. She emitted an involuntary gasp and then when she caught her breath, shrieked so loudly that birds scattered. She whirled and faced me.

"What were you thinking?" she spluttered. "I told you I'd do it myself!" She picked up her cap and tugged it on.

I wanted to apologize, but when she looked at me with those *you-betrayed-me* eyes, water dripping from her sodden, sideways ballcap, I began to giggle.

"You think this is funny?"

"I didn't mean to . . ." I tried to sound serious and contrite, but my giggles gave way to belly laughter.

Renee marched away, her sneakers making squishy noises on the hard gravel path. She jumped into the passenger seat of the vehicle and crossed her arms.

The old lady volunteer pointed at me. "Mister, you're a real jerk." Then she tossed the empty water jugs into the vehicle's bed and sped away. Renee didn't look back. I stopped laughing.

After lunch I lay on a blanket, listening to the creaks of swaying branches and to the crunch of bicycle tires on the gravel path. I couldn't help but think how I'd ruined such a great time with Renee. If only I hadn't tried to act so macho. I just wanted another chance to make things right.

At some point, I fell into the edge of sleep and remembered one of the last picnics that Leah and I shared with our parents, a year or so before she ran off with Richard. We were in the Hill Country, somewhere around New Braunfels along the Comal River. It was one of those Norman Rockwell days—Mom had prepared fresh potato salad and Dad had grilled up steaks. We played spades on a checkered tablecloth and talked about the future. It was one of the happiest moments of my childhood.

I heard the rustling of feet next to me and then whispered voices. "Dad, are you asleep? Trevor and I want to play catch."

I peeked an eye open. "Go ahead."

"No, we want to play with you. I brought my glove, remember?"

"I'm taking a nap."

"Come on, Dad. It'll be fun."

I'd played enough catch with Kellen to know it would never be fun. It was bad enough throwing the ball around in the privacy of our backyard; I certainly didn't want to do it in a public park. "You two start without me." I rolled over and closed my eyes tight.

A minute later, I felt a sharp kick to my thigh. "They're

waiting," Leah said. "Get up and play with them."

"I don't even have a glove. And I got this bandage on my throwing hand."

"Stop making excuses. Come on, the boys just want to hang out with you. Take it as a compliment. Maybe you can teach them something. You're the big baseball nut." She stuck out her tongue at me. "Emphasis on nut."

I trudged to where Kellen and Trevor were throwing ground balls to each other. "So, who's up for a little catch?"

"Told you he'd play with us," Kellen said, then underhanded the ball in my direction and ran over next to his cousin. "We're throwing grounders."

"I see that. Gotta keep your butt down, though, or the ball will roll through your legs. Okay, show me what you've got." Aiming toward Trevor, I sidearmed the baseball and flicked it along the top of the grass.

Trevor shuffled to his right and fielded the ball between his feet, his manner as natural as a player who'd been around the game all his life. He instinctively rotated his shoulders and zipped a return throw which stung my fingers.

"Whoa! Take it easy. Do you see a glove on my hand?" I smiled, then signaled Kellen and rolled a much slower ground ball toward him. He dropped to his knees and smothered it, as if falling on a live grenade. "No, Kel. You need to let the ball roll into your glove."

"I am."

"No, you're not. Do it like Trevor."

Kellen crossed his arms and pouted. This was exactly why I didn't want to play catch.

I tossed grounders for maybe fifteen minutes, with half that time dedicated to demonstrating the correct fielding stance. Surprisingly, Kellen seemed to have improved—at least he kept his knees bent and didn't swat at the ball.

When Trevor said, "Fire it to me, Uncle Jack," I snapped off a throw that landed in his glove and sounded with a *thwip*. It wasn't a serious fastball by any means—Trevor was barely nine—but I hadn't thrown a ball without an arc in forever. It felt wonderful.

"Now me," Kellen said. "I want to catch the Cannon."

"You sure?"

He grinned and pounded his mitt. "Fastball, baby."

My throw couldn't have been any harder than the one I delivered to Trevor, but it was definitely faster than anything Kellen had ever seen. Above chest-high, not a perfect throw but catchable. He extended his arm, palm up, fingers down, and tried to track the ball, but it missed his glove and bounced off his left shoulder. He crumpled to his knees and yowled.

I gave him a quick once-over and determined he wasn't injured. My right hand, however, stung like hell and the bloody bandage hung loosely from my wrist. "You're okay," I told him. "Shake it off." I picked up the ricocheted ball and helped Kellen to his feet. Then I ripped off the remainder of my bandage.

He wiped his eyes with the hem of his t-shirt. "You threw it too hard."

"Maybe you should learn how to catch." I dropped the ball into Kellen's glove pocket. "Stop crying. You're not hurt." Then I walked back to my original position opposite the boys.

Kellen reared back and fired the baseball over my head. "Maybe you should learn how to throw!" He slammed his glove to the ground and stormed off.

I ran after him, grabbed him by the shoulders, and yanked him to a stop. "You're not a baby. Stop acting like one."

He wriggled under my grip. "Leave me alone!"

"Look, I'm sorry the ball hit you—"

"You're not sorry. You wanted to hit me."

I gave an exasperated sigh. "Why would I want to hit you?"

"Because you don't love me." He lifted his eyes and stared right through me. "Mommy always told me she loved me. But you never say it."

His accusation knocked me on my heels, and I let go of his arms. Melanie had once said the same thing, that I didn't express my love to Kellen, that I created the same emotional distance with my son as my father had with me.

"You never say it, Dad," he repeated. "Come on, one time. Tell me you love me."

"Settle down or I swear I'll give you a spanking you won't forget."

"See, you don't love me. You hate me."

"I don't hate you."

"Well, I hate you. It's your fault that Mommy's not here." He pounded his fists against my chest. "I wish you had died instead of her!"

<hr>

For the rest of the weekend, I replayed our trip to the state park. It seemed I'd screwed up everything. Renee Lincoln thought I was a jerk. Leah thought I was a bad father. And Kellen . . . I couldn't believe how much he blamed me, how much he hated me.

On Sunday, Kellen and I stayed on different floors of the house. The only time we saw each other was when I cooked— okay, burned—grilled cheese sandwiches for lunch and when we went to McDonald's for dinner. Our conversation was limited to grunts punctuated with icy stares.

I couldn't wait for Monday to arrive.

That next morning, I drove Kellen and Mitchell to school,

then fought horrendous rush-hour traffic into work. I pulled into the Gemini Devices parking garage forty-five minutes later than usual and found it half empty. Had I missed an email about an off-site meeting?

The elevator, which stank of mildew and bleach, carried me to the third floor. I stepped out into utter chaos. Boxes cluttered the desk of our executive admin, Deb, the most organized person I knew. Her computer monitor was unplugged and facing backwards. The walls which normally held framed brochures of our newest technology were bare except for empty nails.

What the hell?

I passed Scott's office and read his whiteboard: *Thanks a lot, assholes.* "What's going on?" I asked.

"You miss the big announcement?" He glanced at his watch and scoffed. "Of course you did. You're late."

"What announcement?"

"Look around. Figure it out. They just laid off thirty percent of the company."

"You gotta be kidding me. Were you one of the—" I stopped mid-sentence and reread his dry-erase board. "Man, I'm sorry."

Scott poured a drawerful of office supplies into a Xerox box. "You better go find out if you still have a job."

I rushed to my office, a hollow feeling spreading in my gut. My laptop docking station was still there. No note saying "*See me.*" I exhaled with relief, then headed back to talk to Scott.

Martin Eckersley stood in the hallway. Martin was a mealymouth bean-counter who'd been promoted as my boss six months ago. He didn't know the first thing about sales or medicine. He only knew debits and credits, receivables and account aging reports. I'm not sure whether it was his thin mustache—which reminded me of that freaky director John Waters—or his proclivity for accounting, but Martin Eckersley gave me the willies.

"Jack," he said. "I need to talk to you."

☙

By ten o'clock, I was driving home, the trunk of my Hyundai filled with two boxes of personal items, plus the laptop that Martin somehow allowed me to keep. The knotted stomach from getting laid off had given way to a pounding heartbeat that I could sense in my ears and see pulsing on my neck in the rearview mirror. My jaw clenched. I couldn't believe I'd worked six years for them, and the bastards had the nerve to hire a security guard to escort me to my car.

I passed Kellen's school and wondered how I'd break the news to him. Then I thought of how he'd react, probably like my father had when I flunked out of college, a look of disdain etched on his face. *You're a loser. Always have been.*

When I got home, I dumped the boxes onto my bedroom floor, then sifted through their contents, wanting to get this whole thing over with. I didn't need to keep any reminders of what Gemini had done to me. First, I extracted a box of my business cards—didn't need those anymore—and lobbed them into the trash can. I plucked out a commendation plaque that Gemini had presented to me during the company anniversary party three years ago and wondered why I'd brought the stupid thing home. I thought about chucking it as well, but then I closed my eyes and remembered the look of pride on Melanie's face when I'd received the award. I set the plaque on my bed.

Then I pulled out a pair of framed photographs. The first was a kindergarten photo of a gap-toothed Kellen, taken a week after he lost both of his front teeth. The other was a picture of Melanie that I'd taken the afternoon I proposed. In the photo, she sat on the railing of a gazebo, her legs crossed at the ankles, a half-carat diamond on her hand. I'd always been grateful I'd captured the look on her face—part joy, part shock—after I'd given her the ring box. I cradled the photograph to my chest.

Everything's falling apart, I thought. I had a wonderful wife—gone. I had a steady job—gone. And Kellen—not gone yet, but slipping away.

I looked back at Melanie's photograph. This was all her fault. She'd abandoned us. I slammed the photo on the nightstand. The blow shattered the glass and shot out daggers onto the bedspread and into the carpet. When I flipped over the frame, Melanie smiled at me through the cracked glass, the image eerily reminiscent of my view through her smashed windshield. "I didn't mean it!" I cried. Tears streamed down my face as I picked out jagged shards of glass from the frame, slicing my fingers. "I'm sorry, Melanie. I'm so sorry . . ."

Ever since she died, I'd been looking for someone to blame. Not just an impersonal car manufacturer or tire company or road designer. I had searched my broken family, alternately accusing Melanie, Kellen, and myself. But this wasn't our fault. We were the victims.

I finally knew who to blame: God. He wasn't just a hands-off caretaker of the world. He meddled. He screwed up people's lives. Like that pitcher in high school, God threw curveballs I couldn't handle, and He was laughing at me.

Chapter 17

When I awoke on New Year's Day, a part of me thought things would be different. That the nightmare of the previous seven months would have disappeared. That Kellen wouldn't be so trying. That I wouldn't be so dissatisfied with my life.

But as I lay on the carpet next to Leah's couch, my head throbbing because of last night's party horns and countless glasses of champagne—plus a tall glass of vodka splashed with orange juice after everyone else went to bed—I knew that simply flipping the calendar wouldn't change things. There is a certain clarity that sets in when the clock strikes midnight and you're the only one at the party without someone to kiss.

Leah and Richard tumbled out of their bedroom. She headed for the kitchen; he headed for the TV. "You look terrible," she told me.

I managed a wan smile. "Happy New Year to you, too."

While I attempted to figure out which football teams were playing in the bowl game that Richard had turned on, Leah made cleaning-up noises in the kitchen. She emptied the dishwasher; she filled the dishwasher. I heard the crunch of trash being compacted and the clink of glass bottles being collected. I wondered vaguely if I should help her. Then I felt a plastic champagne flute whack me in the back of the head.

"You gonna help?" she said.

I gathered dirty plates from the living room and carried them into the kitchen. Leah stood at the island and knifed off a slab of chocolate cake, then without use of a fork, scarfed it down in three gulps. "So much for my New Year's resolution," she said.

"You swearing off cake?"

"I need to lose twenty pounds." She turned her head toward the other room as Richard cheered something in the game. Then she rolled her eyes and whispered, "Sometimes I think I'd be better off losing two hundred pounds."

I didn't know what to say, so I began rinsing the dirty plates.

"What about you?" she said. "Any resolutions?"

I thought about what I'd written down during my last session with Dr. Mike. I'd skipped the usual nonsense like exercising more and paying off my credit cards. My resolutions were more basic: discover what made Kellen tick, rebuild something that resembled a life, find joy. But I couldn't tell Leah about those. Instead I told her, "I don't know, maybe get better organized."

"Give me a break. Maybe you should make a resolution about Kellen."

"Like what?"

"He wants to—needs to—spend time with you. And you need to spend more time with him." She walked to the refrigerator and retrieved a newspaper article she'd cut out and affixed to the door. She handed it to me. "Little League signups are this weekend. This says they're looking for volunteer coaches and managers."

"So?"

"So maybe you should sign up to be Kellen's coach."

I folded the article and stuffed it in my wallet. "We'll see."

"You're not even considering it, are you?"

I smiled weakly. "We'll see."

❧

On the first Saturday of the new year, Kellen and I bundled up in heavy coats and drove to the baseball park. We walked beneath a banner that read *Sugar Meadow Little League* and past a sign that bore the message *SMLL—Real Baseball.* I always got a kick out of that sign, because the people I saw in our Little League didn't appreciate the fundamentals or subtleties of the game. They measured the quality of their baseball experience by the cost of their equipment and the prestige of their private instructor.

"I want to be pitcher this year," Kellen said. "Just like you."

"No one pitches at your age. They use a pitching machine. Remember that thing with the wheel?"

He hunched his shoulders. "Then I want to be first baser. Or second baser. Not catcher. Derek says you have to wear some ball thing in your pants."

"I don't think you'll be playing catcher."

We stopped in front of the complex's main diamond, the one with the fancy bleachers and the spacious dugouts, the one where the *big kids* played. Caution tape lined the chain-link fence. Inside, a fat guy wearing a navy SMLL ballcap and matching windbreaker pushed an edger along the baseline, spraying a cloud of grass clippings and red clay. The temperature was barely forty degrees, but the fat man's face was covered with sweat, dirt, and dead grass. Then he hopped onto a small tractor called a Gator and drove across the infield dirt, dragging some device that tilled the soil. Games wouldn't start for two months, but Sugar Meadow Little League was already a hotbed of activity.

Temporary signs staked along the sidewalk pointed us to the Little League office. We passed through a steel door that was propped open with a five-gallon bucket filled with used baseballs and entered a cramped room with a dozen other parents and wannabe major-leaguers.

After waiting in line for ten minutes, I found myself face-to-face with a leathery-skinned woman whose expressionless gaze suggested a Botox fetish. "My son wants to sign up for baseball," I said.

"Has he played here before?"

"Yeah. Last year he—"

"Over there." She pointed to another table.

Wondering where she parked her broom, I moved to the other line and eventually registered Kellen.

"That'll be a hundred and thirty dollars," said a man who sported long, brown sideburns and had a thick coat of back hair creeping out of his shirt collar. After I gave him the check, he introduced himself. "Taylor Ferguson. I'm league president. You interested in doing some coaching or managing with us?"

"Nah. Just want to root for the team."

"My dad played baseball in high school," Kellen said. "He was the Cannon."

Taylor Ferguson arched an eyebrow and focused intently on me, as if he were watching a fishing bobber dance in the water, just waiting to set the hook. "Kids would sure learn a lot from someone who's played before."

"Appreciate it, but, uh . . ." I cleared my throat and scratched my head, unable to think of a comeback. Back in the old days, I could at least trot out the *Work-is-so-hectic* excuse.

"I'm not saying you have to be the manager. Maybe just help out a little as a coach."

I looked at Kellen, who smiled up at me with puppy-dog eyes. I gave a sigh and said, "Guess I could help."

Two weeks later, Taylor Ferguson called to remind me of the

managers meeting three days away. "We're still working on identifying all the managers," he said. "It'd be great if you could just attend the meeting. We wouldn't want your son's team to be out of the loop, would we?"

A week after that, he called to advise me of player tryouts on Saturday. "Your son's team needs someone to evaluate the kids. I think I have someone who can manage your team, but he hasn't given me a final answer. He is definitely gone this weekend, though. Thanks for helping out."

The night before tryouts, Taylor called again. "Looks like we're going to need you to tag team with somebody. Glad we can count on you, Jack."

I must confess that I fell for Taylor Ferguson's misinformation and false assurances every step of the way, never imagining it was an elaborate ruse to sucker in yet another first-time manager. But as the reality sank in, I discovered I was actually looking forward to getting out on the field again. Probably no one was more qualified from a baseball perspective—I played well into my senior year of high school and was talented enough that scouts from the Southwest Conference came to watch me pitch.

What was the big deal anyway? Teaching a bunch of third graders how to throw, run, and hit would be easy. And I was one of the few Sugar Land parents who didn't buy into all the spoon-fed ideas of diversity, tolerance, and self-esteem. A few months with me and these kids would understand what baseball was all about.

Oh, and the winning team would receive a huge trophy.

On the morning of tryouts, I showed up at the field fifteen

minutes ahead of time. It was obvious the other seven managers had been there a while, as they rested on lawn chairs outside the third base dugout, clipboards and laptops at the ready, bags of sunflower seeds open at their feet. I didn't have a clipboard, a chair, or the first clue how tryouts were supposed to work.

A lanky man wearing a burnt-orange baseball cap leaned back in his chair and adjusted his sunglasses. "You the other manager?" he asked me.

"Guess so."

He extended his hand. "Clay Baxter."

I gave him a quick wave but no handshake. "Jack Kennedy."

He snickered. "Well, that's easy."

"What?"

"Oh, I'm just a nickname guy. That's my thing. Like Taylor Ferguson—he's Big Fuzzy. Dusty Phillips. Gumbo LeJeune. You know Chuck Moretti, the head of groundskeeping?" He pointed to the fat guy I'd seen at signups. "Everyone calls him Ground Chuck. That's one of mine."

Clay Baxter seemed nice enough, but he reminded me of every slick glad-hander that ended up in sales because he thought schmoozing was a career.

"You get roped into this, too?" I said.

"Nah. I've been coaching Little League for eight, nine years. I've got two older boys. Managed their All-Star teams. See that sign over there? We took district and area both years. Nick's my youngest, but he's probably the best of the bunch."

Ground Chuck walked up carrying a stack of papers. "Here's your tryout list. Rate 'em however you want. Draft is Tuesday night in the league office. I need to know who already has a coach of record."

Everyone's hand went up except mine.

Clay Baxter snorted. "You need to get a running mate, Mister

President."

A smattering of overheard conversations plus Ground Chuck's score sheet helped me decipher the tryout process. Apparently the kids would rotate through several positions, fielding fly balls, grounders, and thrown balls, then take five swings off the pitching machine. I looked to the outfield where all the kids gathered along the fence. I didn't see Kellen.

"Number thirty-four," Ground Chuck hollered, and the first player raced to his spot.

A volunteer loaded a baseball into the feeder chute of a pitching machine, which had been rotated to shoot the ball into the sky. It sailed high over the boy's head. Instinctively, he backpedaled then drop-stepped then sprinted his way to the ball, covering fifty feet in no time flat. He slid and caught the ball over his shoulder. Willie Mays would've been impressed. I know I was.

"Now that's a ballplayer." I searched the score sheet so I could flag this one as a keeper.

"Don't get too excited," Clay Baxter said. "You can't have him."

I shot him a look and mumbled, "We'll see about that." I ran my finger down the page and found number thirty-four. I think I knew the name before I read it: Nick Baxter.

"Wait 'til you see him bat. His hitting instructor used to play with the Red Sox. Told me to buy that new Easton bat. Four hundred bucks, but you gotta buy the best, right?"

I didn't say anything but watched the rest of Nick's tryout with a sense of envy that was at *seven-deadly-sins* level. The kid had it all: rocket arm, soft hands, and a sweet swing that made Ken Griffey, Jr. look like a hack. I hoped Kellen could at least field a grounder without having it ricochet off his shin.

Ground Chuck whistled to alert the next player. "Number sixty-three!"

Clay Baxter leaned over and whispered, "This kid's a keeper. He has a GLM."

"GLM?" I knew baseball acronyms like ERA and RBI, but this was a new one.

"Good looking mom," he explained. "When in doubt, go for the eye candy. My friend says he always drafts a team mom, a dad with a pitching machine, someone who can host a pool party, and as many GLMs as possible. He doesn't even care if the boys can play."

The kids soon blended together, and I didn't bother putting names to the players anymore. An hour had passed, and there were only two or three good ballplayers in the bunch, along with a number of crappy ones and a handful of horrible players. No one could draft a team from this group.

When Mitchell Flint took his turn, he was as gawky and clumsy as I expected, but he looked like he could hit for power if he ever connected. I didn't see Stacy. She was probably lost in the sea of moms and dads standing along the fence, everybody worried their son's precious career was going to be derailed by a poor tryout. I figured I'd draft Mitchell, though, since he was a known quantity and had one of the most important qualities for a Little Leaguer, a major league GLM.

We were down to the last ten players to try out.

"Is this kid yours, Mister President?"

I didn't answer, too embarrassed to admit the truth. The last thing I wanted to do was engage Clay Baxter in a duel using our kids' talents—or flaws—as weapons. I pretended to be in deep thought with my tryout list but peeked over my sunglasses to the outfield, where Kellen promptly missed both popups. He didn't look like a complete dweeb, just another kid playing a sport for which he had no aptitude. At shortstop, he actually made a decent stop of one grounder and threw a rainbow to first base.

Kellen ran to the dugout to find a bat, then strode to the plate wearing a beat-up batting helmet. He banged his bat on the plate as if he were killing spiders. On the first two pitches, he came up empty, swinging late and completely missing.

Clay Baxter chuckled. I suddenly became interested in the materials used to construct the dugout. I couldn't wait for tryouts to be over.

On the third pitch, Kellen unleashed his typical swing, all arms and no hip rotation. The ball dribbled twenty feet from the plate. He swung and missed at the final two pitches with equally disgusting batting form and would have scored zero had I bothered writing it down.

Drafting the team took an entire evening. When I got to heaven, I was going to demand those three hours back.

All eight Peewee managers crowded together in the league office, score sheets and red pens and highlighters of every color scattered across the tables. League president Taylor Ferguson, in a tone reminiscent of a judge issuing jury instructions, explained the draft process. "No pressure, guys," he said, "but your choices tonight will shape how your season turns out."

The first round went as well as I could have hoped. I took Corey Griffin, the biggest stud I'd seen at tryouts. He snagged everything in the field and cranked line drives to the fence. Plus he ran like the wind. I put a smiley face next to his name.

Charlie Sanderson, Kellen's best friend since kindergarten, was on the board as I prepared to make my second-round selection. But Clay Baxter chose him before I had the chance. "That's my kid's friend," I said.

"What, you want me to just give him to you? That's not how a draft works, Mister President."

"I thought this was about the kids."

"Tell you what. I'll trade you—your son's friend for that Griffin kid."

"Screw you."

He laughed. "*That's* how a draft works." He motioned to the league president. "I'm taking Charlie Sanderson. The rest of you are gonna regret letting him fall to the second round."

As the draft continued, my biggest surprise was how much the other coaches already knew about the players. Other than Kellen and his friend Charlie, I recognized only a handful of his classmates, including Derek Leathers and Mitchell Flint. I probably picked those two sooner than they deserved, but I didn't want to end up with a bunch of strangers. And I harbored hope that maybe Kellen would appreciate the gesture.

After choosing my eleventh player, it became clear I'd be stuck with a real loser in the final round. My last pick would be a choice among the remaining five kids, two of whom didn't know which side of the plate to stand on. That left three: Kakazai, Ziang, and Williams.

The only notation on my score sheet for Tyler Williams, other than his grade of zero, was the word *clown*. I tried to remember if he'd been involved in all the horseplay. Then it hit me.

When Tyler Williams found himself in the outfield for the first baseball tryout of his life—his blue jeans and sweatshirt gave that away—he probably didn't realize he was supposed to field two pop flies. When the first ball flew into the sky, Tyler never saw it. Thankfully, the ball landed harmlessly twenty feet behind him. On his final attempt, he held out his glove and circled under the falling ball like a circus clown pretending to catch the acrobat. I cringed as the ball bounced off the top of his head and dropped him to his knees.

"Come on," Clay Baxter said. "Pick one."

So I used my keen baseball intuition and drafted Tyler Williams, because his name was pronounceable and I liked the circus.

I took a final look at the roster for the Peewee Dodgers. Corey Griffin. Derek Leathers. Mitchell Flint. A lot of boys I didn't know. Kellen. And in a moment of draft insanity, our neighbors Patrick and Stewart.

What had I done?

Chapter 18

By Saturday afternoon, the weather was still chilly, with highs in the mid-fifties, but the sky was sunny—it was a great day to practice baseball. I arrived thirty minutes early so I could pick up my team's equipment and subsequently lugged the heavy bag to the field.

I stood at the bleachers waiting for the parents and kids to arrive. If I had my way, I would have skipped the parent meeting altogether, but Taylor Ferguson had insisted managers distribute medical release forms and beg for a team sponsor. One thing I knew was that Gemini Devices wouldn't be sponsoring anyone this year.

"Coach, got a minute?"

I turned to face a black man with a shaved head—Derek's father. The deaf guy. In the months since we met in the school cafeteria, he'd grown a goatee that was flecked with patches of silver. He wore a grey sweatshirt that said *Texas Sports University*. I remembered he was a bigwig at that fancy sports complex. I remembered that he'd moved from Tennessee. I just couldn't remember his name.

"Need another coach?" he said. "Be happy to help."

I'd heard horror stories about fathers who volunteered to coach just so they could ensure their son played all the best positions. It didn't matter the level: Little League, high school, or beyond. Daddy-ball was the worst thing that ever happened to baseball.

"It's just practice," I said. "Don't need any help."

"If you say so . . . Hey, I remember you. We met at the school. It's Jack, right?"

"Uh-huh." All I could think was that I needed to figure out his name or I'd spend the rest of the season referring to him as Black Guy or Deaf Guy. "If you could grab a seat, we need to start."

Deaf Guy clambered up the bleachers. I scanned the other parents. The only friendly face I recognized was Stacy's; she huddled with two women drinking coffee and chatting like old friends. Another lady pushed a stroller and made goo-goo noises at whatever was inside. Captain Carl looked around nervously as if the galaxy were in peril.

A knot of boys played wall-ball at the concession stand, bouncing a tennis ball and racing to touch the brick wall. They were dressed in league-issued grey baseball pants and most wore an old jersey or t-shirt. Two of the kids—Patrick and Stewart, naturally—had elected to dress in the same personalized uniform: baseball pants and a shirt that read *SMeLLy—Real Baseball*. "You guys keep playing," I called. "This won't take long."

Then I addressed the parents. "I'm Jack Kennedy, your manager. Um . . . the league president wanted us to meet before practice . . . Here's a medical release form. Sign it. I'll be handing out a practice schedule next time. Games won't start for a month. And . . . uh . . . I guess that's about it."

The woman sitting next to Deaf Guy asked, "Do you want snacks after practices or just after games?"

"What are we supposed to do?"

"Our old league did snacks and drinks on game days. But not at practice."

"Sounds good to me." Actually, I thought the whole subject sounded ridiculous. We were here to play baseball, not throw a tea party. "Anything else?"

"Who's your team mom?" asked the woman with the stroller.

I'd completely forgotten. Just like you couldn't have high school football without cheerleaders, you couldn't have a kid's sports team without a team mom. "Congratulations," I said. "You're hired."

"No way. I've got a new baby."

It was bad enough getting tricked into managing. There was no way I was going to distribute snacks, organize parties, or hot-glue names on pennants. "We're going to need a team mom," I said, eyeing the parents.

The women averted their gaze. They knew casual eye contact could result in VD. Volunteer Disease. I'd seen it with Melanie; she used to get roped into everything.

"Somebody. Please."

Finally, Stacy raised her hand. "If no one else will . . ."

"Great. Meeting's over."

"Wait—what should we call you? Coach Jack?"

Maybe it was because I grew up in the country, but the idea of being on a first-name basis with everyone—Dr. Mike and Pastor Steve came to mind—was plain wrong. I'd been taught to respect my elders and that included calling them by their last name. I didn't want seven year olds calling me Coach Jack. But I didn't want to go by Coach Kennedy either, having been called President Kennedy too many times over the years.

"Just call me Coach K. Like that basketball coach at Duke."

"Dodgers, get a ball from the bucket and find a partner. Warm up your arms before we start." The boys ran to their bat bags, which were heaped outside the dugout. "And hang up those bags on the fence."

Everyone did what I said, except for a boy wearing a Jeff Bagwell jersey. He sat on the grass and pawed at the contents of his bag. I walked over and said, "You're name's Omkar, isn't it? What are you doing?" He replied something—it could have been English or Hindi—but I couldn't hear him. "Speak up."

"I said I don't have my glove."

"Is this how to get ready for baseball? You wouldn't go to school without pencils, would you?"

Omkar's lip quivered as he tried to form a reply, then the rest of his body joined in. "I'm sorry, Coach," he blubbered.

I heard parents walking by and felt a sense of panic. "Stop crying, Omkar. Let's find your glove. No tears, buddy." I pulled his bat bag onto my lap and rifled through it. No wonder he couldn't find his glove. The bag was jammed with extra shirts and cleats. I removed the clothing, plus a can of bug spray. It looked like someone had packed him for summer camp. Then I saw his glove. "Here. Go throw with somebody."

I looked up to find utter chaos on the field. The kids were arranged haphazardly across the infield, and errant throws were whizzing right and left.

"Hey, guys. Come on, do it right." They looked in my direction, clueless to what I wanted. "Look, it's not hard. Half of you line up on the baseline. The other six find a partner and spread out. That's too far, Kellen. No, that's too close."

The players finally lined up like I wanted but when they began to throw, everything fell apart again. No one—save Derek and the Griffin kid—could throw worth a darn. "Dodgers, come here and circle 'round."

"Do you want us to grab a knee?" someone asked.

"Yeah, grab a knee. Listen guys, I'll teach you about baseball, but you have to listen and work hard. We're going to start with throwing."

I dug into the team equipment bag and extracted a new baseball, hermetically sealed in a plastic bag. I ripped the bag open with my teeth and dropped the baseball into my right hand. It rolled across my palm, and my index and middle fingers spread reflexively across the red stitching. My crooked ring finger and deformed pinky pointed away from the ball as if they didn't want anything to do with it. Then I felt a familiar tingle in my fingertips—four-seam fastball.

I tugged on a catcher's mitt and pounded the ball deep into the pocket. "Let me show you guys how to throw this thing."

Fifteen minutes later, the players had finished warming up. Tyler Williams and Omkar needed a lot of work on their mechanics, but those two wouldn't be fixed in a day. Kellen was obviously hopeless. I looked to the outfield and saw several boys—Patrick, Stewart, and the gangly Luke Appleton—chasing each other in the outfield.

"Boys, get over here. Now!" What I needed was a whistle like my old high school coach used to blow. Coach Richter treated all his athletes like lower-ranked soldiers and used to bark commands when we ran our drills.

The Dodgers raced to where I stood and plopped onto the infield around the second base bag. I channeled Coach Richter and said, "On this team we won't have kids running around and not paying attention. Do you understand?"

No one answered. One of the twins scooped fine red dirt between his fingers and poured it onto second base.

"Stay out of the dirt, Stewart."

"I'm Patrick."

"Stay out of the dirt, Patrick."

I rubbed my temple. "I need everyone to run one lap around this field and think about how you should be practicing. Touch each of those yellow foul poles in the outfield. Go!"

As the boys ran their lap, I looked outside the fence. A number of parents had hung around, but I could read their body language. They were here to judge, not to help.

The boys slid into home plate as they finished their lap, except for Mitchell, who dragged in last, clutching his side. "Now get your gloves and line up at shortstop," I said. They ran to the left side of the infield and fanned out from third base to second base along the edge of the infield grass. "I need one line. Everyone get behind Ryan. Derek, go play first base."

Two boys jostled for the first position in line. Then I realized I had two Ryans: Ryan Baker and Ryan Tiefenbaum. "Baker, you go first. Teefen . . . Teethy . . . T-Bone, you're next. Everyone line up behind Baker and T-Bone. Play's at first. Nobody out."

I hit grounders for a long while, but it seemed I was wasting my time. The ones who could field couldn't throw, and the ones who could throw couldn't field. The exception was Corey. I'd been right about him—he was a stud. Based on what I saw, he was my new full-time shortstop.

"Coach K, I'm thirsty," Derek said.

"Everyone take a two-minute break. Don't goof around. Kellen, I want to talk to you."

"Yes, Dad?" he said as his teammates scampered away.

"I'm tired of you not hustling for the ball."

"I'm trying."

"Move your feet and bend down. Don't let any more ground balls get by you."

"But—"

"No buts, Kellen. Be a leader."

I devoted the last forty-five minutes to batting. It's more

accurate to say I devoted the last forty-five minutes to letting the boys stand around the field while I tossed pitches to kids who couldn't hit. When practice ended, I'd barely made it through half the team.

The boys circled around me a final time and, for once, didn't act silly. Even Patrick and Stewart looked sluggish. I felt exhausted as well, but launched into my post-practice speech.

"Dodgers, I saw some good things today. Corey, great job on infield. Appleton and Derek, you had a couple nice hits. Sorry we didn't get everyone a chance to bat. Spent more time with each person than I thought. Guys, we still have a lot of work to do to get ready for the season."

"Coach K, what happened to your hand?" T-Bone asked.

"Nothing that you'd care about. Everybody needs to stop talking and listen. Now, two more laps around the field."

The boys groaned, but took off toward the right field fence. I flexed my right hand to lessen the pain, then gathered my equipment and exited the dugout. The parents, who'd been so eager to hear everything I said at the team meeting, ignored me. The exception was Deaf Guy, and he was coming my way.

"Are you guys through, Jack?" he said. "I mean, Coach K."

"For today."

"You sure had your hands full out there. They had you outnumbered. If you reconsider bringing on a coach, let me know."

During the forty-five minutes I'd spent throwing batting practice, I'd wished for someone else to toss the ball so I could concentrate on fielding. But I didn't know if Derek's father was the right choice. I could just hear Clay Baxter laughing about how I had a disabled man helping me out. "Appreciate your interest," I said. "But how could you . . . you know . . . communicate?"

He pointed to his lips. "I'm a good listener."

I laughed. "I guess we could use a hitting coach."

"Whatever you need."

Now I'd done it. Not only had I tapped a coach who couldn't hear, I still didn't remember his name. Maybe Kellen knew. Or he could ask Derek.

"One more thing, Jack," he said. "I'd like to have my company sponsor the team. Unless you already have somebody."

"Wow, I completely forgot to talk about our sponsor at the meeting."

"Website said three hundred bucks." He handed me a check.

I thanked him and inspected the company check, feeling a sense of relief. Now our team had a sponsor. And I had a coach. And Deaf Guy had a name.

I reached out to give him my typical fist-bump, but for some reason decided instead on a handshake. "Thanks again, Pete."

Chapter 19

I opened Kellen's bedroom door. The lumpy form under the bedcovers lay motionless, so I nudged him. "Happy birthday," I said and presented him with a plate of fresh pancakes. I'd spent the last half-hour mixing the batter and adding so many chocolate chips and blueberries that the pancakes were more like dessert than breakfast. But they were Kellen's favorite.

He snapped awake. "I knew you wouldn't forget, Dad." His big smile told me I'd made the right decision—I'd been afraid of reminding him of practically burning down the house on my birthday, but I also knew better than to mess with Kennedy birthday traditions: serving breakfast in bed, dining out at a favorite restaurant, and following the golden ribbon. Tradition held that during the night before someone's birthday, a magical fairy would attach a gold ribbon to the bedpost, which the birthday person would then follow through the house all the way to the pile of presents. Melanie had come up with that one.

She'd also come up with an unusual tradition just between the two of us. On the day I turned thirty, I was toweling off after a morning shower when Melanie grabbed me from behind and screamed. I tumbled forward but somehow managed to keep my balance, then wheeled around. "Why the hell did you do that?"

She stood barefoot in her bathrobe and offered up the most innocent look she could. "Wasn't me. That was old age creeping up on you." Then she dropped her robe. The blood in my face moved elsewhere and we danced to the bedroom, where we enjoyed our own special birthday celebration.

Kellen wolfed down his pancakes but couldn't take his eyes off the gold ribbon attached to the bed's footboard. "What did you get me, Dad?"

"Can't do anything until you finish breakfast."

"I bet you bought me a new PlayStation."

I thought about the pile of presents that the ribbon led to. No PlayStation.

"Charlie's dad bought him one. And he's got this game, Wild Wild Racing. It's awesome."

"You're not supposed to guess. That's the rule."

I spied Kellen's plastic alligator on his dresser and remembered the day Dr. Lincoln—no, Renee—gave it to him. Had it really been five months since I'd last seen at her at the state park? Five months since I'd dumped water on her? Five months of wondering what she was up to?

"Can Mitchell sleep over tonight?" Kellen asked as syrup dribbled down his chin.

"No." I took a napkin and cleaned his face.

"Then can I sleep over at Mitchell's?"

"No. It's a school night."

He wolfed down the last pancake and flopped out of bed. He touched the ribbon as if it were an electric fence. "I want to open my presents now."

"Tonight at dinner. After practice. Where do you want me to take you?" I hoped he'd choose Benihana—he always liked the way the chef tossed the knives and built the little onion volcano—because I was craving sushi and a couple of Mai Tais.

"Let's go to Miss Skeet's." He slipped his fist around the gold ribbon and followed it out of the room.

"We always go to Miss Skeet's."

"That's because Miss Skeet's is so good, Dad." The ribbon ended barely ten feet outside his door, not down the staircase and through the first-floor rooms like it usually did. He was lucky I'd found any ribbon at all. Then he looked down at the pile of presents—I believe three constitutes a pile. "Is that it?" he said.

I swallowed nervously. "Get ready for school. Don't forget your Valentines. Happy birthday, buddy."

As I drove the boys into school and overheard Kellen telling Mitchell about the presents waiting for him, I knew I needed to make another run to the store. And that was going to have to wait until I finished answering a jury summons at the Fort Bend County courthouse. I figured that would take a couple of hours.

By the time I found a parking spot, signed in, and watched the video on the importance of jury service, an hour had already passed. The bailiff warned us that the judge wouldn't tolerate citizens shirking their responsibility to society, so I didn't bother asking to be excused so I could go shopping.

"How long is this supposed to take?" I asked the woman next to me, her head buried in a paperback.

"I've been called twice. One time they let me go at noon. The other I was here for three days."

"No way. That won't work for me. I've got an eight year old to take care of." I shrugged. "Single dad."

"Weren't you paying attention earlier? If you have a young kid, you should be exempt—you didn't even need to show up today. Go tell the bailiff or the judge."

I couldn't believe I'd wasted my entire morning.

After receiving the blessing of court personnel, I headed for the front door. My next stop would be Kroger for groceries and a birthday cake. Then on to the mall for some better gifts. I walked outside to my car. It was gone.

I circled the lot, trying to determine if I was turned around and had parked on the other side. But I ended up back where I'd started, next to a pickup with deer hunting stickers splashed on the rear window. I hadn't noticed the handicap-only parking sign before.

Leah wasn't available until school let out, which meant that forking more than two hundred bucks—that I couldn't afford—to retrieve my car from the impound lot didn't happen until four-thirty. I raced to pick up Kellen from his after-school care, performed a quick clothes change at the house, and hurried to the Sugar Meadow fields for five-thirty practice. I never made it to the store.

Pete was unloading an ice chest from his trunk as I walked up carrying my equipment bag. "Thought we weren't doing snacks for practice," I said.

"A little surprise I have for later. Can you give me twenty minutes with the whole team at the end of practice?"

"You bet."

We walked to the fields and stopped at the batting cage. Pete set down a bucket of wiffle balls and a batting tee. "I'll do whatever you want, Jack. Just tell me the plan."

I didn't have a detailed plan, didn't think I needed one. "How about we rotate 'em? You take three at a time, and I'll work with the rest. I'll just holler when it's time to switch."

"That won't work, Coach." He tapped his ear.

"Right, sorry about that. I keep forgetting you're deaf. Must be a pain in the butt."

"You flunk anatomy?" He smiled wide; his white teeth seemed even brighter against his dark skin. "I'll admit being deaf is inconvenient, but I don't dwell on it. God took away my hearing, and I just try to accept His will."

"Took it away? You weren't born deaf?"

"I'm post-lingual deaf. I was born hearing but when I was about Derek's age, I caught spinal meningitis. A common side effect is deafness."

Now I understood why Pete's speech hadn't been so affected. What I didn't get was how he could be sanguine about losing something so important to him. Then I thought about my mangled fingers. Being casual about them was hard to do considering how much they'd messed up my life's plans.

Patrick and Stewart whizzed past and I wondered if they were up to date on their Ritalin. We followed them to the dugout and gathered the players. "We have another coach," I said, pointing to Pete. "He's going to work with you on hitting."

"Are you Derek's dad?" someone asked.

"Yes, and you can call me Coach Pete. Today we're gonna swing off the tee and do soft-toss with the wiffles."

"And everyone has to wear a helmet, even in the cage. Right, Coach Pete?" He didn't reply and I saw his face was turned away from me. I tapped him and repeated, "Right, Coach Pete?"

"That's right," he responded deftly.

"One more thing. When you talk to Coach Pete, you have to look him in the face. He has to be able to read your lips. That's because Coach Pete is deaf." A collective ooh rose from the boys. "Now pair off and go throw your warm-ups."

I emptied the equipment bag and set the catching gear against the fence. Then I carried a ball bucket and bat out to the plate. Returning to the dugout, I found Patrick rummaging through bat bags. "What are you doing?" I asked. "Get back out there and warm up."

"My glove broke," he said. He handed me his fielding glove; its fingers were hanging loose, not secured to the glove's webbing like they should have been. A long, leather lace had been pulled through its holes and hung from the pinky.

I inspected the lacing more closely and could see what looked like tooth marks. "What the heck did you do, gnaw through it?"

"It's so boring warming up, Coach K. And Stewart never throws it good."

"So you ate your baseball glove?"

He looked dejected, then suddenly brightened. "That means I can get a new one!"

"Hold on," I said. "I know your glove looks ruined, but you don't need to throw it away. You just need to repair the broken laces. I can tell your dad how to fix it—it takes some time, but you'll be happy with the result."

He looked at me as if I were speaking Portuguese. "Check Mitchell's bag." I said. "I think has an extra glove." As Patrick scurried off, I realized I was in need of a glove, too. Although I could still catch a few of the kids' throws barehanded, throws from the likes of Corey and Derek were starting to hurt. I tried to remember what happened to my old baseball glove. I knew I'd seen it since Melanie and I changed houses, but not for a few years.

An hour later, the players had rotated through the infield and the batting cage, the practice clearly more productive than our first day. Derek was the last batter, and I saw he'd returned to the dugout and was drinking Gatorade.

"You done batting, Derek? Tell your dad to join us. Everybody in!"

A stampede of players thundered across the diamond and flopped to the ground at my feet, in a semi-circle around third base. Patrick flicked Stewart's cap off his head before hiding on the other side of Mitchell. Coach Pete walked over with a tee, a bat, and a rolling ice chest.

"Coach Pete wants to talk to you."

Pete ran a towel across his sweat-covered head and dropped it at his feet. "I'm worn out, guys. You sure looked good in the cage. I wanted to show you something else today. Who wants to learn the secret to hitting?"

"Me!" the boys yelled and shot their hands into the air.

Pete picked up a baseball and balanced it on the tee. He stood facing the team. "Who can tell me the most important part of your body for hitting?"

"Your feet?" Appleton guessed, probably because I'd mentioned his tendency for *happy feet* during the last practice.

"Your hips," Corey said.

"Those are both good answers. But they're not the most important. It's not your hands or your eyes, either."

"Your butt!" Patrick said, which caused the boys to laugh hysterically. The human butt was the single funniest punch line to any kid's joke.

Coach Pete thumped his chest. "It's your heart. I don't care how perfect your hands are or how well you keep your eyes on the ball. You gotta want to hit that ball as hard as you can. Now here's the way a lot of you swing."

Pete took his stance beside the tee and swung meekly, knocking the ball against the adjacent fence. "See? It didn't do much." He teed up another ball. "This is the way I want you to hit." He whipped his bat around and struck the ball so it banged off the fence and deflected behind him. The boys sat in awe.

"Don't be satisfied with making contact. Swing for impact. Like this."

Pete donned safety goggles and reached into the ice chest. He extracted a large grapefruit and placed it on the tee. Then he waved the boys back a few feet, twirled the bat in his hands, and obliterated the grapefruit into a mist of rind and pulp with a single powerful swing.

I watched twelve jaws simultaneously drop. Almost immediately, hands flew in the air and voices cried, "Me first!"

"We're going to take turns—everyone will get a chance, just relax—and each of you can blast away." Pete opened the ice chest, filled to the lid with grapefruits. The boys squealed.

Over the next twenty minutes, each boy took powerful swings at the defenseless fruit. "Impact!" Pete hollered as each swing met its target. Parents and kids from other teams looked on from outside the fence as the Dodgers hooted and cheered.

"There's one grapefruit left. Coach K, want to do the honors?"

I had to admit—it looked like fun. Pete tossed me the safety goggles, and I shifted my body to the other side of the tee, so I was facing the outfield fence instead of the dugout. I moved the tee about ten feet away from the kids.

"Watch out, guys," I said with a smile.

I may have been known for my arm, but I swung a pretty good stick as well. As long as the grapefruit wasn't dipping and breaking to the outside corner like a frickin' curveball, I knew I'd pulverize it. I took a hard swing—in an instant, the grapefruit turned into a shower of pulp. A deflated cover of yellow-orange rind traveled a hundred feet before landing in the outfield past second base.

"Holy shit!" Corey exclaimed. "I mean holy moley! That was the best one yet."

Coach Pete stood to the side, a satisfied look on his face. He winked at me.

"You guys enjoy that?" I asked, and was answered with a

unanimous cheer. "Me, too. Now before we leave, I want to make sure we know everyone's name."

I placed my good hand above the head of each player while the group collectively chanted, "Corey . . . Ryan . . . Derek . . . Kellen . . . Ryan . . . Patrick . . . Stewart . . . Tyler . . . Luke . . . Omkar . . . Zachary . . . Mitchell!"

"Do we have a cheer?" Kellen said.

I looked at the players in their blue Dodgers caps. "Let's do *One-Two-Three Big Blue*. Everybody, hands in. Omkar, you lead us."

In a hushed voice, Omkar said, "One . . . two . . . three . . ."

"Big Blue!"

❧

Kellen and I went straight from practice to Miss Skeet's. We were both starving, so I ordered some chips and queso to tide us over until our food was ready. Kellen sat at the table, practically drooling over the three presents. I'd bought two of them: a Duncan yo-yo like I used to play with and a DVD of the latest Pixar blockbuster. The other gift was from my parents.

"Don't open anything until we eat," I said. "Want to play video games?"

"Can I?"

"Here's two bucks. Happy birthday."

Kellen ran off and I sipped my beer. My gaze fell on a plastic sign on the table. The sign showed two buxom blondes wearing tight midriff tops, one emblazoned with *Miss Skeet* and the other with *Margy Rita*, plus advertising copy that said *Perfect Pair*. Subtlety was not a major objective at Miss Skeet's. I flipped the sign around and saw a picture of a brunette holding a heart-shaped plate of onion rings. It was accompanied by the text *Give a Special Valentine this February.*

I guess that's why I felt so miserable—Valentine's Day had always been special for Melanie and me. Our first date had been on Valentine's Day. We watched *Witness* and afterwards debated its merits over pizza; she proclaimed it one of the best movies ever. I told her Kelly McGillis was way too hot for an Amish woman and Harrison Ford was horribly miscast as the cop. We spent the rest of the evening chatting about our favorite films and discussing our dreams for the future. Melanie and I married three years later.

Then when Melanie was pregnant with Kellen, I'd rushed her to the hospital when contractions woke her up. Eighteen hours later, she still hadn't fully dilated, so it looked like she wouldn't deliver until after midnight . . . which would make my new son a Valentine's Day baby. She didn't appreciate the beauty and symmetry of having her child born on Valentine's Day—our special day—and when I told her I hoped labor would last another two hours, she declared I should shove a watermelon up my butt and hold it until the clock struck midnight.

I smiled at the memory.

Kellen returned when the money ran out, and we settled into our cheeseburgers. "I had a blast at practice, Dad. Did Coach Pete know it was my birthday?"

"Nope."

"He's so cool, letting us bust those grapefruits." Kellen chomped on curly fries, then asked, "Are we eating cake here or at home?"

"I'm sorry, Kellen. I meant to get you a cake. Just didn't work out."

He gave me a pitying look, then grabbed the first present and ripped it open. He peered at it, confused. "What is it?"

"It's a yo-yo. You can do all kinds of tricks—"

He was already opening the next present. "Oh, this is what I'd wanted for Christmas. Looks good, Dad."

"Maybe we can watch the movie together this weekend." I felt an overwhelming sense of embarrassment. How could I have bought such lame gifts for Kellen, especially on his first birthday with just the two of us? I glanced around and hoped no one at the restaurant was watching.

Kellen reached for the long cylinder wrapped in blue paper. "It's from Grandma and Grandpa." He opened one end and slid out a bright blue aluminum bat. "Now that's what I call a real present!"

He wasn't being mean, I know, but his words hurt just the same. "Let me see it," I said. The bat was a Louisville Slugger TPX Omaha, longer and heavier than the one his mom and I had given him only fourteen months ago. Below the sweet spot of the barrel, a label claimed the Omaha was constructed of Scandium XS alloy, with ultra-light weight and enhanced trampoline effect. Whatever that meant. "You'll need to write them a thank-you note," I said.

We didn't stick around Miss Skeet's much longer. When Kellen arrived home, he took his bath, then crawled into bed and called me to tuck him in. I wanted to apologize for messing up his birthday, to offer reasons why he didn't get a birthday cake or any decent presents from me. But I knew the judge had been right this morning when he told us, "Don't offer excuses. Just do your job."

"That new bat's gonna make me a great hitter," he said, snuggling under the covers. "I love you, Dad."

My eyes watered but all I could say was "Good night." I went downstairs and opened a beer. And thought about my life's spiral into a world I'd never imagined, one devoid of employment, of hope, and of happy birthdays.

❧

"We're going to be late," Kellen said, shaking me. Kids liked to say they hated school, but the truth was they didn't know anything else.

Completely disoriented, I lay in the recliner instead of on my bed. My eyes looked out to blinding sunlight, so I squinted and covered my face. My head ached terribly. "What time is it?"

"After seven o'clock. I've been ready for fifteen minutes, but I didn't know you were still asleep."

I fished out the cell phone from my pants pocket and punched speed dial. "Stacy, do you think you could take the boys to school?"

The voice on the other end assured me that she could be over in a few minutes. I thanked her, hung up, and lumbered to the bedroom.

"Are you sick?" Kellen asked.

"I just need to sleep."

A little after noon, I woke up feeling like my old pitching wheelbarrow. My head clanged with every step I took into the bathroom. I downed four extra-strength Tylenol, then went into the kitchen to make lunch. Six empty Bud Light cans dotted the counter. That explained the headache.

A legal pad lay on the kitchen table. A closer look told me Kellen had written his thank-you note. "*I had a good birthday. I got a cool bat. We went to Miss Skeets and I played games and Dad drunk beer. Nobody slept over. That suked. Love, Kellen.*"

This wasn't the kind of note my parents needed to read. I crumpled the paper and threw it in the trash.

Chapter 20

The five weeks of preseason passed quickly. My team had improved a ton, but it wasn't clear how they'd stack up against other teams in real competition. The schedule guy hadn't done us any favors—we were starting the season against Clay Baxter's Pirates.

At eight in the morning, Kellen climbed onto my bed and exclaimed, "Today's our first game!" His royal blue jersey was tucked into his baseball pants and he stood shoeless in royal blue socks. A matching Dodgers cap rested askew on his head. "Where are my cleats?"

I'd never been a fan of the Los Angeles Dodgers—Kirk Gibson's World Series walk-off homer notwithstanding—but I had to admit they had the sharpest uniforms in major league baseball. Even without his cleats, Kellen looked like a real ballplayer. "Go check the garage," I said. "They were caked in mud after that last practice. Don't put 'em on until we leave, though."

Kellen dashed toward the bedroom door, then stopped mid-stride. He spun around. "Who are we versing today?"

"The Pirates."

"That's Charlie's team."

"Uh-huh." I didn't tell him that one of Charlie's teammates

was a kid named Nick Baxter or that Nick's dad had probably been honing his team's skills to championship form. I didn't want Kellen to be nervous. I was nervous enough for both of us.

The only time I developed a case of nerves in high school was when reports surfaced that baseball legend Coach Gustafson was traveling from Austin to watch me pitch against the Columbus Cardinals and also to check out their first baseman, some six-foot-six country boy with twenty home runs. I'd developed a queasy stomach in the locker room, but once I took the hill I was all business. I never looked to the stands, never checked to see whether Coach Gustafson showed up, and never worried about facing Country Boy. By the time I exited the game in the seventh inning, I'd given up only three hits and fanned eight. Country Boy went 0-for-3 with two strikeouts.

When Kellen rushed off, I crawled out of bed and staggered to the bathroom. I couldn't shake the bad feeling I had about today's game. I leaned over the toilet, gagged, and threw up. And hoped things would turn out the same as they had against the Columbus Cardinals.

❧

Sugar Meadow Little League marked the transition between preseason practice and regular season games by flying a brand-new American flag at the park entrance. I passed the flagpole that rose from a bed of crape myrtles and noticed the crisp fabric flapping and snapping above me. When I reached the field, I heard the ping of an aluminum bat and then the cheer of the crowd. I cocked my head to see a boy about ten years old rounding first and heading to second. He slid in ahead of the throw, then popped up and dusted off his pants. His buddies in the dugout immediately launched into a series of sing-song chants. I leaned on the fence and closed my eyes, taking in the sounds.

I watched the older kids for a couple of innings, then became bored when three separate pitchers threw seven straight walks. With an hour before we'd play, I wandered the park to find Kellen and tried not to think about our upcoming game.

Cameras were everywhere. Something about the dawn of a new baseball season makes parents want to snap photographs to preserve the smiling face and clean uniform of their child. But no matter how many pictures they took—and my folks never took any because they didn't own a camera and saw no reason to archive childhood moments—they would never capture the actual experience of playing the game.

Baseball is about stories, not pictures.

What photograph could ever describe the time I turned a triple play for the Red Legs? It was a highlight-reel play, my quintessential Little League story retold and refined through the years, but the only photograph that existed was in my mind. I used to regale Melanie with the details: last inning, bases loaded; me at third base, rocking forward on the balls of my feet; the line drive to my right; the chalk burning my eyes and nostrils after the ball landed in my glove; the blind reach to tag out one runner and then a throw to first to nail the other. I'd tell her how my teammates tackled me and pounded me on the back and carried me to the dugout. I could describe every nuance of the play to her, but couldn't fully explain the way it made me feel. She wouldn't have understood.

That was the baseball experience I wanted for Kellen, to win a game with his glove or his bat, to slide into home with the winning run, or to strike out the final batter. I knew if Kellen applied himself, he might have such an opportunity. However, I wasn't going to coach with a camera around my neck.

❧

"Let's go, Dodgers," I said as the team playing ahead of us vacated the first base dugout. "Hang your bags on the fence."

I looked across the diamond and saw Clay Baxter hitting fungoes to his team. Charlie Sanderson, decked out in scuff-free catching gear and custom-painted helmet, caught the relay throw and flipped it to his coach. I turned to T-Bone. "You're catching today. Got your cup?"

He shook his head. "I don't like catching."

"I didn't ask if you liked it. We need a catcher."

"My cup's at home."

"You're supposed to—never mind." The rest of the team was milling about the dugout. "Grab a seat," I told them. "Who's wearing a cup?"

Appleton raised his hand. "What's the batting order?"

"Don't interrupt. Come on, guys. Who's wearing a cup? Mitchell? Corey?"

Baker stood and slightly spread his legs. He made a fist and rapped his knuckles against his crotch, creating a hollow noise that sounded like a woodpecker attacking a plastic tree. "I can catch," he said.

I yanked the clipboard from the fence. "Now I have to change everything." I scribbled the defensive adjustments, left the batting order intact, and made a final check to confirm that my weakest players would still get their minimum playing time. "Okay, listen. Here's the lineup. Appleton's leading off and playing first. Derek, you're—"

"Look at that man on the tractor!" Tyler pointed to the field.

I followed everyone's eyes and turned my head to see "Ground Chuck" Moretti dragging the field with his Gator. A rake screen attached to the tractor's rear was smoothing the dirt and, as a byproduct, kicking up a cloud of dust. Ground Chuck swerved a tight circle around second base, leaning out the open left side of the Gator and looking down to make sure he didn't hit the bag. My team was enthralled.

"Yes, it's fascinating," I said. "Now let's talk about the lineup. Everybody bats—that's the rule. Appleton, you're leadoff. Derek, Corey, and T-Bone, you're after that. The rest of you check the clipboard. Be ready when it's your turn to hit."

Two umpires wearing matching navy shirts entered the field from a gate near the third base dugout. The heavier man carried a facemask and his college-aged counterpart held a Gatorade. "Managers, meet me at home plate."

I felt like a prizefighter confronting my opponent in center ring. My throat felt dry but my upset stomach had disappeared.

The home plate ump rubbed up a brand-new baseball with dirt from the batter's box. "Coaches, I understand this is your first Peewee game. We're going six innings or an hour and a half, whichever comes first. You know there's a five run limit per inning, and the mercy rule is in effect."

"Can you go over the rules for the number of pitches?" I asked. "League handbook made it seem complicated."

Clay Baxter rolled his eyes.

"Get an adult to feed the machine. Up to five pitches per batter. No balls and strikes; we just keep track of the pitches. If the batter swings and misses three times or doesn't put the ball in play by the fifth pitch, he's out."

"And foul balls?"

"Unlimited on the last pitch. Anything else? Pirates, put your team on the field."

I'd hoped that with the kids a year older, the level of play would be higher in Peewee than in Rookie ball. That was wishful thinking. My team scored four runs in the first inning, and only Derek's bloop single over the second baseman made it out of the infield. So much for a month of batting practice.

In the bottom of the first, the leadoff Pirates hitter swung at his first pitch and grounded to Corey at shortstop, who made the routine throw to Appleton at first base for the out. Our crowd cheered as if Corey's play would end up on ESPN. They weren't as excited when Mitchell and Patrick proceeded to let two easy ground balls roll under their gloves, putting runners at first and third with only one out and their cleanup hitter, Charlie Sanderson, at the plate.

"Want to move the outfielders back?" Pete said. "Stewart's pretty close."

"Fine. Whatever." I was more worried about getting my third baseman's head in the game than the position of my outfielders, who couldn't catch anyway. "Mitchell, pull hitter. Wake up."

Pete tapped me on the shoulder. "The outfielders?"

"Do whatever you want."

Charlie Sanderson shanked two foul balls down the first base line, and I felt relieved that his timing hadn't reached mid-season form. On the third pitch, he lifted an easy pop fly in front of the mound. It dropped into Derek's glove like a dead bird. Derek pulled out the ball and held it up. No one paid any attention to the runner from first, who hadn't tagged up. Except me.

"Throw it to first!" I stepped out of the dugout and onto the grass. "Double play!"

Derek spun and Appleton ran toward first, glove extended. Derek fired the ball ten feet over Appleton's head, and it came to rest along the cyclone fence fifty feet beyond the base. Kellen never budged from his position in right field, and I'm not sure he even knew what was happening. I grabbed my forehead and wanted to yell out to Kellen, but even if I managed to rouse him, he was too far away to be of any help. By the time Appleton sprinted to the loose ball, one run was in and the other runner had advanced to second base.

"Son of a bitch," I muttered and spiked my Dodgers cap to the ground. "We should be out of this inning. That's a bunch of crap."

"Take it easy, Coach," Pete whispered. "I don't know what you said, but the boys in the dugout can hear everything."

We escaped the inning with no additional damage, so we continued to the second frame leading four to one. I returned to my spot as third base coach, Pete went to first, and Captain Carl made another appearance as commander of the pitching machine. I reviewed the notes in my spiral bound scorebook, checking the statistics from the previous inning and looking ahead to the next few batters. My dad taught me how to keep a scorebook by the time I was ten years old; it added an extra dimension to watching, not to mention managing, a game. Plus, there was magic in those symbols and numbers.

Zachary Reed, a kid who singlehandedly filled the bleachers with parents, step-parents, grandparents, and siblings, led us off with a groundout to the pitcher. I wrote 1-3 in my scorebook. When Stewart popped up to the second baseman, the notation was simpler: 4.

With two outs, Kellen made his batting debut as a Dodger, first taking practice cuts with his blue Omaha bat and then launching into his spider-killing routine at the plate. In response, Clay Baxter moved back his outfielders.

Our dugout chanted, "I say Kellen, you say hit. Kellen . . ."

"Hit!"

"Kellen . . ."

"Hit!"

"Kellen, Kellen, Kellen . . ."

"Hit, hit, hit . . ."

"Hit, Kellen, hit!"

The message didn't transmit, as Kellen swung at but missed the first pitch. The swing was all arms and no hips, causing Clay Baxter to call, "Everybody up!" Kellen fouled the second pitch wide of the baseline, then whiffed on his third and final pitch.

"Good cut," someone called from our stands.

"Good Lord," I muttered. I licked the tip of my pencil and wrote a capital K—swinging strikeout—in the scorebook next to Kellen's name. Back when I pitched on varsity, the JV team used to wave *K* signs every time I struck out an opposing batter. Then someone would mark the strikeout by taping a *K* sign to the wall of the press box. That tradition ended the day we played a team of mostly black kids, after I struck out three batters in two innings and didn't get another strikeout the entire game. Police showed up to quell the near-riot, and school authorities issued apologies after the game for the accidental racist message.

By the fourth inning, my Dodgers had built a nine to three lead and had shrugged off a Nick Baxter inside-the-park home run which plated Charlie. According to league rules, everyone had to play at least two innings—the person who wrote that had never seen my team. "Tyler," I said, "go to left field. Omkar, go to right. Stewart and Kellen, you're sitting."

We held on to win by a score of ten to seven. After the final out, my guys threw their caps and gloves into the air before lining up to shake hands. They practically skipped across the infield grass, with Pete and me at the end of the line. I gave a fist bump to each kid on the other team, then found myself facing Clay Baxter. He didn't look as forlorn as I'd hoped. "Good game, Mister President," he said. "We'll be ready next time."

After the game, I assembled the players under an oak tree near the batting cage. The parents joined us and one of Zachary

Reed's mothers passed out the post-game snacks, Goldfish crackers and Powerade.

I gestured for Coach Pete to speak first. He asked, "How does it feel, guys?" and was met with a chorus of cheers. "Just wanted to say you all looked good and played hard. This is going to be a fun season. Coach K?"

I set down the bucket of balls and parked myself on the lid. "Dodgers, I'm real happy we won, but don't get cocky. There's a lot we still have to work on. Your hitting was decent today, but defensively you were terrible. I think we had eight or nine errors. And you better learn to get your head in the game."

I paused and stared at the players. Everyone was looking around, obviously thinking about something else. "Hey, listen when I'm talking. Now don't forget, practice Monday and then game on Tuesday. Be here an hour before game time."

"One more thing," Coach Pete said. "Let's do *Big Blue*." He led the boys in the cheer, then doled out high-fives and fist bumps.

I was standing by myself, basking in our first win and waiting for Kellen to return from the restroom. Luke Appleton's dad, a former SMLL board member who now managed his older son's Major team, marched up and pointed his finger in my face. "Coach K, you were out of control today."

"What's your problem?"

"It's just a game. You're treating the boys like crap. And you're not getting everyone in the game like you're supposed to."

"I'm following the rules. Don't tell me how to coach." We'd played one lousy game, and I was already tired of parents whining.

"Realize you're a role model out there," he said. "Stop being a dick."

Chapter 21

After leading the Dodgers to their fourth straight win, I could sense a shift in the way parents were treating me. Appleton's dad had stopped complaining and the applause from the bleachers had gotten louder. Granted, not one parent had come up and thanked me, but they weren't openly hostile anymore. For Little League, I figured that qualified me as a rock star.

But it did nothing to improve my standing with Kellen.

On Friday evening, I stood in front of Pete's house and pressed the doorbell. Kellen stood alongside, carrying a leather football covered in SpongeBob SquarePants wrapping paper, plus a sleeping bag that had come unrolled and dragged behind him. I was finally going to get a night to myself—thank God for sleepover parties.

The door swung open and Derek's mom waved us in. She and I hadn't talked much, but I knew her name was Vanessa. She led us through the family room and out to the patio, where a dozen or so boys—practically all Dodgers—were munching on snacks. T-Bone sat on a chaise lounge, wearing only swim trunks, attempting to make his belly button look like it was talking. Omkar stood next to him, laughing and dropping M&Ms onto T-Bone's stomach.

"I didn't know Derek had a pool," Kellen told me. "I hope you brought my suit."

"Uh . . ."

The birthday invitation Kellen brought home the week before was long gone. All I knew was that Derek was turning eight, the party was a sleepover at his house, and I needed to buy a present. No one had told me anything about swimming.

"The water's probably too cold," I told him.

"Actually, it should be nice," Vanessa said with a lilt in her voice that made me think she'd grown up in Tennessee or Alabama. "We've been heating the pool for a couple days. If the boys don't want to swim, they can always use the hot tub."

"Dad, they've got a hot tub! Can you go get my swimsuit? Please?"

All I'd wanted to do was drop Kellen off and get on my way, to enjoy one evening without having to worry about all the mommy things. But it seemed I could never get time to myself.

"I'm sure Derek has an extra pair of shorts," Vanessa said. "Kellen can borrow one of his."

I considered her offer. That was certainly the easiest option. Of course, Kellen would probably turn all mopey and blame me for ruining his fun. "No, that's okay," I said. "I'll run home and get his stuff."

"Thanks, Dad!" Kellen raced away.

Vanessa opened a bag of tortilla chips and dumped them in a bowl. "Coach K, when you get back, stay for dinner. We have tons of food."

"Oh . . . well . . . I have plans." Of course I hadn't made any specific plans for the evening. I just needed some *Me* time.

Twenty minutes later, I returned to Derek's house with Kellen's swimsuit and goggles. I walked through the front door without knocking and carried the swim gear back to the pool.

When Kellen saw me, he broke into a big smile and flashed me a thumbs-up.

"You're welcome," I said. "Have fun. Listen to Derek's parents."

I told him goodbye, then wandered through the house to find Pete. He was sitting in front of an open refrigerator, an ice chest at his side. I tapped him on the shoulder. "What are you up to?"

"A surprise. For later." Pete looked around as if he were smuggling diamonds, then opened the ice chest. It was full of grapefruits and oranges. "After dinner we're gonna break out the batting tee."

I laughed. "So you've combined the birthday piñata with Gallagher's sledge-o-matic?"

"Pretty much. By the way, stick around. We're cooking boogers."

I did a double take, then realized he meant *burgers*. "Thanks, but—"

"All the Dodgers are coming."

I didn't have the heart to tell Pete that four days a week with the boys—and seven with Kellen—was enough for me. Just then, the doorbell rang. Pete didn't notice it. After a moment, it rang again.

"The door," I said. "I'll get it. Hey, make sure these guys get some sleep tonight. We've got a game tomorrow. Five o'clock." Pete gave a nod and I figured this was the perfect opportunity to make my escape. I opened the front door and found Mitchell and Stacy standing there.

Mitchell bounded in, a silly grin pasted across his face, and gave me a fist bump. "Hey, Coach. What's up?"

I jabbed my thumb toward the pool. "Everyone's out back."

After Mitchell dashed away, Stacy stood there holding an overnight duffle, a sleeping bag, a pillow, and a present that looked suspiciously like another football. She wore a snug blouse and low-rider jeans, and when she leaned over to place everything except the present onto the floor, I thought I saw the flash of a black thong.

"Earth to Jack," she said. "I could use a hand."

My eyes zipped back to her face and I could feel a rush of warmth to my cheeks. I grabbed the duffle bag and the sleeping gear and schlepped them to the game room, wondering if Stacy knew how embarrassed I was. Then I waited a good five minutes to make sure she'd left.

When I came down the stairs, Stacy was chatting with Vanessa. I tried to slip quietly past them, headed toward the door.

"Oh, I didn't know you were still here," Vanessa called. "I was just talking to Stacy about the party. You two ought to join us."

The look in Stacy's eyes was that of a cornered animal. I could tell she would rather be anywhere but in a house full of kids. She pretended to scratch her cheek but instead shielded her mouth to send me a message: *Help.*

"Actually, we were going to grab some Mexican food," I said.

"Thanks for the offer, though," Stacy told Vanessa, then gave her a hug. "Hope everyone has a good time. See you tomorrow morning."

The door closed behind us and we walked to our cars. "What *are* you doing tonight?" I asked.

"Absolutely nothing. I just want to drink some wine and take a bubble bath." Stacy beeped open her little red Mazda Miata.

"That's better than me. I was going to start on my taxes."

"And I thought I was pathetic. Look, it's the weekend. Are you still up for Mexican food?"

❦

Since Stacy lived close to Pete's family, we dropped off the Miata back at her house and she climbed inside my car. Ten minutes later, we parked in front of Pappasito's Cantina. Eleven minutes later, we stood at the bar holding beer bottles.

I lifted my Corona. "To Fridays!"

Stacy clinked her bottle against mine. "And no kids!"

As we killed time waiting for our table, grazing on tortilla chips and queso, we talked about how we'd come from similar country roots and how we'd ended up in suburbia. "If you'd told me five years ago," she said, "that I'd be a single parent, I would have thought you were crazy."

"So what happened?" I said, vaguely recalling something about a messy divorce.

"It's a long story. Short version is that Jeremy traveled a lot and had too many layovers, if you know what I mean."

"Ouch."

"Uh . . . yeah." Stacy finished her beer and flagged down the bartender. "Frozen margarita. Salt. Two limes. And a shot of Grand Marnier. What about you, Jack?"

"I'm set." I knew I could down three beers without feeling any effect, but since I was driving, I'd better play it safe. Maybe one more drink. Over dinner.

"No, I mean, it's been about nine months, right? I know how tough it is to be both mom and dad."

I'd spent the last year thinking about how unique my situation was, how no one could understand what I was going through. But Stacy knew. She knew the frustration of never having a moment's rest. She knew the grief of losing a marriage. She knew the loneliness.

"Changed my mind," I said. "I'll have that margarita. And I'd rather not talk about the past anymore. It's too depressing."

She shrugged, smiling. "Then let's have some fun."

Minutes later, we sat underneath the painted mural of a Mexican bullfighter, our table covered with a sizzling platter of fajitas and abundant servings of guacamole, sour cream, and pico de gallo. Stacy filled a tortilla with grilled shrimp, then drizzled melted butter and salsa on top. She took a bite and moaned. "I haven't had shrimp in forever." I gave her a curious look and she replied, "Mitchell's allergic to shellfish."

"Really? I knew about the peanuts."

"We have to be so careful. That's why we hardly eat out anymore." She took a napkin and wiped salsa from her chin. "Thanks for getting me out of that party tonight. This is so much more relaxing."

She raised the margarita glass to her lips and ran her tongue along the salty rim. I have no idea if she was teasing me, but I felt a stirring that I hadn't known in a long time. And I remembered the thong.

By the time we'd finished eating, Stacy was working on her third margarita while I was still nursing my first. I sucked on my lime wedge, feeling happier than I had in months. Tomorrow would mean returning to life with Kellen and coaching Little League, but for now—with the team GLM across from me—I had zero plans and zero responsibilities.

Stacy upended her glass and shook it until the last remnants of frozen margarita slid into her throat. "Let's get out of here," she said. Then she reached over and stuck her straw in my glass to slurp down what I had left.

"You're drunk," I said.

"Oh, I'm not drunk. I'm just in a good mood." She fumbled a pocketbook from her purse and dropped it on the table. She giggled and said, "Well, maybe a tiny bit drunk."

I drove Stacy home, grateful I hadn't gotten as hammered as her, and pulled in behind her Miata. "Had a great time tonight," I said, throwing the transmission into park. A weird déjà vu surfaced, a reminder of long-ago dates where I didn't know if I was supposed to tell the girl goodbye in the car or walk her to the porch. Driven more by manners than anything, I went around and opened the passenger door.

Stacy took my hand and got out. She gave me a quick hug—standard suburban-issue, all arms, nothing below the shoulders—and then a peck on the cheek. She cocked her head at me. "It's only eight-thirty. Come inside. I think I owe you a margarita."

The logical part of my brain—or maybe it was the little angel on my shoulder—told me I should get on my way. Go back to my house. My empty house. Stacy weaved as she tottered toward the front door. Another voice suggested I should walk her inside, make sure she's okay.

When I entered the foyer, I stumbled over a pair of sandals. Stacy stood barefoot in front of a CD collection that was stored in three metal towers. "These were all Jeremy's," she said. "Choose whatever you want. I'll make us some drinks." She spun and I was pretty sure there was an extra button open on her blouse.

I tried to convince myself that I was imagining things. Stacy wouldn't be hitting on me. We were just friends. But I also knew I hadn't seen that cleavage at dinner.

"Let's hear some music," she called from the kitchen.

I pored over the CDs, selected some classic rock that I grew up with, and inserted them into the stereo. The sound of ice crushing rang from the kitchen—she'd found her blender. I could use that drink. Wait a minute. What the hell was I doing here?

With the bluesy guitar riffs of ZZ Top pounding from the speakers, I went to find Stacy, determined to tell her I had to leave. She stood at the kitchen island, singing along with the music, her bottom swaying from side to side. As she turned to me, I noticed her hair was mussed up and she was biting her lip like a model. She reached a glass toward me. And then she slipped.

I felt a splash across my chest. She tumbled toward me and I somehow caught her, then we slid awkwardly to the floor.

"You okay?" she said.

"You okay?" I said.

We lay there on the floor, soaked with alcohol, and began to laugh. Stacy rolled onto her side and I noticed another button was undone.

I didn't want to think about the past, didn't want to think about the future. I pulled her tight and drew her into a hard, deep kiss.

And didn't go home.

Chapter 22

I stood on a mound, my high school uniform hanging sloppily on my skinny frame. The batter was Larry Wayne Tucker, who had been my best friend through sixth grade until he stole ten dollars from me at the Lee County Fair. He smiled through darkened teeth and spit a stream of tobacco juice at me. My pitch sailed high over the backstop.

In the next moment, I was pitching again, but now the batter was Kellen, wearing his blue Dodgers cap with the intertwined L and A. No helmet. I squeezed the ball tight, afraid he might get hit by a wild pitch. Tate Gillum, my high school nemesis, stood laughing in the dugout.

Kellen swung and the ball flew high into a white sky. I looked up, but the light blinded me and I couldn't locate the ball. It was a popup just off the mound. I attempted to catch it with a tiny circus net. Just as the ball came into view, I collided with a previously nonexistent tree and staggered backwards. The ball splattered on the ground—it was a blood-red grapefruit.

The doctor above my gurney wore a medical gown and full mask, yet I knew he was Coach Richter. Stacy Flint stood next to him holding a rib-spreader, her blouse opened to the navel. My high school coach was preparing to perform surgery on me, and all I could think about was how he'd butchered a watermelon into unrecognizable red and green chunks during our team picnic.

"Jack."

Shafts of sunlight streamed through the half-moon bedroom window and attempted to pry open my eyelids. Nature's alarm clock. My head hurt but I recognized the voice, which wasn't as pleading as it was last night.

"Morning," I said, peeking one eye open. Stacy stood dressed in a pair of running shorts and a white t-shirt, her hair pulled into a ponytail. Droplets of perspiration beaded on her forehead.

"Wake up," she said. "It's nine o'clock. The boys need to be picked up in half an hour. I'm gonna take a shower. There's fresh coffee in the kitchen."

I lay in bed, clearing my mind of the strange dream and trying to piece together the events of the previous night. I remembered getting drunk, getting naked, and getting laid. And although I knew I should probably feel guilty, I didn't. I hadn't had anything resembling human contact in months.

Suddenly I realized my newly awakened libido was interested in a reprise. My clothes were somewhere, but they weren't necessary in the short term. I followed Stacy into the master bathroom. She shrieked when I opened the door.

"Jesus, Jack, don't scare me like that!" She grabbed a bath towel and wrapped it around her.

"Just wondering if you wanted to take advantage of a little free time this morning."

"No," she said. "Look, last night was wonderful. God knows I needed it—"

"Me, too—"

"But we don't have time to mess around."

She adjusted the towel, careful to cover her breasts, but didn't know the mirror behind her revealed her naked backside until she saw me checking out her reflection. "Cut it out. There's a time for seeing each other naked, but this isn't it. You know last night was a one-time deal, right?"

I hadn't really thought about why we ended up together in bed. Wasn't love, even I knew that, but there must have been a reason we couldn't keep our hands off each other. "Where are my clothes?" I asked, realizing my predicament.

"I put them in the dryer. They should be ready by now. I'll pick up the boys and bring Kellen to your place."

Get out—that's what she was saying. Not that I could blame her. She'd have a hard time accounting for the presence of a man in her house, especially her son's baseball coach. I retreated from the bathroom.

"Thanks for drying my clothes," I said. "I'll be gone by the time you're done."

Back home, I tossed my clothes in the hamper and stepped into the shower. I kept replaying the evening, not just the sweaty parts, but our discussion of how hard life was as a single parent. Maybe that was our common bond, maybe that's why we needed *somebody*.

The phone rang as I toweled off. "Dad, can I play at Mitchell's house for a while? His mom says it's okay."

"No, you have chores to do at home, son."

"It would only be for a couple hours. Mitchell's mom said she could bring me home after lunch."

"You have responsibilities here. You can't ignore those by playing over there." The irony of my statement hit me immediately and I felt my face flush. After a pause, I said, "Fine, but you need to be home by one o'clock. We have to be at the fields by four. Game today."

I hung the wet towel on the shower door and faced the mirror. It didn't reflect a flattering picture. My brown hair was tousled, with wild cowlicks that reminded me of waves on a choppy lake. The weight that I'd dropped last summer had come back with a vengeance, and I no longer had a thirty-eight-inch waist. After combing and shaving, I pulled on my *SMLL—Real Baseball* t-shirt and noticed how tight it fit across my chest. At this pace, I would be an unrecognizable blob in a few months.

The clock chimed ten-thirty, and I knew I'd have another couple of hours to myself, which wasn't much different than most weekdays when I drove Kellen to school and returned to the house alone. Not working had initially been liberating, but six months later, I couldn't stand watching cable TV all day. My plans to organize the house and garage had failed miserably. It seemed every time I opened a drawer, reminders of Melanie lay everywhere, and I couldn't bear to move them or throw them away. So the house was frozen in time, unable to change.

I thought I'd use the two hours to organize Kellen's bedroom, which had devolved into a total mess. I went upstairs and opened Kellen's door, which had a poster of Roger Clemens taped to it. Clemens and I were basically the same age and he was in the prime of his career. The poster showed the Rocket in action, driving his legs and grimacing as he delivered a pitch. He could have been the heir apparent to fellow Houstonian Nolan Ryan in the hearts of fans, but he seemed destined to play as a worthless Yankee forever. We could have been Longhorn teammates. Now we were worlds apart.

Kellen's room looked worse than I remembered. Dirty clothes littered the floor, but I wasn't touching those—gathering laundry was his responsibility. One corner near the window was piled with toys and games. In the opposite corner, the surface of his assemble-it-yourself desk was strewn with trophies and a pile of papers. The only clean spot in Kellen's room was the surface of his dresser, where his toy alligator presided over the chaos.

I began cleaning off the desk. First I gathered two summer reading trophies—Kellen was proud of his ability to read, which he'd mastered by kindergarten, although he didn't have a trophy for last summer . . . because Kellen hadn't checked out any library books. One trophy was covered with a gooey red substance, probably the remnants of a strawberry Pop-Tart.

I shifted the papers to wipe up the Pop-Tart and noticed the top page contained a letter. *"Baseball is so fun. Derek has a party next friday. We got him a football. Love, Kellen."* This couldn't have been a school assignment; in fact, it reminded me of Kellen's thank-you note to my parents.

The other papers were also letters from Kellen, some one-sentence missives such as *"I got a B+ on my math test"* and others that covered half the page. One note read: *"School started back today. It was very cold outside. Dad yelled at me to hurry but it wasn't my falt. The ziper on my jacket got broke. Dad yells a lot. I miss when you were here. You hugged me and said I was your favrit boy in the world. Are there kids in heaven? Love, Kellen."*

Christ. He was writing to Melanie. I thought about the letter I'd written her on the day I considered ending my life. I'd been so desperate, so unable to imagine my world could get better. Was Kellen going down the same path?

I read every letter, starting with what looked like the first one back in June. With each note, it appeared Kellen thought his mom would somehow answer him. I thought he had accepted his mom's death, but it was obvious that my son had a tenuous grip on reality.

I slumped against the bed and rubbed a hand across my forehead. What was I going to do?

Chapter 23

Stacy and I had been delivering our respective kid to each other's doorstep for months. But when I saw her steer her red Miata into my driveway, and then watched Kellen and Mitchell hop out, I felt a wave of apprehension. I opened the front door and the boys ran toward me. "Guess what I found at Mitchell's," Kellen called. My stomach lurched—had he discovered what Stacy and I had done last night?

"It's a new can of tennis balls. Mitchell and I are gonna go play wall-ball with Patrick and Stewart. And then Mitchell's coming with us to the game. Derek's party was so much fun!"

"Uh . . . that's good."

"What about you, Dad? Did you do anything fun?" As my mouth hung open, he said, "You didn't watch my DVD, did you?"

I absently shook my head, then stood and gaped as the boys raced inside. When I turned around, Stacy was coming up the sidewalk. Goose flesh appeared on my neck and forearms, and my tongue thickened. "Uh . . . hi, Stacy."

"You're not gonna get all weird on me, are you?"

Of course I was. I'd been in the middle of a giant freak-out since I came home. Not only was I dealing with Kellen's secret letter writing, I was having to reevaluate my questionable behavior. What kind of man screws the mother of his son's friend?

She handed me Mitchell's bat bag and clasped my elbow as she made the transfer. She gazed at me with kind eyes and said, "I'm not expecting anything from you."

"Stacy, we shouldn't have—"

"I'm sorry about what happened. Not about last night itself, but about the confusing signals." She waved a hand at me. "I don't want a relationship. And I don't think you want a relationship. Can we just be friends? Pretend that nothing happened?"

"Something did happen," I said.

"I know. But—"

"It can't happen again. Can we just not talk about it?" I took a deep breath and tried to regain my composure. "I understand I'm taking Mitchell to the game."

"Is that okay? I have some things to do." She pulled car keys from her purse, then said, "Let me put this in his bat bag." She produced a silver cylinder the size of a thick highlighter. "This is Mitchell's epi-pen. For his allergies. He should always have one handy." She glanced around and slipped me a gold-plated watch. "Here. Found this in the kitchen. Don't think Kellen saw it, though."

I slipped my watch into my pocket and waved an awkward goodbye.

❧

By the time I reached the fields, I'd pushed away thoughts of my complicated life. That was the thing about baseball. No matter how messy the real world was, once you stepped between the white lines, life became simple: home or visitor, safe or out, win or lose.

I walked by the batting cage where Appleton stood waiting to hit. Coach Pete tossed wiffle balls to Kellen and hollered, "Impact!" with each swing.

"Come on, Kellen," I said. "Plant your feet. Do it like Coach Pete taught you." I peered inside the fenced cage, where Captain Carl was feeding balls into a pitching machine and Corey was banging each one back at him. "That's it, Corey," I said. "Show 'em how it's done."

I took a long walk to the outfield to observe the boys warming up. When I stepped on the dry infield dirt, I pawed at the red clay. I felt like sprinting to second base and executing a pop-up slide but suppressed the urge. In the thick outfield grass, I took measured steps and daydreamed about laying out for a batted ball. And I thought of "Moonlight" Graham stepping between the lines of Ray Kinsella's Iowa cornfield and getting another chance to live his dreams of playing baseball.

The field lights sounded a loud click and bulbs buzzed. Four pairs of boys were playing catch in left field, when suddenly Stewart rushed his brother and delivered a haymaker punch to the head. Patrick shrieked and fell to the ground. Stewart saw me running toward them and took off for the outfield fence.

I knelt at Patrick's side. His lip was split open, blood gushing out of the wound. He dragged his hand across his mouth, then saw the red smear and yowled. "Coach K, Stewart hit me!"

"Why were you fighting?"

He didn't answer but spat blood in the grass. "I'm telling my dad. Stewart's gonna be in big trouble."

I helped Patrick up, then whistled sharply to Stewart. "Get over here!" We marched to the batting cage—Patrick intermittently spitting blood, Stewart intermittently offering excuses—and found their father.

The calm, cool Captain went nuts. "What did you two do? Let me look at your face. You're gonna need stitches."

"Carl, it's just a busted lip. I don't think he needs stitches."

He whipped his head around. "Don't tell me what to do, Jack. What, you think because you're the manager, everyone has to bow down to whatever you say?"

"That's not what I'm saying—"

"Because I don't have to put up with it. My kid's more important than your big ego." With that, Carl dragged his sons toward the parking lot.

I stood there slack-jawed. It was as if Captain Carl had thrown his own haymaker and caught me upside the head. I found Pete and told him about Patrick and Stewart, but kept quiet about Carl's comments.

"You do know that Ryan Baker's at his grandma's funeral," Pete said. "We only have nine players now. If we lose another, we'll have to forfeit."

Forfeiting would have been better than playing the game.

"Everything's goofed up," I told the players. "A lot of you will be playing new positions. Be sure to check the clipboard. Now, who has a cup?"

As the boys farted around getting ready, I looked past them and saw Stacy walking up the sidewalk. Why couldn't I have found an anonymous barfly to sleep with instead of her? As I was processing that thought, I noticed two people following Stacy. I recognized them immediately—who wouldn't recognize their own mother and father?

Pete waved his hand in front of my face. "Umpires are waiting."

Dazed, I walked toward home plate, glancing over my shoulder to the bleachers, where Stacy plopped down in front of my parents. The field umpire, a heavy-set man with a white beard, led the pre-game introductions. I didn't hear a word he said because I stood staring at the home plate umpire. Decked out in the obligatory navy shirt and grey pants, the home plate umpire also wore a narrow-brimmed navy cap which hid short, brown hair. The casual observer wouldn't have even known she was a woman.

When the other umpire finished talking, she said, "My name's Renee. Let's have a good game. Dodgers, put 'em on the field."

I knew I only had a brief moment to talk with her, so I gestured to Pete in the dugout. *Clipboard*, I mouthed, then pointed toward the infield. What was left of my team ran out to their positions and began tossing practice throws around the bases.

"Renee?" I said. "I don't know if you remember me."

She cocked her head and gave me an inscrutable look. "You're the guy from Brazos Bend."

I couldn't read her face, couldn't tell if she still harbored a grudge. "I wanted to apologize right after it happened," I said, "but you left so fast. I . . . I really am sorry."

"We'll have to talk later. It's game time. You're on the clock."

I retreated to the dugout and leaned my forehead against the chain link fencing, then watched Renee as she backpedaled to her umpiring position. Would she accept my apology?

Pete poked me and said, "Want to hear something funny? That's my doctor out there."

"Renee Lincoln?"

"Yeah. You know her, too?"

"She treated Kellen last year." I didn't want to get into the whole story of Kellen's stress-induced breathing problems or the whole fiasco at Brazos Bend.

"I just love her," Pete said. "Real smart. And a sweetheart. Too bad I'm married."

I tried to concentrate on the game, but couldn't focus. When I looked to the field, I saw Renee and worried about how I'd messed up a good thing with a nice lady. And when I looked to the bleachers, I saw Stacy and thought the same thing. Then I thought about Melanie, about how forgiving she'd been, about how I could talk to her about practically anything. Which made me think about Kellen's letters. So much for baseball being an escape from my complicated life.

When the Diamondbacks finally stopped killing the ball and registered their third out, my team ran to our dugout and I loped to the third base coaching box. According to the scoreboard, we trailed four to nothing. I didn't remember any of their runs.

"Where's your coach pitcher?" Renee said.

I looked at the empty mound. Captain Carl had manned the machine for our first four games, but he was gone to the hospital. I needed someone else. "Give me a minute," I said, then darted into our dugout, through the gate, and out to the bleachers. "I need someone to run the pitching machine," I told the parents. "It's not hard. It can be a mom or dad, doesn't matter."

The parents stared back, apparently still afraid they could catch VD during the season. Then one man slowly raised his hand. "I'll do it."

Alarm bells rang in my head. Not him. Not my father. "You just sit there, Dad. Enjoy the game. I need a parent."

"I am a parent. And a grandparent." He patted my mom's leg, then stood.

"No, Dad. I don't need you."

A voice came from the field. "Coach, need a pitcher out here."

My father stepped off the bleachers. "Maybe you don't need me, but they do."

I escorted him to the mound and flashed back to my high school days when we used to practice pitching on the weekend: me on the Giddings mound, Larry Wayne behind the plate, my dad standing beside me, telling me to watch my leg lift, maintain my balance, and follow through. Now the roles were reversed—I had to show my dad how to pitch. I demonstrated how to raise the ball so the batter could see it and how to drop it slowly into the pitching machine. "Timing's real important," I said.

"I think I can figure it out."

When Captain Carl pitched, he always seemed to put the ball where the kids could hit it. My dad's pitching, however, was inconsistent, and I'm sure it's because he oriented the ball differently for each pitch. Even two of my best hitters, Appleton and Derek, struck out swinging at pitches in the dirt.

Going into the bottom half of the third, we trailed 10-1. This had been a terrible game for my parents to attend. If they'd come to any of our first four games, they would have seen a victory. Not this time. I looked to the bleachers and my breath caught. Mom was talking to Stacy. They were smiling and pointing to the field, but I had this odd feeling they were talking about me.

Kellen walked to the plate. He pointed to his grandfather and then to his blue bat, and broke into a smile. "That's my grandpa," he told Renee. She smiled back and gave him a thumbs-up.

My dad lifted the ball, then dropped it in the machine. The pitch passed at Kellen's ankles. The next pitch passed at his eyes. "Dad," I called, "put the ball in the same way every time." He pitched again, ignoring me. This time the ball traveled down the center of the plate. Kellen swung and missed.

When Dad received the return throw, he dropped the ball into the machine without first showing it to Kellen. Which meant the ball whizzed past Kellen so fast he didn't have a chance to swing.

I raised an arm. "Time, Blue."

Kellen met me halfway down the third base line. I leaned over and said, "Last pitch, Kel. Gotta swing. Remember, quick hands." Then I called to my dad, "Do it the way I showed you."

Kellen trudged back to the batter's box, having drawn no confidence from the offensive timeout. Dad lifted the ball with his right hand, then slowly dropped it into the feeder chute. The ball sailed down the middle of the plate, but Kellen ducked his front shoulder and retreated from the batter's box. The crowd groaned.

I couldn't believe it. He'd just turned away, afraid to even try to hit the ball. I spat on the grass and ripped the scorebook from my pocket. I took my pencil and scrawled a backwards K— caught looking—beside Kellen's name. A swinging strikeout I could almost understand. He wasn't that good a hitter. But simply watching the final pitch? "Pathetic," I grumbled, and scribbled another backwards K, this one obliterating the first letter of his name. Kellen with a K.

After the last two kids in the lineup made outs, I returned to the dugout to watch the fourth inning. My father ignored me, instead spending his time talking with Coach Pete. I couldn't take it anymore. "How could you strike him out, Dad? I showed you how to pitch."

Dad didn't say anything but turned slowly, like Clint Eastwood used to do when called out by the villain. "Are you blaming me for Kellen striking out? You think I'm costing you the game?"

"I just want you to do your job."

"That's a funny thing to say, son. Especially from someone who won't even look for a job."

Chapter 24

Greenish-black clouds boiled in the morning sky, obliterating the daylight. "Look outside, Kel," I said. "I bet we're not gonna play our ballgame today."

In the other room, Kellen remained oblivious to the darkening clouds, concentrating his attention instead on Hot Wheels Turbo Racing. "Then let's go see a movie."

"I'd rather go to the batting cages." I was tired of watching Kellen grow more timid with each at-bat. He hadn't tattooed a ball yet in six games. The worst part was how he didn't seem to care about improving. "We can work on your hitting."

"Do we have to?"

"Yes. And get off your butt. You're wasting your life away with those stupid video games." A flash of lightning lit up the windows on the north side of the house, and a loud clap of thunder immediately followed.

"They're not stupid." He slammed the controller to the carpet, where it bounced against the TV stand and snapped off its plastic joystick. He kicked the game console, which caused the game to flicker and the TV to turn a blank blue. Then he stormed up the staircase.

"Get back here and clean this up."

"No!" He slammed his bedroom door, and I heard the loud

click of a lock. Heavy drops of rain splattered on the windows.

I blasted out of my kitchen chair. Kellen hadn't had a spanking in years but certainly deserved one with his little tantrum. At the landing of the stairs, I paused, forcing myself to take long, deep breaths. Because I knew if I spanked him now, I might just whip his ass. "Open this door," I said through clenched teeth. "Do it now or I'll break it down."

After a moment, Kellen unlocked and opened the door. His eyes brimmed red, and a rivulet of tears streaked his face. He met my gaze and hung his head, resigned to the sentence I would mete out. "I'm sorry, Dad."

His contrition caught me off-guard. I wanted to be mad at him. Hell, I'd worked myself up into a righteous rage and he deserved both barrels. At the same time, I knew he was probably as frustrated with the rainy weather as I was.

"Look," I said, "you can't throw things just because you're mad. I'm sorry about the rain, but there's nothing I can do about it. Doesn't mean we're stuck here, though. Let's get out of this house."

We weren't the only people to believe Texas Sports University would be a perfect refuge from the rain. The parking lot was crammed with cars. Pete sure had himself a nice setup, a private health club combined with public amenities available for rent. He was probably rolling in the dough.

Kellen and I sprinted through raindrops and into the front door. Five batting cages ran along one side of the brightly lit room. In the far back, people in safety harnesses scaled rock walls. A snack bar, with neon signs touting *Drinks* and *Sandwiches*, was situated beyond the front desk.

"We want a batting cage," I told a twenty-something woman at the front desk. I used the royal *we* because Kellen didn't want anything to do with baseball these days, considering he dragged his bat bag like he'd been sentenced to some sort of death march.

"We have three cages already reserved by teams," she said. "You're free to use one of the coin-operated cages. There's a bit of a line, though."

Sheets of rain poured down the windows. The sloping steel roof echoed the pounding storm; it sounded like we were trapped inside a drum kit during a furious solo. "We're not going anywhere," I said, alluding to the rain. "Guess we'll wait."

Suddenly Kellen pointed to the area with the rock wall. "Look, it's Coach Pete!" He ran over and gave Pete a high-five. I knew Kellen was a big fan of Coach Pete, as were all the Dodgers. At first I thought the boys were simply excited about the novelty of a deaf coach. Kellen had told me that they often played a trick where they'd mouth words but not speak them, and Pete could always understand them. But it wasn't the uniqueness of Pete's disability that caused my team to greet him with high-fives, down-lows, or soft fist bumps at practice. They genuinely liked him.

"Waiting to bat, I see," Pete said. "I can give you a priority status on a cage, but it'll still be a few minutes. Kellen, can you hold on a bit? I promise to get you in as fast as I can."

"I don't want to bat," Kellen said, and I shot him a glare. "Dad made me come here."

"Tell you what. Derek's in the back at the new racquetball courts. Want to hang out with him?"

"Can I?"

"Let the boys play," Pete suggested, "and we can talk baseball in my office."

Compared to the upscale furnishings and equipment found downstairs, Pete's office was spartan. The second floor contained a bank of cubicles, each a cramped booth with just enough room for a desk and two chairs, one for the *fitness specialist*—salesman—

and the other for the *prospective member*—out-of-shape sucker. Just as casinos relegate their security personnel to the upstairs, far from the lights and glitz below, this unglamorous room was where the heavy lifting occurred, where rich, overweight visitors were quietly strong-armed out of their money and welcomed to the fraternity of the fit.

"Don't worry, I'm not going to sell you a membership," Pete said, reading my mind. "Have a seat."

I plopped down in an aluminum chair with red fabric over minimal padding. I knew it wasn't meant to be comfortable, because the idea was to get customers to part with their money sooner rather than later. I'd sat in a similarly cramped chair months earlier when I bought my car, but the salesman never knew how motivated I was to get rid of the stinky Lexus and to escape his smarmy personality.

"Heard anything about a makeup game?" Pete asked.

"The scheduling guy already sent an email. They're waiting to see how much rain we get."

"Hang on." Pete raised his left palm to me and unholstered a buzzing device from his belt.

I was confused. It made no sense for a deaf man to own a cell phone. I watched him flip open a small LCD screen to reveal a miniature keyboard. He pressed the tiny keys with his thumbs. When he finished, I pointed to his phone. "Is that one of those PDAs?"

"Yeah. Combination cell phone and pager, plus it handles my email and instant messaging. For us deaf folks, it's a real lifesaver."

As Gemini's senior sales rep, I'd lived on my cell phone. Before they canned me, management had even discussed equipping me with a Blackberry, a move I had resisted. The device may have been wireless, but it struck me as another means to tie me down, an inflexible umbilical cord to the company. I couldn't imagine such a device being a source of freedom. Pete's phone was the deaf equivalent of the wheelchair.

"Any chance you'll be able to hear again?" I blurted out, then felt instantly embarrassed.

He didn't answer right away. "Probably not," he finally said. "Although I've been talking with my doctor—you remember, that umpire lady."

"Sure . . . Renee. What did she say?"

Pete's eyes widened and he flashed a lopsided, curious grin. "Renee?"

I felt heat rise up the back of my neck. "Doctor . . . uh . . . Lincoln," I stammered. Pete stared me down, and I knew if he was selling health club memberships, I'd probably cave and buy three. I finally cracked under his gaze. "We've crossed paths a couple times outside her office."

Pete squinted at me, judging my truthfulness, then said, "I was supposed to have a cochlear implant seven years ago."

"What happened?"

Pete looked wistfully past me. "They couldn't do the surgery. You see, my ear canal has a lot of bone that formed after I lost my hearing. It's called ossification. Kinda like someone pouring concrete into an open hole. Unfortunately, it's common for people who lose their hearing to meningitis. My doctor in Tennessee had to abandon the idea of an implant."

"And Dr. Lincoln?"

"She examined me when I moved here from Tennessee. Just a routine visit. She's talking about options with new technology."

"I hope it works out for you."

"Whether it's God's plan for me to hear or not, I don't know." He shrugged his shoulders, then exhaled deeply. "What about you, Jack? I don't mean to pry, but what happened to your hand?"

I shifted my misshapen right hand into my lap and then down behind my leg. "Long time ago. It's nothing."

An air of uneasiness filled the room. I was afraid to say anything that might draw even more attention to our respective physical problems. Pete seemed equally uncomfortable. So we sat there staring at each other.

As the silence grew, I began to think I'd really pissed him off, either by talking about his disability or by refusing to talk about my own. I remembered how Melanie used to get mad when I'd shut her out. I'd never shared with her the whole story about my hand: how I injured it, how immature I'd been, how disappointed I still was with myself.

Finally, I said, "You wanted to discuss baseball?"

Pete didn't respond, and I hoped it was because hadn't seen my lips move. I was about to repeat myself when he said, "Thanks for letting me help coach the kids."

I sighed with relief, glad to steer the conversation back to normalcy. "Glad you volunteered. The boys sure are killing the ball, and that's mostly due to you."

"All I did was simplify things. Tried not to get caught up in *squashing the bug* and stuff like that."

"Well, it's working."

Baseball was a subject I could talk about all day. I could discuss the different philosophies of hitting instruction, describe how to throw a cut fastball, or argue that trading Joe Morgan to the Cincinnati Reds was the dumbest thing the Houston Astros ever did. Because talking about baseball made me happy.

"I can't believe we're five and one," I said. "We have a good chance to take that first place trophy, especially if Clay Baxter's kids can lose a few. Now if I could just get Kellen to snap out of his funk . . ."

"You shouldn't be so hard on Kellen."

"I'm not tougher on him than anyone else. Sometimes I get on him if he's not trying hard, but that's all." I didn't tell him the truth: that Kellen had been a huge disappointment to me.

"If you want, I'll take some extra time with him on his hitting. And Jack," Pete said, nervously scratching behind his ear, "no one except you really cares if the Dodgers take first place. We're not playing as a team. I'm worried some of our players are on the outside looking in."

I didn't know where Pete was going with this. His son had played almost every inning in our six games. Derek was my utility ballplayer and had seen time at three different positions in the infield. He couldn't possibly be angling for more playing time. "Did Derek say something?"

"No, Derek's fine. He's having a great time. I'm worried about guys like Tyler and Omkar. They play so little that they don't even feel like part of the team."

I fidgeted in the uncomfortable chair. "Nobody has said anything to me. I know those guys play a lot less than the other kids but, come on, they really suck. You know that's true."

"Honestly, I don't care how good or bad they are. I just want them to improve . . . and to be part of the team."

"Nobody's said one damn word about how I'm managing," I snapped, "except for you. Everyone's happy we're winning."

"You're wrong. You hear what you want to hear."

"And you don't hear anything, so get off my ass."

"I may not hear," Pete said, shaking a finger at me, "but you don't listen."

Chapter 25

I had just returned to the house after carpool duty when my cell phone rang. Caller ID showed a number I didn't recognize, but it originated in the 214 area code, which meant Dallas. "Jack! How are you doing? It's Scott."

"Long time since I heard from you." The reality was that I hadn't thought about my former coworker in months. "You in Dallas now?"

"Been here about five months."

Which meant he got hired not long after Gemini laid us off. I still hadn't found a job, although it was probably more accurate to say that no job had found me, because I hadn't done more than post my résumé online and go on two unproductive interviews since January.

"How are things in Houston?" he said.

"Nothing shaking here. Unfortunately."

"I might have good news. I work for Tarrant County Medical Solutions now, and my boss is looking to hire two or three salesmen. Pay is similar to what we made at Gemini and, of course, the work's basically the same. It'd be a new set of doctors and hospitals, just like when we started back at Gemini. Might be fun."

"I don't know. How soon?"

"My boss is on vacation, but he wants to start hiring right after Easter. Email me your résumé and I'll hand-carry it to him when he gets back. It's a slam dunk if you want the job."

"Okay," I said slowly, trying to wrap my head around the news. "Wow, this would be a big change."

I hung up, my mind spinning. Could this be the break I needed, that Kellen needed, to move forward? All I knew was that staying in Sugar Land in a perpetual state of uncertainty and grief was sucking the life out of us.

❦

April fifteenth had been circled in red on the refrigerator calendar for a long time. My federal tax return was due, and this was the last year I'd be filing jointly. But that wasn't why the date was circled. Today was Easter Sunday and Leah had made me promise to attend church with Kellen. I stood in the kitchen, arranging the last of the chocolate treats in Kellen's Easter basket, wishing I could just skip to Monday and avoid today. Because the red circle wasn't for Easter, either.

April fifteenth was Melanie's birthday.

It helped that the trappings of Easter provided some distraction. My parents always used to drag Leah and me to sunrise service every year. Mom would buy me a new clip-on tie, which appeared in my Easter basket along with a chocolate bunny, colored eggs that still reeked of vinegar from the decorating, and a small bale of artificial grass.

Where I grew up, the traditional Easter service was always held outdoors when the weather cooperated, and there was often a slight chill in the air before the sun rose. German farmers stood around in their suits, shaking hands with each other, uttering more words than they probably did in a month: "He is risen!"

and its rejoinder, "He is risen, indeed."

Each worship service was predictably the same. The senior pastor recited the Easter story and the congregation responded with unusual vigor. We belted out traditional hymns, making sure each alleluia was sung with at least ten syllables. And after church, we'd head home for Easter dinner and, later, sit outside to listen to a ballgame on the radio.

For the first time since Melanie's funeral, Kellen and I walked into Merciful Savior to worship. Kellen clutched my left arm, and I knew he too was remembering that horrible day. "You'll be okay," I told him.

Pastor Steve greeted parishioners in the narthex. He wore a long, chalk-colored robe; brilliant-white paraments with intricate gold designs hung around his neck and down his chest. His balding dome was sweaty, a testament to having performed two services already. "Glad to see you, Jack," he said, shaking my arm and covering it with his free hand, as if giving a hug. "He is risen!"

My response was programmed and automatic. "He is risen, indeed."

I broke free from his grasp and made my way with Kellen through the crowd. We eventually found Leah, her family, and— to my surprise—my parents, sitting in a pew near the front. Two large crosses formed from Easter lily arrangements flanked the altar; they reminded me of the funeral sprays months back. Behind the crosses, the praise choir gathered in flowing scarlet robes.

I bent down and kissed my mother on the cheek. For a country woman, she dressed impeccably. She wore a teal dress with white shoes and matching purse. Her silver-white hair was teased high, which gave the illusion of a dollop of light meringue. My father towered next to her. His diagonally striped tie barely reached the top of his navel—Mom's fashion sense had never rubbed off on him. "Happy Easter," he said.

I was sure he hadn't forgotten their last trip to Sugar Land: the horrible baseball game, the argument that carried from the field to the parking lot, the tears in my mom's eyes as they drove away. Kellen slid between them, giving me maximum distance from my father.

The congregation swelled as latecomers rushed in. It was my first worship service in a long time and I felt like a visitor, even though we'd been members for six years. The youth pastor, who wore his stringy brown hair in a ponytail, strapped on an electric guitar and rocked out on a version of *Jesus Christ is Risen Today*, which served as the prelude. The drummer, a high school kid whose idea of dressing up was to wear new tennis shoes, came in on the toms and snare after the opening guitar solo. This was not your father's worship service.

A half-hour later, Pastor Steve strode to the pulpit. His sermon resembled his typical pabulum, almost New Age in its message, and my thoughts began to drift.

"She's dead, and I'll never see her again," Pastor Steve said, and I snapped to full alert. "I was there when she died and when they laid her lifeless body in the ground." He paused. "But the promise of Easter is that death is not permanent. I know I will see my mom in heaven."

It was eerie. Pastor Steve, whose sermons were normally forgettable and unremarkable, was suddenly clear and, dare I say, dynamic. I sat with rapt attention and absorbed his words, all the time thinking about Melanie.

"Easter means change," he continued. "For Christians, every day is a new day, with yesterday forgotten. So how will Easter change you?"

My mind spun, and I suddenly needed to escape. I clambered

over Richard's and Leah's legs toward the side aisle, then hurried to the rear of the church. In the restroom, I splashed water onto my face.

Eventually my breathing slowed and I regained my composure. I looked in the mirror— my eyes were red and puffy. A young boy opened the door and rushed in to use the urinal. I wiped my face with a paper towel and left.

When I returned to the narthex, I saw the congregation lining up for Holy Communion. That was too much. I couldn't eat the holy meal only a few feet from where Melanie's casket had been stationed months earlier. Instead of returning to my seat, I escaped to a side hall and pretended to read the bulletin boards, killing time as I waited for the worship service to end.

A familiar cry told me they were finished. "He is risen!"

"He is risen indeed."

"Lunch is ready," Leah announced, and the Kennedy clan moved to her cramped dining room, where six chairs surrounded an oblong table. A folding table stood nearby, with two steel chairs tucked underneath.

"Marissa, you're sitting with the adults," Leah said.

Marissa nudged her brother. "You losers have to sit at the kiddie table." She was fifteen, and her status in the family had just been elevated. The promotion wasn't due to a sudden surge in her maturity. In fact, Marissa's behavior annoyed my sister on an almost daily basis. I knew that Marissa only sat at the big table because we had a vacant chair.

"Jack, would you take these into the kitchen?" Leah lifted off the glass lids from two Corning dishes.

The smell of baked beans rocked me. I gasped, the odor

instantly transporting me back to that June day. The crock pot. The Lexus. The accident.

No one noticed my reaction. I hurried to the kitchen with a lid in each hand, and when I returned, my father stood to say grace. My silent prayer was that the day would pass quickly.

After lunch, Marissa vanished to her room to escape the family. Trevor and Kellen were involved in a rousing game of basketball in the driveway, and Richard was poisoning his lungs on the patio. The rest of us sat in the living room.

"I didn't know you and Mom were coming down for Easter," I said.

My father sat in a recliner with his legs propped up and his eyes half-closed. If Dad was going engage in conversation, I knew there was only a small window of opportunity after the meal. "Your sister's idea," he said. "Leah asked your mother a month ago. We had to find people to cover for us at church." That was no small task. Mom headed the ladies' guild and the women's auxiliary. Dad served as lay minister and assisted in the distribution of the Sacrament on Easter morning.

I remembered Scott's phone call and wondered what everyone would think about me taking a job so far from the family. I could guess my Dad's reaction—he'd criticize whatever choice I made. "Since you're all here," I began, and their eyes turned toward me. "I received a call from a friend three days ago. He has a job opening for me."

"That's great, dear," my mom said, tugging an afghan over her short, skinny legs. "I knew everything would work out."

"The job's in Dallas."

I was surprised by my father's response. "Could be worse. Could be some God-forsaken place like Oklahoma."

My mother popped him on the shoulder. "If you hadn't stopped at that restaurant in God-forsaken Oklahoma, you might still be washing your own clothes." Back in the mid-fifties, Dad's car overheated on the way to a fishing trip with his buddies. While he waited three hours for a new water pump, he struck up a conversation with a tiny, big-haired girl at the country diner next door. She was a real spitfire, and it took only a year for her to be persuaded to marry him and move to Texas.

Dad gave me a serious look and said, "Son, do whatever's necessary for your family. If you're in Dallas, so be it. Just don't come back here a Cowboys fan." Then he smiled.

"Leah?" I asked, not sure if I wanted her to wish us well or beg us to stay.

"You need a change. Melanie would've agreed."

Suddenly I realized why my parents had skipped their country church to be with us on Easter. Today was Melanie's birthday and everyone had been concerned about how I'd react. The truth was that I felt horrible, maybe more than usual on this anniversary, but no one realized I was reminded of Melanie on an almost daily basis. Anything might trigger a memory: seeing a Camry on the freeway, standing in line at the grocery store and hearing someone talk about a bunco party, or even being served baked beans for Easter dinner. I'd lived with these unwanted stimuli for almost a year.

"Everyone knows it's Mel's birthday. I appreciate you keeping me busy, so I'm not going crazy. But I understand she's dead and she's not coming back, just like Pastor Steve said. I have no idea what she'd think about moving to Dallas."

"We love you, son," Mom said. "We miss Melanie, too."

"This job isn't about me running away. I just think Kellen needs an opportunity to grow up where he's not constantly reminded about what he's lost."

No one said anything, but Leah wiped her eyes and Dad pulled out a handkerchief and blew his nose.

Then Richard came in and flipped on the TV, zipping through the channels. His selfishness and ignorance of events around him was incredible. Mom and Leah moved to the dining room, whispering as they walked, and began poring over photographs for a family scrapbook that Leah was putting together. My father nodded off in the recliner.

I sat there and wondered if joining Scott was really an excuse to run away from my past, my broken life. Pastor Steve had asked how Easter would change us. Watching my son shoot hoops outside the window, I had my answer. We would move to Dallas.

Chapter 26

In its infinite wisdom, Sugar Meadow Little League had decided that our rainout would be made up as a Saturday doubleheader. A few minutes before one o'clock, two umpires walked onto the field. I recognized the red-haired man as one of the dads from Kellen's old Yankees team. The other umpire had olive skin, gorgeous eyes, and a shy smile—I hadn't seen Renee at the fields for weeks.

"It's great to see you again," I told her as the other umpire left to rub sunscreen onto his face. I'd secretly hoped to get another chance to chat with Renee before we moved.

"I was wondering when I'd run into you again."

"Kinda surprised you find time to umpire Little League." I knew I sounded awkward—I felt awkward—so I said, "You know, being a doctor and everything."

"It's all about balance. It's not right to work all the time." Renee's words were familiar. Melanie used to tell me the same thing.

My eyes were drawn to the infield, where the Cubs manager, a man with muscles bulging out of his *SMLL—Real Baseball* t-shirt, ran around with a kid slung over his shoulder. They were both laughing. Ernie Jenkins was one of those rah-rah guys, leading cheers and acting like everyone's best friend. He arrived at home plate with the boy still across his shoulder, legs kicking in the air. "Take it easy on us today," he told me. "Aren't you guys in first place?"

"Yeah. I'm not sure how." I gave him a sheet of paper and said, "Here's our lineup." I'd spent an hour on it yesterday, trying to devise the optimal defensive alignment and batting order.

"I don't have one for you," he said. "We just kinda wing it."

I wanted to insist that he go back and write out his lineup, but I didn't want to look like a jerk in front of Renee. "We need a batting order, at least. For the scorebook."

"Tell you what. I'll just bat 'em according to jersey number. Will that work?"

I didn't say anything but simply nodded. Then I walked back to the dugout with the clear understanding of why the Cubs had won only two games all season.

In the top of the first, Appleton started us off with a meek ground ball to the pitcher, who tossed him out easily. Derek got us on track with a hit, but then he stumbled over first base and had to settle for a single. When Corey and T-Bone reached safely on infield hits, the bases were juiced with only one out. I looked over at Ernie Jenkins—he was juggling baseballs in the dugout, paying no attention to the fact that we were about to open a can of whoop-ass on them.

"Nail one, Baker," I called from the coaching box.

Captain Carl dropped the ball into the pitching machine, and it zoomed to the plate. Baker smashed a line drive directly at the first baseman, who instinctively lifted his glove . . . and somehow caught it.

"Get back!" I called to T-Bone, who had leaned with the swing and had broken for second.

T-Bone dove back to the bag. He was too late, as the first baseman beat him there to complete the double play. Ernie

Jenkins flew out of the dugout, cheering and pumping his arms, and chest-bumped the first baseman. The kid had a goofy grin, but probably didn't understand what had happened.

"Don't worry, guys," Coach Pete said. "Hats and gloves, let's shut 'em down."

I was livid. Poised to score at least three runs, we'd pissed away a perfect opportunity. Now the Cubs had all the momentum. As I feared, they struck with a big rally, scoring five runs before we knew what hit us. I knew we needed to get on track quickly, or we'd be out of this game . . . and out of first place.

We didn't fare any better the next inning. After a pair of groundouts, Kellen strode to the plate. "Come on, Kel," I muttered. "Get a piece of it."

Three weak swings later, Kellen headed back to the dugout. I flipped my scorebook open. Once again, it was Kellen with a K. At least he didn't get caught looking.

I stood next to Pete in the dugout as the Dodgers went on defense. "You gotta help Kellen with his hitting. It's driving me crazy."

"Between games," he promised. "Be patient. Kellen's hitting will come around—probably not today, maybe not even this year—but he'll get the knack of it. Eventually."

"Do what you can."

Three innings passed and we trailed twelve to zip. Nothing short of a miracle would save us. We'd reached the top of the fourth, and we needed to score three runs or the mercy rule would kick in. My worry now was to get the Dodgers thinking about baseball again. We couldn't afford a letdown in the second game.

Mitchell led off the inning with a huge double to left field. It bounced twice and hit the fence. Our stands went wild, as if one hit would make a difference. That meant Kellen was due. Please, not again.

"You can do this, Kellen," encouraged Coach Pete. "Impact, not contact. Big tough swing. Here we go."

"Impact," I repeated and clapped my hands.

Had our mantra produced the desired effect, Kellen would have ripped the ball. Instead, he swung as usual, a looping motion with no hip rotation. However, he did make contact, a ground ball that found its way toward the hole at shortstop. I couldn't tell if the ball had eyes and would trickle through to the outfield grass.

The shortstop crossed to his right and knocked it down. The baseball lay momentarily on the dirt and the kid barehanded it, firing a long rainbow to the first baseman. Kellen beat the throw by a step and a half. It was his first legitimate hit of the season—I felt an overwhelming sense of relief.

"Out!" boomed Renee Lincoln, and I looked up, incredulous, at the woman whose right arm was raised in a fist.

"No way!" I raced from my coaching box to where she stood in the grass behind shortstop.

"Get off the field, Jack. Only players allowed out here. And the ball's still live."

"How can you call him out? He beat it by two steps."

"Settle down. Stop yelling."

"I'll yell if I want. My team's getting their ass kicked, and you make a call like that?"

She had been moving away, but with my last outburst, turned back sharply. "Leave. Now. I don't want to eject you, but if you keep it up, I'll have no choice."

"He's safe," I growled.

"Go."

"He's safe. This is ridiculous. He's safe!" I stormed off the field and Pete stopped me as I barreled into the dugout. "Can you believe that?" I said.

"The call doesn't matter," he said flatly. "We're losing by twelve runs. See the boys' faces? Look in the stands. You're acting like a baby in front of everyone."

I covered my mouth with my hand so Pete couldn't see my lips. "Bite me."

The game ended three batters later. I fumed in the dugout while the boys ran out to get their post-game fix of sugar and caffeine. "The bright side," Pete said, packing the equipment in preparation for moving to the opposite dugout, "is that we have thirty minutes before our next game. Maybe they'll have time to forget."

I shook my head. "They shouldn't forget. We just dropped out of first place."

Pete put a hand on my shoulder. "You need to let it go. Blowouts happen."

Of course he was right, but I still hated losing. After a moment, I left the dugout and joined the team. I sat on the ball bucket and looked at the kids. Everyone was quiet and staring at the ground, either too afraid or too embarrassed to look at me. As much as I wanted to vent about their half-hearted play, I realized this wasn't the time.

"Dodgers, just forget that game. Baseball's like that sometimes. Hang in there." I paused, feeling the weight of what I was about to say. "I'm sorry for acting crazy out there. Just because I disagreed with the call—"

"I beat the throw, Dad."

"Yes, you did. That was a good hit, son. But I was wrong to argue. I'm sorry. Let's all try to start over. Remember, next game's a tie score—nothing to nothing."

I felt better, yet I knew another person deserved an apology. I looked around and saw Renee standing outside the third base fence. I waved to attract Pete's attention. "Could you work with Kellen on his hitting? I need to talk with . . . you know."

Renee stood alone, leaning on the fence, staring at another game in progress. I felt terrible that I'd let my emotions get the best of me.

"I want to apologize," I told her.

"Too late for that." She crossed her arms, and I could see her fists clench. "Get the hell away from me."

I heard the sound of an engine and turned to see Ground Chuck driving his Gator toward our field, where he'd drag the dirt in preparation for the next game. There wasn't much time to apologize.

"Look, I'm sorry," I said. "I shouldn't have lost my temper. You didn't deserve to be treated like that."

"Got that right. It's guys like you that ruin Little League."

I wanted to say more, to try to convince her of my sincerity, but I knew she didn't give one whit about my intentions. Walking slowly back to our field, I knew I'd screwed everything up. What was wrong with me? Yelling at Renee like that, then hoping she'd simply accept my apology. I was such a jackass.

I stepped into the empty third base dugout and looked toward home plate, where Pete stood behind Kellen, positioning his elbow and shoulder in an attempt to improve his batting stance. Then he clapped his hands and pumped his fist in encouragement. I felt lucky to have someone like Pete.

The sound of an approaching engine and metallic clacking drew my head to the left. A small green and yellow tractor had circled wide around third base, the driver's attention focused on the noisy rake attachment. Ground Chuck was headed for home, toward Pete and Kellen.

"Heads up!" I shouted.

No one heard me.

❧

I had one chance to avert disaster: intercept the tractor. I bolted from the dugout. When I reached the baseline, Kellen looked up. So did Pete. Ground Chuck turned forward and gaped.

Suddenly I realized the danger facing me. I was in a pickle, a hot box . . . a rundown. Ground Chuck loomed closer, and then he turned the wheel hard to the right.

The flat front bumper struck my legs just below the knee, my right leg absorbing the initial blow. I heard a loud pop, then found myself suspended in the air, feet above my head.

My left shoulder made a sickening crunch as the ground rushed toward me. Dirt filled my mouth and nostrils. Then I was flat on my back.

I tried to call out Kellen's name, but my breath had been knocked out. Daggers of pain shot through my side. I felt a steady pressure on the back of my right thigh.

"Nobody touch him," Pete called, then knelt next to me. "Jack, are you hurt?"

"Kellen," I said faintly. As I inhaled, a sharp stitch filled my chest. Maybe I'd landed on something.

"Get the kids off the field," I heard someone say, then Kellen's screams rang in my ears. Oh God, what happened to him?

Bright sunlight shone across my face, flickering as the bobbing of heads produced momentary shadows. I could hear Ground Chuck's voice. "He just jumped out in front of me. Someone call an ambulance!"

I didn't need an ambulance. Just needed to stand up, shake it off. When I shifted, another pulse of pain shot through my body.

"Don't move," Captain Carl ordered, in a thin voice that was nothing like his Star Trek hero.

Minutes later, I heard Renee's voice. "Give him some room. Jack, where does it hurt?"

I took shallow breaths and forced my body to say, "Tell me about Kellen."

"He's safe."

"By two steps. Already told you." I had to close my eyes as the world began to spin around me.

"I mean, he's not hurt. Just you. Stay still. Let me check you out."

Soft hands touched my scalp, massaging my skull as they traveled down my face and neck. A thousand pinpricks stung when she brushed my forehead. She palpated my neck and shoulders. I flinched.

"Left shoulder. Could be dislocation or a fractured clavicle."

My world turned fuzzy. Didn't my niece play clavicle in the band? I couldn't move my left arm.

Her hands moved to my waist and hips. No pain, thank God. Down further, my right leg throbbed. I felt my left leg being examined. But my right leg was the one that hurt like hell. A thought flashed—did I still have a right leg?

Renee returned to my head, leaning over my face. Her fingers wiped dust from my mouth. "You're pretty banged up. An ambulance is on its way—"

"I want Kellen—"

"You need to go to the hospital."

I opened my eyes and stared into Renee's face. "Find my son."

She nodded and I heard muffled voices. A moment later, Kellen appeared next to me. "Daddy?"

"Let me see you, Kel. Are you hurt?"

He looked down toward my legs, opened his mouth, and let out a blood-curdling scream. "No, Dad! Please don't die!" I saw Pete put his arm around Kellen and pull him away. As a grey fog slipped over me, I could still hear Kellen crying.

Seconds passed, maybe minutes, maybe hours. Then I felt more hands on my side, turning me. A heavy board slid beneath me. Hands slowly rolled me to my original position. Foam blocks surrounded my head, as if someone were forcing my skull into a football helmet.

"They're immobilizing your neck," Renee explained.

"I'm sorry," I mumbled. "I'm so sorry."

Straps tightened across my forehead, securing me to the neck brace. Suspended in the air once more, I floated on a gurney into an ambulance. Renee climbed in and held my hand.

A wave of warmth washed over me, and the voices dulled to a murmur. Blackness enveloped me.

Chapter 27

Thank God for morphine. Lying in my bed at St. Mary's Catholic Hospital, I jammed my thumb against the medication pump button. The nurse had assured me I couldn't overmedicate myself, so I decided to wring out every drop of morphine from the IV.

It had been three days since Ground Chuck literally turned my life upside-down, one day since they wheeled me into surgery to reconstruct my unstable right knee. The door to my room opened and Leah walked in carrying a bouquet of flowers. "Afternoon, Superman." She placed the flowers onto a rolling food cart, next to two colorful arrangements of lilies, chrysanthemums, and carnations. "Who sent the other flowers?" she asked.

"No idea."

She plucked a card from each vase. "One's from Sugar Meadow Little League. The other says, 'Coach K, We hope you feel better. We miss you. Love, The Dodgers.' That was nice of them." She turned her eyes to me. "You look better. How's the leg?"

"Throbbing." I pushed the happy button again.

My orthopedic surgeon swung open the door. Dr. Powell had large ears and a red, bulbous nose that reminded me of W.C. Fields. "Let's see how that knee's doing today."

He carefully pulled back the gauze covering my right knee. A four-inch scar ran vertically from the middle of my kneecap to the upper shin, which had turned a lovely shade of blue and violet, tinged with green. Two small puncture holes on opposite sides of the knee made me look like a vampire victim. Hinged braces immobilized my right leg. Dr. Powell probed and prodded the immediate area around the incision, then bent my knee.

A sharp pain shot up my leg and radiated across my hip. I gasped. "Don't . . . please."

"Pain's normal, unfortunately. Has the nurse shown you how to use the PCA system?"

"Yeah." I rolled my head back and squeezed my eyes closed, trying to will the pain away.

"I need to check your other injuries." Dr. Powell undid my pale-blue gown to expose my left shoulder and lightly pressed my collarbone. Then he lowered the gown below my chest, unveiling a spreading purple blotch below my right nipple, and carefully examined my side. He removed several x-rays from an oversized envelope attached to my chart, slipped them in the illuminating viewbox on the opposite wall, and peered at them through reading glasses.

"Your left shoulder had a partial dislocation, but that's better than a broken clavicle. You got lucky with those two fractured ribs. Didn't puncture a lung."

Lucky? I didn't think so. "What about my leg?"

"Remember what I told you about the *unhappy triad*? Not much in your knee is original equipment anymore."

My memory was vague, but I knew the surgery had been long and complicated. I'd suffered a blown-out anterior cruciate ligament. Torn medial collateral ligament. Tear of the medium disco-something-or-other. They drilled holes for the arthroscopic instruments, attached a graft from a tendon in my leg, and reconstructed my right knee. "Will I be able to walk again?"

"Of course you will," Leah said brightly. "Right, Doctor?"

Dr. Powell nodded. "I'd have you up on that leg today if you could use crutches. But that shoulder's gonna give you fits for a while. Afraid you'll be confined to a wheelchair or the bed except when you're doing leg exercises. And those start now."

While I flexed and extended my knee at his command, attempting to practice relaxation breathing like Melanie had done during labor, I thought about the difficulties that lay ahead. Walking, driving, and shopping were going to be an ordeal. How could I take care of Kellen like this?

"When will I get better?" I asked him.

"You'll need the crutches for at least a month and the knee brace through the summer. Probably Christmas before you lose the limp. However, your prognosis is excellent." He seemed downright giddy.

After he left, I shifted uncomfortably in the hospital bed. The bulky leg brace was clearly going to be annoying. I manipulated the controls to elevate the bed to a sitting position, but then my ribs fired a warning shot. I grabbed for the PCA button and told Leah, "I don't know how I'm gonna do this by myself."

"You're not. You have family. I'll be here for you, and Mom and Dad said they'll stay as long as you need them."

I tried to imagine living in the same house with my parents again, dealing with my mother's constant doting and my father's silent disapproval. God, it was going to be just like growing up.

I was afraid to pose the question, but did anyway. "How's Kellen?"

"Better. Mom and Dad are watching him. They'll come by after lunch. Kellen didn't want to go to school."

I blew out a measured breath. "He was like that after Melanie died. Hates being singled out and having people treat him weird."

I contemplated how I could ease his stress, then had an idea. "You know where I keep all those mementos of Melanie? There's a dark blue towel in there. Have Mom and Dad bring it to me."

"By the way, Kellen wrote you a note."

"Oh God, not one of his letters."

She handed me a page of paper. "It's real sweet. Read it."

The letter said: *"Dear Dad, thank you for saving me from being runned over. You are my hero. Don't worry Gramma and Grampa are taking care of me. Love, Kellen."*

"What did you mean," she said, "not one of his letters?"

Kellen's obsession with writing notes to his dead mother wasn't something I wanted to publicize. At the same time, Leah—or worse, Mom or Dad—might stumble across one of them. They deserved the truth so they wouldn't be blindsided. "It's kind of odd," I said. "Kellen occasionally writes notes to Melanie, like a diary."

"Oh, I know about that."

"Guess you found one. Sorry, I should have told you."

"I've known for a long time. He writes letters to Melanie so he can work through his emotions."

"What? I don't understand."

"You know I'm in counseling with Dr. Mike, right? Richard won't go and he won't even talk with me about it. Just eats me up inside. Well, Dr. Mike told me to write letters to Richard to tell him how I feel, even though I know he'll never read them. It helps me get things off my chest. I suggested Kellen do the same thing after Melanie died."

"You?" My mind was spinning. My sister had gone behind my back and driven Kellen into a world of psychological mumbo-jumbo. "Leah, can you go? I need to rest."

"Are you in pain?"

"Yeah." It was an understatement, on so many levels.

The afternoon passed slowly. Mom and Dad came by for a brief visit, promised they were taking good care of Kellen and told me to feel better. I tried to take a nap but never could get comfortable, so I settled for watching game shows on the overhead TV.

Around four o'clock, the day nurse, a middle-aged woman with lifeless eyes, methodically changed my IV. "Describe your pain on a scale from zero to ten," she said in a dull, monotone voice.

"Six, maybe seven." My pain level had reached ten on Saturday night, but had stayed steady between four and seven once they started giving me drugs. I was pretty sure the morphine bag had hung empty for a couple of hours—my entire body throbbed.

As soon as she replaced the bag, I pressed the PCA button repeatedly, like a hurried executive in front of an elevator, not wanting to be cheated out of any medicine. Thankfully, the drugs began to flow. Morphine and saline. Tequila and lime juice. I didn't care. Anything to dull the pain.

Dusk eventually crept in, and an orange glow washed over my hospital room. Due to Sugar Land's flatter-than-flat topography and a dearth of buildings taller than two stories, my west-facing window had a perfect view of the setting sun. Another day had slipped into oblivion.

The banging of multiple fists on the door startled me. Then the door flew open. Three boys—one black with short, curly hair, another heavy-set wearing glasses, and a freckled blonde— entered, ignoring all semblances of decorum and manners. The two adults who followed them didn't appear to care about the noise.

"Hi, Coach K," Mitchell practically shouted. "We brought you some presents."

Stacy, who carried a teddy bear and a bunch of blue helium-filled balloons, shushed him. "Sorry, Jack. We didn't mean to barge in. Is this an okay time?"

"Yeah. It's good to see friendly faces." I craned my neck to see Kellen, but he hung back behind Coach Pete.

Stacy cleared a spot on the shelf for the bear and the balloons, setting them next to the three flower arrangements, which had been moved from my food tray to make room for my as-yet-uneaten dinner. I'd wanted to eat—was hungry, in fact—but the meal consisted of roast beef that tasted like shredded erasers, overcooked mashed potatoes, and slimy Brussels sprouts.

She approached my bed and gave me a platonic kiss on the cheek, taking care not to aggravate my injuries. "There's one balloon from each Dodger. Did you get our flowers?"

I pointed to the yellow and white arrangement. "Thank everyone for me."

She smiled and retreated to the opposite wall, next to the x-ray viewbox. The boys circled my bed and gawked at my broken body, which was mostly covered by a tan blanket. Derek and Mitchell pointed at me and whispered to each other. Kellen stood quietly.

I reached out my right hand, grimacing at the fresh pain in my ribs, and rubbed his back. "Good to see you, son."

Kellen didn't reply; he just stared at me and swallowed air.

"Come here," I said, crooking my finger. When he leaned close, I whispered, "Don't worry. I'm gonna be okay."

He began to breathe rapidly, then raised a hand to his chest as if he were reciting the Pledge of Allegiance.

"Are you feeling squeezy?" I asked, and he nodded back

frantically. I reached under the covers and extracted the Yankees towel, then pressed it into his hands. "You remember when Mom said you can use this if you feel nervous? Well, I know you're growing up and everything, but I want you to have this in case you need it."

His hands tightened around the towel, then slowly relaxed. His breathing fell into a normal rhythm. "Aunt Leah told me you have a scar."

"It's nasty, but it's also pretty cool-looking. Wanna see?" I peeled back the blanket and the boys' eyes widened. I pointed out all my injuries and, after a few minutes, noticed that Kellen's face was no longer taut.

"We have another present for you," Pete said. He sheepishly stepped forward and presented me with a brand-new baseball, its red stitching winding around it like a ribbon. I twirled the ball in my fingers as if fumbling for the proper pitching grip, then noticed all the signatures written in black ink.

"It's from the boys. They signed it for you at practice." His voice quavered and his eyes welled up. A solitary tear ran down his brown face, along his broad nose, and into the thicket of mottled black and grey hair of his goatee. "I'm sorry," he mouthed silently.

"Can you give us a minute?" I asked Stacy.

She quickly ushered the children out of the room, promising them candy from the vending machine. Pete remained fixed at the foot of my bed. "It's all my fault," he said.

"No, it was an accident. It just happened."

"It happened because I wasn't paying attention. I put both of you in danger. If only I wasn't deaf." Pete wiped his eyes with the back of his hand.

I knew how helpless he felt. Been there, done that. Since Melanie's accident, I found myself questioning everything. If only

I hadn't been speeding. If only I hadn't decided to work that Saturday. If only I hadn't selfishly claimed the new Lexus for myself, pawning off the smaller Camry on her. *If only* a lot of things, and she might still be alive.

"It's not your fault," I said. "Wasn't anyone's fault."

Pete nodded and I felt like he could read my mind as well as my lips. He'd become more of a friend in three months than anyone else I'd known in Sugar Land. Even realizing his limitations, Pete had stepped up to help me and the rest of the team. And when I needed a kick in the butt, he'd been the one to deliver that as well. Melanie would have liked him.

Around two in the morning, I awoke and couldn't get back to sleep. So I just lay there in bed and contemplated everything. Life had seemed perfect only a year ago—now I was laid up here in the hospital with both a body and family in need of healing.

The one thing I'd come to hate over the past year was nighttime. During the day, I could muddle my way through, put up a brave front. Like today, when it seemed everyone I knew came by to wish me well, I could allow myself to exist in that alternate reality, where life was manageable because I had my friends and family.

But in the middle of the night, when no one was there to hear my lies, I'd feel the terrible emptiness. Because she was gone.

I tried to focus on anything besides Melanie, and found myself thinking about the Dodgers. The baseball from Pete lay next to me, and I brought it to my face. I read the signatures, noting all the kids I'd come to know: Baker, Derek, Mitchell, Corey, T-Bone, Appleton, Tyler, Zachary, and Omkar. Even Patrick and Stewart, who were starting to grow on me. Kellen's name was there too. Someone with sloppy handwriting had printed "*Get well, Coach K.*" The K was backwards, which I knew was normal for kids this age, but I kept staring at the signature. Then it hit me.

I deserved the backwards K . . . because I'd been caught looking. I'd been caught looking in the rearview mirror, unable to save Melanie. Since then, I'd been afraid to move forward. God had thrown me curveballs, but the bat had remained frozen on my shoulder—I'd been caught looking at life.

The pain in my body grew mercilessly through the lonely night. I reached for the PCA control and held it in my deformed hand. Pain was normal, Dr. Powell had said. Healing only came after enduring the pain. Instead of pressing the button, I let it fall to my side.

Chapter 28

When the insurance company decided enough was enough, the hospital released me. Carrying my crutches, Mom walked alongside my wheelchair as I rolled through the hospital entrance doors. My parents' car was parked in the patient pick-up area, its doors and trunk open and ready to be loaded.

I was unsure how to navigate the twenty feet or so, then Dad leaned down and offered his arm. "I've got you, Jack. Just hang on. We'll take it slow. Let me know if you need to stop."

I rose tentatively from the wheelchair, slid the crutches under me, and shuffled slowly to the curb. His hands helped fold me into position and pour me into the car. My father, the gruff son of a bitch, was actually gentle. He wasn't the man I knew. Or thought I knew.

He reversed the process when we arrived home, unfolding me from the car, supporting me, and leading me inside. I collapsed onto my recliner in the family room.

"Here's your crutches, honey," my mom said, leaning them on the wall beside me.

My eyes were already closed. "I think I'll take a nap."

She draped a blanket over me. "You do that. We'll go buy some groceries. What do you want me to make for dinner?"

Mom's home cooking. That was the best medicine. "Anything, Mom. Anything at all."

My parents had been gone only ten minutes when my cell phone rang. The phone lay on the kitchen table. Thirty feet away. Ugh.

I lowered the recliner footrest, making sure not to jar my leg, and pulled the crutches under me, spreading them wide for support like two legs of a tripod. The phone stopped ringing, but I was determined to stand. I concentrated on keeping my balance while gathering the crutches under me, then slowly rose. Finally, I limped into the kitchen.

The first thing I noticed on the freshly scrubbed kitchen table was a letter. I was tired of stumbling across Kellen's notes, but like passing a traffic accident, I couldn't keep from looking. The page read: *"Dear Dad, I am happy you are home from the hospittal. I miss you soooooo much. Love, Kellen."* He'd colored a pair of stick figures, one larger than the other, and a rudimentary house. The sketch reminded me of the one he'd done for Dr. Mike at our first visit. But this time we were smiling.

Melanie would have posted this on the refrigerator, I thought, then caught myself. This kind of stuff was my job now. I shoved the cell phone in my pocket. Then I picked up Kellen's note and hobbled to the refrigerator, where I affixed the paper to the door with butterfly magnets.

Easing back into the recliner, I checked the call log: six missed calls and two new voice messages. Each one originated from the same number in Dallas. I skipped the voicemails and dialed Scott's number.

"Jack, why haven't you returned my calls?"

"It's a long story." I spent ten minutes explaining the circumstances that put me in the hospital and another five describing the ordeal of coming home. "Doctor says I should be fine after my recovery, but I can't move to Dallas for at least a month."

"You didn't get my messages?"

"Not yet."

"My boss couldn't wait any longer. He hired someone already. I tried, buddy."

When I hung up, I banged my forehead with the cell phone. My eyes fell on the signed baseball on the coffee table. For the past few days, it had reminded me not to get caught looking anymore. But how could I move forward if life kept knocking me on my ass?

❦

My first physical therapy session was almost over. As I lay on my back, digging my heels into the table and tightening my hamstrings, I plotted the death of my therapist.

She had started me with what she claimed were easy exercises. I flexed and pointed my toes, which stretched my calves. I straightened my leg and tightened the muscles on top of my thigh, which stretched my quads. I squeezed my butt muscles together, which stretched—well, let's just say it stretched my imagination. But when she had me raise my leg and hold it six inches above the padded table for a count of ten, I decided she must die. An agonizing death.

"That's all vor today, Meester Kennedy," she said, sounding as if she'd seen *Young Frankenstein* one too many times. "We verk on your quads more next time. Have a guday."

Leah wouldn't be back with the car for another hour—she'd scheduled an appointment with Dr. Mike—so I hobbled to the exit door and turned down the hallway. I needed to find a place to eat my lunch . . . and to plan a painful revenge for Frau

Blücher. I entered the atrium a little after noon, looking for a secluded spot. My crutches clicked like a metronome across the ceramic tile, and I found a table next to floor-to-ceiling windows which looked out on a decorative pond.

Kellen and I had walked by that pond months ago when he needed to visit the doctor. *The doctor* . . . I stared out the window. I couldn't believe how hurtful I'd been to her at that game. Even in the throes of my tantrum, I knew I was wrong to yell at her . . . but had continued anyway.

What I didn't understand was why Renee acted so kindly after the way I treated her. I remembered how she took care of me before the paramedics arrived, held my hand on the ambulance ride, and kept me awake by singing a loud and purposely off-key version of *Take Me Out to the Ballgame*. If I ever saw her again, I'd apologize the right way.

Minutes passed, but the feelings of guilt didn't. I grabbed my crutches and set out for a lonely walk around the atrium, finally stopping at a bank of vending machines. One thing I'd decided while lying in the hospital was to get in better shape—no more junk food. I fed a dollar into the machine and punched the button for Diet Coke.

As I shuffled back to the windows, I saw Renee sitting at a table by herself. I shouldn't have been surprised, since her office was in the same building, but I froze. As sure as I'd been that I wanted to apologize, I was suddenly scared to death. I spun before she could see me. Then I rushed away as best I could. I flopped into my chair to complete the escape . . . until my crutches crashed to the ground and everyone in the atrium turned and looked at me.

A moment later, Renee appeared at my table. I was petrified that she would sit down, equally petrified that she would leave. "Can I join you?" she said, then sat down before I could respond.

"When did you get out of the hospital?"

I stared for a moment before answering. "Uh . . . Thursday. They ended up doing a total ACL and MCL reconstruction. And they fixed my menista . . . uh . . . minimal—"

"Medial meniscus?"

"That's it."

She popped open a Sunkist and emptied her lunch bag onto the table. "You doing physical therapy here?"

"Three days a week. I'm just waiting for my ride." I opened my sack lunch and pulled out a PBJ sandwich and a bag of carrots. Suddenly I felt like a middle-school boy, alone in the cafeteria and joined by the prettiest girl in school. As I chewed on the carrot sticks, I gathered my courage.

But before I could apologize, Renee said, "Sorry I didn't come visit you in the hospital." Her eyes were cast down—she seemed keenly interested in opening her potato chips. "I . . . uh . . . had a tough workload. A few surgeries."

Well, that threw me. I hadn't expected her to visit. "You shouldn't be apologizing to me. I was totally out of line at the game. And if it helps, I'm really sorry about dumping ice water on you, too."

"Water? Oh . . ." The corners of her mouth twitched up, then back down. "That was a long time ago." She stared into her lap and drummed a finger on the table. "It's just that . . . I feel like I contributed to the accident. You know, we argued about that call at first base, and—"

"I shouldn't have charged the field—"

"Stop." She inhaled deeply and glanced out the window. "Look, I blew the dumb call. My mouth said 'Out' even though I saw the runner beat the throw. Then when you argued, I didn't back down."

"I was way out of line."

"True, but if only you'd have been with your team, maybe the accident wouldn't have happened." She brushed a lock of brown hair behind her ear. As I looked at her, something about her struck me as different, but I couldn't put my finger on it.

"Look, Renee, you didn't do anything to cause this. Sometimes accidents just happen." I tried to push back a memory of a horrific car crash that had also been classified as an accident.

"You're sweet," she said.

"Believe me, I know." I looked into Renee's eyes and somehow knew she was a good listener. So I took a long drink of Diet Coke, exhaled, and told her the ordeal of eleven months ago. It was a story I had told superficially many times over the past year: taking two cars to Kellen's team party, the blowout and crash into the tree, and the investigation into the cause of the collision. Of course, the accident was never blamed on Melanie, the car, or even the tire itself. The final report identified a nail puncture as the likely cause, with low tire pressure and high speed as contributing factors. As I told Renee what had happened, the pain flooded back, more acute than ever.

I was still rambling when Renee took my hand and gently squeezed it. "No one should have to go through that. Losing someone important to you." Her voice trailed off, and I could sense she was holding something back.

We sat in silence, but I had all these questions about what made her tick. Eventually, she gathered the remnants of her lunch and placed them in a paper bag. She lifted an uneaten candy bar and placed it in the breast pocket of her blouse, patted it with her hand, and smiled. "For later. I need to get back to work."

As she stood, it finally clicked. Now I knew why she looked different. She wasn't wearing her white coat. I'd always seen Renee in some sort of uniform: a doctor's coat, park ranger outfit, or blue umpire shirt. Now here she was, a woman with no disguise. "Where's your lab coat?" I said.

"Probably on a hanger in my office." She fixed her gaze on me. "What? Do you think I wear my coat all the time? A doctor is only part of who I am." She walked toward the trash can, twirled, and tossed a perfect fadeaway jumper with the wadded-up paper sack. Then she blew imaginary smoke from her index finger.

"Is this where you usually take your lunch break?" I blurted.

"Unless I have morning surgery. I like to come here and look at the ducks. Keeps my mind clear for afternoon patients."

"Well, I'm going to be here three days a week myself. I'd enjoy sharing lunch with you, if you don't mind"

"Are you asking me on a date?" she teased, smiling broadly.

I took a deep breath. "Absolutely."

Chapter 29

On Wednesday, Frau Blücher had the day off, which meant I'd been assigned to the less sadistic physical therapist, who released me five minutes early. When my session ended, I hurried as fast as my crutches allowed to the atrium.

Renee was already sitting at the far table, staring out the large window toward the pond. As I approached, I could see her birthmark—what had previously looked like the state of California actually included the Baja peninsula as well, a blotch of red running from behind her ear, down her neck, and disappearing into the collar of her blouse.

"What's up, Doc?" I said with my best Bugs Bunny impression, shaking the back of Renee's chair. "You beat me here today." I laid my crutches across one chair and sat in another.

"I don't know about doing lunch today," she said.

"You gotta try this coffee cake from my mom. She's a blue-ribbon chef for this stuff." I reached into the plastic grocery bag that served as my lunchbox.

Renee smiled wanly and turned back toward the window. "Maybe another time."

My fingers loosened on the Tupperware containing Mom's crumbly dessert, then moved to the rectangular box I'd carefully wrapped this morning. I pulled it out of the bag. "Got you something."

"I said I'm not hungry."

"Would you please turn around?" When she twisted around to face me, I said, "This is for you."

"Jack, you shouldn't have."

"What do you mean? It's just a little gift. Open it."

She placed both hands on the table, her fingers splayed wide, her arms tense. "I just . . . want . . . some privacy."

Something was definitely wrong, but I wasn't sure what I'd done or said to upset her. I was sure, however, that she didn't want me around. I slipped the gift back in my grocery bag, pulled my crutches under me, and backed away. "I'm just gonna sit over there. Don't worry, I won't bother you. Hope you feel better."

I crossed the atrium and found a table far from Renee, then extracted the contents from the grocery bag. As I bit into my peanut butter and honey sandwich, I thought about the times we'd seen each other. In her office. At the state park. On the baseball field.

And every time, I'd screwed things up.

I flicked the sapphire-colored ribbon on the wrapped box. What was I thinking, giving a present to someone who'd only recently become my lunch companion? I'd bought the thing at the mall because I thought she might like it. That had obviously been a mistake.

My bag of pretzels and a banana disappeared in short order, but I didn't have the heart to eat Mom's coffee cake. I watched Renee sitting by herself and wanted to go give her a hug. Then I thought that if an inexpensive gift was pushing the boundaries, a hug would definitely be the wrong move.

So I gathered my trash and crutches and retreated from the atrium. After popping into a nearby restroom, I checked my watch because my folks were supposed to pick me up after lunch.

An hour to kill, maybe two if Mom was navigating, and I hadn't brought a book. Wait a second—this building was full of waiting rooms stocked with magazines and newspapers. All I needed to do was go back to where all the offices were located.

And if I happened to see Renee again, I told myself, that would just be a coincidence.

As I neared the atrium, that squeezy feeling rose again. My chest tightened and I could feel my breathing quicken. *Don't screw this up.*

Renee was still sitting at the far end of the atrium. Her elbows were propped on the table, and she held her head in her hands. Even from here, I could see her staring into nothingness.

"I came to apologize," I said, limping up next to her. "Sometimes I don't think."

"You didn't do anything wrong. I just want to be alone."

"Well, if you need to talk with someone . . ."

When she looked up at me, whatever strength that had been sustaining her drained from her body. In a tremulous voice, she said, "I miss my dad."

I didn't know what was going on, but I could tell she was in pain. Quickly I sat next to her. "Tell me."

She collected her thoughts and exhaled a few times. Then she said, "Dad died fourteen years ago today. You see, it was just him and me for most of my life. Mom passed away from cancer when I was four, so he was the only parent I ever really knew."

"I'm sorry."

"Everyone goes through it, I know. Losing a parent . . . that's nature's way." She was silent for a long while, then took a sip from a Dr Pepper can. "He's why I became a doctor."

Renee stood abruptly. "Will you walk outside with me?"

❦

The little pond outside the professional building didn't resemble the big lake at Brazos Bend in the slightest, with its blue-green dye and man-made shoreline—not to mention a fountain that rivaled Old Faithful—but I just knew that Renee spent a lot of free time there. We walked along a decomposed granite path that ran next to the pond and under the shade of willow trees and Bradford pears.

An empty concrete bench appeared around a turn in the path. I wouldn't have minded stopping to give my armpits some relief from the crutches, but Renee seemed intent on walking, so we passed it by.

"Where are we going?" I asked.

"A little farther. I want to show you something."

Just as my shoulders began to burn from the strain, Renee stopped and pointed to a tree next to the path. An old birdhouse, constructed from rough-hewn cypress and decorated with interweaved twigs, hung from the trunk of a pecan tree.

"My dad and I built that bluebird house together. Sort of a father-daughter thing. When I moved to Texas, I brought it with me." She play-shushed me. "There's another one at Brazos Bend. Don't tell anyone."

I crisscrossed my finger across my chest. "It'll be our secret. You said he's the reason you're a doctor. Was he one, too?"

She reached out and ran her finger along the hole that formed the birdhouse door. "That's exactly one-and-a-half inches in diameter. Perfect size for a bluebird. If it's any bigger, starlings or grackles can take it over. You don't want that. Bluebirds need a safe place to raise their family."

I wasn't sure what to say.

We stood there a couple of minutes, and she rambled on

about how a parent bird carefully builds the nest, how the fledglings are cared for. Finally, she said, "My dad was an accountant."

"Oh."

"But he used to be a carpenter. He taught me how to build things. We probably made fifty or more of these birdhouses. I'm sorry, I'm just babbling."

"It's okay." I threw an arm around her shoulder. "What are friends for?"

I felt her tremble, and then it all spilled out.

"When I was a senior in high school, Dad and I built a huge deck in our backyard. We didn't even need a deck, but I think he just wanted to spend time with me before I graduated and went off to college. So I was his assistant.

"The first week, we sank the piers and hung the joists. Dad wasn't in any hurry, and he took time to check the plumb and level of each piece of lumber. Then we nailed down the deck boards. I can't remember how many there were, but I know I lugged every single one because of his lame arm."

I raised an eyebrow.

"He was shot by the Viet Cong during a helicopter run. Ever heard of Operation Junction City?"

I shook my head.

"That's why he gave up carpentry as a career. And then my mom got sick . . . Anyway, the morning we built the railing, he asked me to check the workshop for some more nails. When I returned, he was on his back and clutching his lame arm. I thought he fell. But it was much worse."

"His heart."

"I didn't know what to do. He was dying. I ran back to the house and called the ambulance. I tried CPR—the only training I had was watching that old TV show with those two paramedics—but I wasn't doing it right. The doctor said he suffered a massive heart attack and was probably already dead when I tried to revive him. I can't help but think I should have done more."

"So that's why you became a doctor."

∞

"Try the dewberry," I told Renee, pointing to the slice of coffee cake with purple-black filling.

She bit off half and gave a slight moan. "Jack, this is even better than her apple coffee cake. Your mom ought to open a bakery."

"I know, right? Told you she's a great cook."

She stuffed the remainder in her mouth, then glanced at her watch. "Look at the time! I have to get back to the office. Thanks for listening to the stuff about my dad."

"Anytime." I reached into my grocery bag and pulled out a box wrapped in silver paper with a blue ribbon. "Renee, please let me give you this. As a friend."

She looked carefully at the present, then back at me. "Has anyone told you that you look like this crazy coach at the Little League fields? You're much nicer than him, though." Her mouth spread into a wide smile. And then, like Kellen on Christmas morning, she tore apart the wrapping paper with abandon.

"I love it!" she exclaimed as she lifted the ceramic figurine from the box.

"It's a great blue heron. But I guess you knew that."

Renee deposited the figurine back into the box, then pointed at me. "Stand up." As I fumbled for my crutches, she said, "Never mind, just stay there." She leaned over and wrapped her arms around me. And surprised me with a kiss.

Chapter 30

After three weeks of physical therapy, I could feel the strength returning to my leg. And three weeks of lunchtime chats with Renee had lifted my spirits as well.

On Sunday night, I celebrated my newly restored driving privileges by taking Kellen to Sugar Land's best pizzeria. He'd never been to Bella Moglie, because the restaurant with its kitschy decorations and gooey, Chicago-style stuffed pizza pies had been the special place that Melanie and I used to frequent. I requested the usual table in a booth decorated with posters of Sophia Loren, the same booth where Melanie and I had sat with dazed grins, marveling at the ultrasound picture—on second thought, Kellen *had* been to Bella Moglie.

I ordered a half-cheese, half-pepperoni pizza while Kellen cast furtive glances toward three of my favorite arcade games from the 1980s: Ms. Pac Man, Asteroids, and Galaga. "After we eat," I said.

"What?"

"I see you checking out the video games. Relax, you can play them later. Why don't we sit here and talk?"

I folded my hands in my lap and looked at Kellen. He propped his chin in his right hand and stared back at me, then began bouncing his leg under the table.

"What are you doing?" I said.

"Um . . . waiting to eat pizza."

"No. With your leg."

"Nothing." The bouncing stopped. Kellen stuck his pinky in his mouth and chewed on the fingernail. His eyes darted around the room, and the bouncing started up again.

"Are you trying to annoy me?"

"You're mad at me, aren't you?"

"I'm not mad. I'd just like us to have a nice chat." I hoped to steer the conversation toward the notes Kellen had been writing to Melanie. With another grief therapy session scheduled for tomorrow—the last one, I hoped—I didn't want to give Dr. Mike a reason to extend things. Besides, I was tired of hearing Kellen brag about Dr. Mike's latest adventure.

"Coach Pete said I should tell you something, but I'm supposed to make sure you're not already mad."

I rubbed my temples. "What now?"

Kellen lowered his head and mumbled, "I lost my baseball glove."

"You what?"

"See, you're mad."

I gritted my teeth and forced myself to breathe through my nose, while I imagined the earnest look on Pete's face as he cautioned Kellen to tread lightly with me.

"But it's okay, Dad. You don't have to buy me another one. I'm not going to play baseball anymore."

I probably should have seen it coming, with all his complaints about having to attend practices and games, but I'd always figured the joy of being on a baseball field with friends trumped any feelings of inadequacy or fear. "I'll buy you a new glove," I said. "You're not giving up baseball."

"I just don't like it anymore."

"That's not the point. You made a commitment to the team. You can't be a quitter."

In a small voice, he replied, "But what about you?"

Leaning on my crutches, I pressed open Dr. Mike's office door. Kellen trotted in ahead of me. "Guess what happened to my dad."

Dr. Mike took a long look at me. "Trampoline accident?"

"No," Kellen said, laughing.

"Skateboarding down the stairs?"

"You're funny, Dr. Mike. He hurt it at my baseball game. Tell him, Dad."

I hobbled into the office and related the familiar story of getting flipped by the Gator. By now I'd become an expert on such terms as *cruciate ligament*, *hamstring autograft*, and *anterior dislocation*, so I sprinkled them into my explanation, which tended to make the injuries sound more life-threatening than they had been. As always, I ended my story by saying, "At least the groundskeeper didn't score."

I waited for Dr. Mike to laugh, but the killjoy just looked at me. "Sounds painful."

Kellen flopped down Indian-style on the couch, and I sat next to him. "I was hurting right afterwards, of course. Real hard to breathe." Images of those lonely nights in the hospital popped into my mind: coughing with three broken ribs, clanging my knee brace against the bed rails, pressing the misnamed *happy button*.

"Hope you feel better. Okay, who wants to go first today?"

I shook my head. "I don't want to split up anymore. Besides, I think this'll be our last session."

"Why do think that, Jack?"

"It's time. It's been almost a year."

Dr. Mike leaned back and opened his palms. "I'm not sure that looking at a calendar is the right way to evaluate this. Kellen, what do you think about our talks? Do you still have some things you want to discuss?"

Kellen didn't say anything and I held my breath, hoping he wouldn't mention the letters to Melanie. Suddenly he said, "It's not fair." He pointed at me. "He won't let me quit baseball, but that's what he did. And he was my coach."

"Hmm. Tell me more about that." Dr. Mike lifted a finger to silence me.

"Dad was my coach—he was the head coach. And then he got hurt."

"Is that why he had to quit?"

"He was in the hospital for like a week, I think, but then he came home. He can go crutching on the sidewalk and to the mailbox, and he does stuff inside our house. But he never comes to the baseball field. Never. Coach Pete and Mitchell's mom always drive me."

I wanted to jump in, explain how draining it had been to accomplish simple tasks, how I couldn't sleep because of the pain in my chest, how I couldn't take five steps without becoming exhausted. But part of me knew the real reason I stayed away.

Dr. Mike looked back and forth at us, and scribbled in his notebook. "Kellen, why do think your dad stopped coming to the baseball field?"

"Because he thinks I'm a terrible player. He's not proud of me at all."

"Cut that out. You have no idea what I've been through."

"You think I'm the worst kid on the team."

"Son, I'm gonna . . . You're not being fair . . . I busted my butt out there for you." As much as I enjoyed baseball, it sure had a way of kicking me in the nuts. After Melanie died, I thought Little League would ease the pain of losing her. But all it did was magnify the problems between Kellen and me. That's why I quit.

Kellen was crying now. "I can't do anything that makes you happy. Why don't you love me?"

I couldn't understand his reaction. It was as if he'd bottled up these crazy thoughts for years, and now he was dumping them at my feet. "Stop being so dramatic."

He turned to Dr. Mike. "My dad was gonna leave me. He got a job in Dallas."

"Kellen, you knew all about moving to Dallas. That's why we packed those boxes."

"No. You were moving to Dallas and I was gonna be left here. To live with Aunt Leah."

"Kellen James Kennedy, what in the hell are you talking about? What gave you that idea?"

"I heard you talk on the phone. You said it was going to be 'just you and him, like old times.'"

My mouth fell open. Kellen was sobbing into his hands.

I grabbed him into my arms and pulled him close. "I'd never leave you, son. We are a family." I lifted his head. "Look at me. I'm sorry—it's just a big misunderstanding."

Just then, I knew why he could believe such an outlandish idea. I took a deep breath and met his eyes, then said the words I'd swallowed for years. "Kellen, I love you."

After our session ended, we scheduled a follow-up appointment, then headed straight from Dr. Mike's office to the local sporting goods megastore.

In the big picture, the disappearance of Kellen's baseball glove wasn't surprising. He was eight years old; losing stuff came with the territory. He'd lost countless socks and shoes through the years, library books, homework, you name it. Experts say it costs a half-million dollars to raise a child. I think most of that is replacing everything they lose.

"This will be your last glove for a long time," I told Kellen, giving him the stern *Dad voice* so he knew I meant business.

"I'll take care of it. I promise."

He tried on a number of gloves and finally selected an eleven-inch Mizuno with brown webbing and a closed back where he could insert his index finger. A wide, black strap cinched across his hand provided a snug fit. "I don't know, Dad," he said. "I like this one, but it won't close right."

"Don't worry. That's normal." I tossed a bottle of neatsfoot oil and a lacing kit into the shopping cart. "We're gonna go home and break in your glove."

"I don't want to break it."

"Break it in. Get it ready."

Back home, I changed into an old pair of medical scrubs and Kellen donned his SMLL t-shirt. He dragged three lawn chairs into our garage, and I propped up my right leg on one of them. Kellen spread old newspapers over a pile of boxes, no longer destined for Dallas, in the middle of the garage.

I laid the new glove on the makeshift operating table. "Time to break it in."

"I don't know how."

"That's what I'm going to teach you."

My son was about to learn one of life's important secrets, passed down from father to son across generations. My dad taught me how to break in a glove years ago and I often wished I'd paused to savor that time together. Our ritual always began with the firm application of glove oil and continued with a week of playing catch every day.

My coaches and teammates used to follow varying rituals which had been shared by their fathers. Coach Richter swore that dunking a new glove in a bucket of water for two hours, letting it dry, and then lathering it with shaving cream was the ideal method. Larry Wayne stuck his glove in the oven to soften it. And Hunter Doyle smeared his glove with cow manure, then his dad ran over it repeatedly with their tractor. I never knew the science behind it, but I remembered that no one ever wanted to borrow Hunter's glove. And he did field like shit.

Kellen's glove lay stiff on the makeshift table like an oversized, petrified hand. I squirted a stream of oil into the pocket, which immediately turned a deep chocolate. With my good three fingers, I rubbed the oil into the leather. The glove appeared wounded, a dark, blood-like splotch spreading across its tan skin.

"Ew," Kellen said. "What are you doing?"

"It's normal. Oil seeps into the leather and softens it up. Makes it easier to close."

"Let me try."

"Here you go. Don't put too much in one spot. A little goes a long way."

I held the glove and Kellen squirted the conditioning oil. He quickly learned to work in the oil and didn't worry when small drops fell like tears and stained an unworked section. He conditioned every square inch of leather, lubricated the hinges to help the glove close, and then looked to me. "Am I done?"

"Good job," I said and tossed him an old rag. "Let it soak in some more. And help me clean up."

Kellen gathered the saturated paper towels and newspaper and placed them in the trash can. Seeing him act so dutifully, I felt a welling of pride. He'd come so far from the crying boy who tore apart his stuffed animals and kept his distance over the past year.

My boy was becoming a responsible young man. Then I watched him set down the rag and wipe his oily hands on the front of his t-shirt. Maybe not a young man, but definitely all boy. And more resilient than before.

"Look!" Kellen pointed to the wall. He chased after a gecko, which scampered across the garage floor and up a steel shelving unit. In his excitement, Kellen knocked two bicycle helmets and a bicycle pump off the shelf. "Sorry, Dad," he called, not really meaning it, as he picked up speed and chased the gecko around a stack of boxes. He promptly collided with the stack, and a box splattered on the floor, its contents spilling out: hand tools, a Frisbee, and an old baseball glove.

"Stop!" I wasn't angry, but knew I had to nip this in the bud before the garage returned to a state of chaos.

"It's a big one," he said.

"Yes, I know. Fascinating. Help pick up this stuff." Spying the mitt on the floor, I said, "And bring me that old glove. Maybe we can fix it, too."

He looked at the flat, dirty thing on the concrete. "Dad, I don't think anything can save that."

The brown blob was my old fielding glove, a Rawlings model that I'd used in high school. Shaped like a thick potholder, with a broken lace between the third and fourth fingers, it was flattened from years of neglect. "You can always fix a broken glove," I said.

Kellen was unimpressed. "Why don't you just buy a new one?"

That was the typical, spoiled-suburban response that had grated on me for years. Break a lace? Throw away the glove . . . or the shoe. Scratch a car? Trade it in for a newer model. Spouse getting old or boring? Ditto. In modern-day suburbia, there wasn't a great appreciation of the imperfect.

"We can do this, Kellen." I inspected the glove more closely. Its laces were actually broken in two places and the remainder had stretched so far that the glove lacked responsiveness. The dry leather inside had cracked like a drought-ridden field, heat and age conspiring to destroy it. This was my Brooks Robinson signature glove—he was the greatest third baseman of all time. He never gave up on hard-hit balls to the hot corner, and I wasn't giving up on my glove either. "Hand me the lacing kit from the bag," I said.

I'd bought extra rawhide lacing and an awl in case Kellen's glove needed repair, but my old glove was definitely the correct application for it. The Kennedy doctors spent the next hour performing surgery on the patient. Brooks Robinson needed a replacement of all his ligaments and tendons. Even his medial meniscus. I carefully cut out the old laces and employed the awl to thread new leather into an intricate cross-stitch. Kellen assisted as I pulled the laces tight and made strong knots.

"The patient's gonna live," I said. "Now he needs a transfusion."

We worked side by side to pour life-giving oil into my Brooks Robinson, completing its slow but steady transformation. I tightened the laces once more and considered our accomplishment. We'd taken two fielding gloves of limited usefulness and returned them to their potential. Broken-down to broken-in. Then I pounded a ball into each glove's pocket to preserve the shape and wrapped each glove with a wide rubber band that Kellen had retrieved from the kitchen.

I placed the two dark-brown gloves on a shelf. "We've done all we can for now. Next, we'll play catch. Before you know it, they'll seem normal."

Chapter 31

"Derek's here," Kellen said as we pulled into the parking lot. "I'm gonna show him my new glove."

I turned off the engine. "Remember, keep a ball in the pocket when you're not using it. Can you hand me my crutches?" But I was talking to thin air; Kellen had already streaked away. I sat in the car another minute, wondering if coming here was the right decision, finally realizing that I didn't have a choice. Slowly, I extracted myself from the car, hopped to the rear door, and pulled out those infernal crutches.

As I limped along the sidewalk, which was still wet from an afternoon shower that hadn't been strong enough to cancel practice, a jumble of emotions hit me. Of course I felt guilty for abandoning the team and nervous about how everyone would treat me, but at the same time I felt a sense of peace—that I belonged out here. Making my way toward the practice field, I pushed away the negative memories and thought instead about Opening Day: the brilliant blue of clean Dodger uniforms, the look on Appleton's face after he hit a stand-up triple, the loud cheers after the victory.

I paused to rest my arms and wondered why coming here today felt different. A pair of older boys ran past me into a dugout and tossed their bat bags onto the ground. Then two men walked by, one rolling a pitching machine, the other lugging an equipment bag across his shoulders and carrying a bucket of balls. Suddenly I understood what had changed—I'd come to the ballfield with no gear, no clipboard. No baggage.

Kellen and I had negotiated a compromise while conditioning our gloves: I'd buck up and help Coach Pete however he saw fit, and Kellen would work harder on his game. And neither of us would complain about it.

I still had reservations, though. What kind of help could I possibly provide? I was unable to put significant weight on my leg. I couldn't hit grounders or throw a ball while leaning on crutches. And I'd come to despise those things, the way they bruised my palms and forearms and chafed my armpits. When I was through with the crutches, they were going straight into the trash . . . or on top of a bonfire.

A baseball whizzed past my ear and I looked up. There weren't any players warming up between the fields—they were the usual culprits, heaving warm-up tosses to each other without regard to pedestrians.

"C'mon, Cale, stop throwing like a girl. Hit my mitt!" The voice came from a pitching cage about fifty feet away. I looked over and spied a boy wearing an LSU t-shirt, which hung low over his baseball pants. Curly hair peeked out under his ballcap; his head slumped down. He stood quietly on the pitching mound at the far end of the cage, slowly swinging an empty glove. Closer to me, a man with several chins and a doughy middle sat on an overturned bucket. He sported a catcher's mitt on his left hand.

"Throw it hard, boy," the man growled with a thick Louisiana accent, "and keep it inside the cage this time."

I watched as the kid, maybe ten or eleven years old, toed the rubber from the stretch position. With exaggerated movements, he brought his feet together, then lifted his front leg in such a way to seriously compromise his balance. Just when I thought he would stumble backward, his back foot propelled him upward and he catapulted another ball over the fence. It rolled to a stop at my feet.

I leaned over and picked up the ball, then hobbled to the other one and picked it up as well. I navigated my crutches around a mud puddle and toward the pitching cage. When I flipped the balls over the top of the fence, the boy mumbled, "Thanks." He didn't meet my eyes.

"Last time," the man said from behind the plate.

"Fastball?"

"I don't care. Anything I can catch. Those last two throws were horrible." The words fired from his lips like poison darts through a straw.

I rested on my crutches and watched the gangly kid try to throw another pitch. This time the ball skipped three feet in front of the plate and ricocheted off the bucket. The man's legs flew off the ground as he tried to protect himself.

"Sorry, Dad!"

The boy's father grumbled and began to collect stray balls at the rear of the cage. "We're done!"

I don't know why I decided to jump into this tender father-and-son moment, but the words escaped my mouth before I considered the implications. "Can I offer a couple suggestions?"

The man stopped and eyed me warily, as if I were a salad with low-fat dressing. "You think you could help my Cale pitch bettuh?"

"Well, I can't show him too much on account of my leg, but I saw a few things in his delivery. If you don't mind."

The man turned his head and spat a stream of tobacco juice, then wiped his chin with the back of his hand. "I'd appreciate it.

Cale's pretty wild." His thick Cajun accent seemed artificial, and I half-expected him to say they needed to leave so they could go "rassle some gatuhs down on the bayoo."

I stepped into the pitching cage. "Okay, let's start with basics. How do you hold your fastball?" I handed Cale a ball and he grasped it with a claw-like grip, his thumb and pinky underneath the ball, his other fingers spread like talons on top.

"Let me show you a four-seam fastball." I opened my right hand and he dropped the baseball into my palm. I spun the ball until my index finger and middle finger formed a V across the widest span of the seams and my fingertips rested on the top row of stitching. My thumb and crooked ring finger lightly framed the ball on its edge.

"What happened to your hand?" the boy asked.

"It's just an old injury," I said, and motioned toward another ball on the ground. "You try now. Make a V on the horseshoe and hold the ball kinda loose."

Cale hesitantly picked up the ball and moved his fingers to where I showed him. "Like that?"

"Yes. Remember, don't squeeze too tight. Trust your grip."

I stepped him through the fundamentals of the delivery, spending most of the time working on his balance. Coach Richter always used to tell me I had a strong arm, but the reason I was so effective was that I maintained good stability on the mound. "When you're out of balance," he'd said, "nothing's gonna go right." Cale soaked up my instruction and attempted everything I suggested. His dad listened intently, not saying a word. I was becoming more apprehensive about having butted in but didn't know what else to do except continue the impromptu lesson.

"Okay, let's put it together. Take the mound and throw a pitch to your dad. Don't worry about how hard you throw it. Don't care if it's a ball or a strike. Just grip it like I showed you, get good balance, and push with your back leg."

Cale took a big breath and gathered himself to work out of the stretch. He came to the set position, lifted his leg high, and flung the ball to his dad. Although the pitch wasn't technically a strike, certainly too high for a Little Leaguer and probably out of the strike zone for an adult as well, his father was able to catch it without leaving the bucket.

"That's a lot better," the man said excitedly. "Do it again!"

Cale pawed at the dirt with his right foot as he stood next to the pitching rubber. Confidence oozed from this young player, and when the next pitch hit his dad's mitt perfectly down the middle of the plate, I swear Cale grew several inches taller.

❧

Two women met me as I left the pitching cage. "I can't believe you're back out here, Coach K," said one of the women who I'm pretty sure was Corey's mom. "Oh my gosh, that day you got hurt—"

"Ryan still talks about it," said Mrs. T-Bone. "Didn't you have surgery? You should be home resting."

I wasn't surprised by their reaction. Most of the parents had been supportive, especially early on when they'd found out my wife had died. It was only when the season started that they began turning on me, begging me to play their kid in the infield, complaining about the way I handled the lineup.

"How are you feeling now?" Corey's mom asked.

"I'm on the mend."

I looked to the outfield, where the Dodgers were warming up, and saw Kellen catch a throw and then flip the ball into the air with his glove. He barehanded it and zipped a throw back to Derek. Kellen was goofing around, but in an *I'm-still-paying-*

attention kind of way. I could deal with that.

I found Coach Pete outside the dugout; actually, he found me. "About time you showed up," he said, his face missing its usual smile. "Where have you been? I told you that none of the other dads were going to be here."

"I was helping some kid pitch. Sorry, time got away from me. How can I help?"

Pete parked his hands on his hips. "You're a baseball coach. Just get on the field—you know what to do." Then he turned on his heels.

I stared at him as he left. What had gotten into him? I stuffed the crutches into my armpits and followed. When I reached the dugout, I caught the faint odor of bubble gum and Gatorade. I paused, then stepped out onto the damp grass.

Just then, my crutches flew out from under me.

I tumbled down and landed on my butt, my left leg curled underneath. My first thought was that I'd blown out my right knee again, but it felt fine. My shoulder felt fine, too. I pulled myself up the dugout fence, then leaned over for the crutches.

Pete raced to my side. "You hurt?"

I chuckled. "What is it with me? I can't stay on my feet out here. Don't worry—I'm not hurt. Embarrassed and a little muddy, but that's okay."

"Jack, don't come out here. It's too dangerous."

I wiped my hand along my left leg, smearing off mud. "I'll be fine."

His arms were crossed. "You're not getting out on this wet field."

"I said I was okay, Pete. What crawled up your butt?"

He shook his head and said, "You want to help? Man the batting cage."

As I wandered through the dugout and into the batting cage, I tried to figure out what Pete's deal was. The only thing that made sense was that he wanted to stay the manager. But he didn't know that I'd spent the past month dwelling on how bad I'd screwed up this whole Little League thing. I wasn't trying to wrest control back from him.

The cage's chain link door opened, and Patrick entered. I knew it was Patrick because he bore a mole on his left cheek and shuffled his feet when he walked. His brother Stewart tended to skip as he walked, plus his hair was longer. Funny thing was that for years I couldn't tell them apart.

"Okay, Patrick," I said, "let's bunt two." I dropped the ball into the feeder chute, and he squared away. He flicked the ball effortlessly toward what would have been third base. On the next pitch, he bunted it perfectly toward an imaginary first base. "Good job. Now swing away."

Patrick spent the next five minutes denting the fence with hits, then gave way to Tyler Williams. The thing that killed me about Tyler was that he had a great stance before he started his swing. Then everything went to hell.

"Tyler, let the ball come to you," I said. Over and over.

I worked with Tyler for what must have been thirty pitches. Finally he started to get the hang of it. I was prepared to shoot another half-bucket of balls, but then he started connecting. When he hit a line drive off the L-screen, I whooped, "Smack-o-rama! Let's end on that."

Tyler bounced out of the cage. Three boys with helmets stood ready to bat. Two down. Ten to go. I took a deep breath and got back to work.

An hour later, I'd finished running all the kids through bunting and hitting. My legs were sore. My armpits were sore. I drank water from the fountain and sat on the bleachers. Pete coached the players through baserunning drills and cheered them on in a relay around the bases. As I watched the boys scurry under a sky darkening from pink to deep-red, I felt physically exhausted. Yet somehow working with the kids had recharged me.

It had been so long since I'd felt alive.

❦

After practice, Coach Pete gathered the players around him. They talked for a few minutes out on the field, then walked en masse to where I sat in the bleachers. Pete said, "Coach K, we have a question."

I glanced from face to face, trying to figure out what I'd done wrong this time.

Coach Pete broke into a smile. "The guys are asking if you can be their manager again."

"I don't get it. I thought you wanted to keep managing."

"Are you kidding me? Come on, Jack. This is your team." He turned to the players. "Who wants Coach K to be manager again?" His question was met with a dozen raised hands.

I moved the crutches off my lap and placed them next to me. "If . . . and this is a big if, guys. If my doctor says it's okay . . . I'll talk to him tomorrow . . . if he agrees, then I'll be thrilled to be your manager." The kids cheered, but an uneasy look passed over Coach Pete's face.

As the players gathered their gear and rushed to find their parents, I hung near Pete and our sons. "Pete, can I talk with you a minute?" I told Kellen and Derek to go watch the twelve year olds play, then I said, "What's up with you today?"

"Nothing."

"I can tell you're stressed out. Is it the kids? Is that why you're throwing me back into the fire?"

Pete shook his head. "No, it's not the kids."

"Then what?"

"Promise not to say anything to Derek."

"I promise. Tell me."

"I have a doctor's appointment tomorrow, too."

Chapter 32

"What's wrong?" I asked, then dropped my voice. "Is it . . . serious?"

He waved his hands. "It's not life or death, if that's what you're asking. Dr. Lincoln's running some tests tomorrow. She's trying to find out if surgery might be an option."

I patted him on the back. "That's great news."

"I don't know what I want the tests to say."

"You want 'em to say that you'll be able to hear again, right?"

He shook his head. "Jack, how do you think of me? If you had to describe me to someone, what would you say?"

The words Deaf Guy and Black Guy came to mind, and I felt embarrassed. "You're a good friend . . . that's what I'd tell people. There's something eating at you, Pete. What is it?"

He leaned against the fence and sighed. "I've been deaf for thirty years now. But ask me how many deaf friends I have. I don't have any. There's this attitude in deaf culture—you're either *big d* or *small d*. Deaf with a big d means you're extra proud to be deaf. They're usually born without hearing, attend a deaf school, and sign. See, I'm using *they*. Because I'm small d."

"I don't get it, Pete. Is this like black people treating each other different because of how dark or light they are?"

"Something like that. But my deafness . . . I'm okay knowing

I'll never hear again. I've accepted it."

"But you're afraid you'll always be small d."

"I *will* always be small d. Especially if I attempt surgery."

"So what's wrong with getting the surgery and not being deaf anymore?" I knew the answer as soon as I said it. "You don't want to be thought of as a traitor."

He nodded. "But then I think about Vanessa and Derek. How I could be a bigger part of their lives if I could hear."

I waved my mangled hand in the air. "You've never said much about my hand," I told him. "Why is that?"

"It's just part of who you are, I guess."

"Let me tell you. When I injured my hand back in high school, I was an idiot. I didn't get treated right away and ended up with permanent nerve damage and these hideous fingers. There's nothing anyone can do to fix it now. But if some new surgery could restore what I lost, I'd have to seriously consider it."

I placed my hands on his shoulders. "I want to tell you something, Pete. You're one hell of a father. And I'm sure you're a great husband. Everyone already knows you're a good coach. Whether you hear or not doesn't change any of that."

"Thanks, Jack. I appreciate what you're saying. And just so you know, I'm not coaching again after this season."

"Why? I just told you—"

"New career plan. I'm training to be an umpire."

"You're joking, right?" But the look on Pete's face told me he was dead serious. I laughed. "Well, you just might be the first umpire who's both blind and deaf."

⚭

For a long month, I'd dealt with the frustrations of using crutches: chafing in my armpits, a dull ache in my palms, and the constant fear that I might topple over at any moment. But this morning had been the last straw. As I climbed into my car to drive to the orthopedist, I tossed my crutches into the passenger seat. One of the crutches struck something—the center console, I guess—and bounced back at me, popping me right in the eye.

"Please tell me I'm done with these stupid things," I told Dr. Powell.

"That's what we need to talk about," he said. He methodically examined my knee, ribs, and shoulder, then pored over my x-ray films. He pointed to the viewbox and said, "Your shoulder shouldn't have any long-term damage. And your knee looks brand new."

"So can I get rid of the crutches?"

"You're healing up fine. But you still need crutches." When I slumped my shoulders, he said, "But only for a couple more weeks. Let's try some baby steps. Time to put some weight on that leg."

I stood at the edge of the examination table. A moment ago, I wanted to discard my crutches. Now I was afraid to. Slowly, I shifted my weight off the crutches and onto my feet. There was pain in my right leg, more dull than sharp, but tolerable. I took a breath and then a step. And then another.

"How does it feel?" he asked.

"Scary, exciting. I won't take walking for granted again."

"Don't overdo it, but I want you to exercise that leg. Use those crutches—at least one of them—but you can walk on it as long as pain allows."

When I left his office and headed to the atrium, I didn't put any weight on my right leg. Or my left leg. I felt like I was floating on air.

I couldn't wait to tell Renee the news about my knee, but it took half an hour for her to arrive. She finally sailed in, her white coat trailing like a cape behind her. "Sorry," she said, catching her breath. "Crazy morning."

"I thought you stood me up," I said with a wink.

"No way. I had a difficult case first thing. Then all my patients backed up."

A difficult case? I'd promised myself that I wouldn't butt in, wouldn't press her for details about Pete, but I couldn't help myself. "Did Pete come see you this morning?" When she looked confused, I said, "Pete Leathers? Friend of mine? He's deaf."

"Oh, yeah—Pete. No, I haven't seen him." She perched on the edge of a chair.

"He said he was coming in for tests today. Checking to see if he's a candidate for surgery. What do you think?"

"Jack, you know I can't talk with you about my patients. It's confidential."

I ran my fingers through my hair and tried to determine if she was shooting straight with me. "I was hoping for good news."

"The only news I have is that I can't stay for lunch today. Can I take a rain check?" She placed her hand on mine, and again I felt the spark—the connection—that she always seemed to generate.

I thought about how much I'd come to anticipate our lunches, how physical therapy had been bearable only because I could see Renee afterwards. The brightest part of my week had been those precious few hours talking with her about nothing . . . about everything. Suddenly I realized that losing the crutches meant that I might lose Renee as well.

"Come with me Friday evening," I said. "Let me take you out to celebrate my new leg. My doctor says I can put weight on it now."

"That's great! About your leg, I mean."

"What about Friday?"

A slight blush tinged her face as she considered the offer. Then she scooted over and pecked me on the cheek. "Friday sounds wonderful."

To say that I'd been looking forward to the weekend would have been a huge understatement. Of course, I was anxious about the Dodger's final game on Saturday—we were tied with Clay Baxter's Pirates for first place. But all I could think about was my date with Renee. I hadn't been on a date in fifteen years.

Kellen was sleeping over at his cousin's house, which meant I could stay out as long as I wanted. I'd told him that I was having dinner with a friend, afraid to reveal that my dinner companion was not only a woman, but also his doctor. Kellen and I were taking tentative steps to heal our relationship; I didn't want to further complicate things.

On Friday at seven o'clock sharp, I arrived at Renee's apartment complex. She buzzed open the steel security gate, and I drove in past a sign instructing visitors to park in a remote lot or risk being towed. No way was I going to hobble from God-knows-where when there were plenty of empty spaces, so I decided to take my chances with the tow truck.

I checked the directions she'd written down in sloppy handwriting—was that a 153 or a 158? I reached apartment 153 first and knocked. No answer. Then I clicked over a few doors to apartment 158, my nerves growing more frayed in anticipation of seeing her. Again I knocked. Again no answer.

My stomach began doing loop-de-loops, and I pulled the directions from my pocket. On closer inspection, I decided the 5 was probably a 6, so I headed over to try that building.

Standing in front of apartment 163, I took one look at the

concrete patio and knew that I was in the right place. Rising from
the dirt of a whiskey barrel, a shepherd's hook held a fancy tube
feeder filled with sunflower seeds. A hummingbird feeder, decked
out with at least a dozen red plastic feeding stations, hung from a
hook in the ceiling. And resting on top of a long table was what
could only be described as a village of birdhouses—tiny
handcrafted buildings with round windows and wood shake
shingles, each house painted in a different brilliant color. They
reminded me of the secret birdhouse she had shown me at the
pond.

Renee opened the door wearing khaki capri pants and a teal
blouse. She had tucked her hair behind the ears and wore a hint
of makeup, which highlighted but didn't overpower her features.
She was, in a word, radiant.

"Wow," I said. "You look . . . nice."

"I'm almost ready. Come in."

I swung forward with the crutches and entered her tiny
apartment. She disappeared back into her bedroom and I scanned
the living room. The furnishings were sparse but tasteful: a
cream-colored leather sofa, crystal table lamps on the end tables,
and a floral side chair. An oval coffee table centered the room,
covered with photo books on the Museé du Louvre and
Everglades National Park, a paperback copy of *The Type E**
Woman, and a Lladro figurine of a female physician. A framed
alligator poster hung above the sofa, and I remembered the
plastic toy she'd given Kellen—he treated it like a gift from a
foreign dignitary.

I sat on the floral chair, my mouth dry and hands clammy,
hoping I wouldn't spoil things tonight. Renee breezed into the
room, and I noticed the silver brooch affixed to the collar of her
blouse. "You must really like alligators," I said.

"They remind me of home. You haven't lived until you

discover an eight-foot gator under your swing set."

I laughed. "Kellen sure likes the one you gave him. He named it Swampy."

"Swampy. I like that. Kellen seems like a good kid."

"He is. You ready?"

She opened the door for me and I hobbled through. "Thank you," I said.

"For what?"

I gave her a wink. "For not living on the second floor."

It seemed that the entire population of Sugar Land had the same idea about dining out. Inside the crowded entrance of Harry's Grille and Steakhouse, their hostess informed us it would be an hour's wait and encouraged us to enjoy the bar. Then she handed Renee a paging device with red LEDs.

Renee gave me the pager. "You take it. I hate these things. They remind me of being on call. And don't worry, one of my partners has me covered."

I led her outside and followed a path of lighted citronella torches to a lush patio, where a waterfall trickled down boulders of moss rock. We sat in wrought-iron chairs behind a copse of red-flowering crape myrtles, my crutches next to me.

Confirming that we were sufficiently secluded, I said, "Want to see me walk?"

"Don't show off for me. Seriously."

"Dr. Powell says I can walk as long as I'm careful."

"But—"

"I won't be stupid. Watch." I stood up with the aid of my crutches, then slowly lifted them parallel to the ground. I took a stiff baby step with each leg.

She grinned. "Good job, Frankenstein."

"Be nice."

"Okay, I never would've thought you'd be walking four weeks

out."

"Probably because I'm such an incredible human specimen."

"Yeah, something like that. Now sit down—you're scaring the children."

"Hush. Me no walk now," I grunted, and returned to my seat.

Over the next half-hour, I came to believe that asking out Renee Lincoln was the smartest thing I'd done in a long time. I was grateful we'd already dispensed with the standard *where-are-you-from* and *what-do-you-do* questions. I already knew she grew up with her dad north of Orlando and, after his death, attended medical school in Florida. Two years ago, she'd joined three old farts in private practice in Sugar Land. And now she was on a date with me.

"Coach K!" The voice came from across the patio.

I looked up to see Omkar Durani, a Dodgers ballcap askew on top of his head, dashing toward me. "My mom didn't think it was you, but I did. I saw your crutches."

"Hey, Om," I said. "Good job yesterday with your hitting. I bet you get a base hit next game."

"Thanks for your help, Coach K. Smack-o-rama!" He gave me a high-five and rushed back toward his parents.

I turned to Renee. "I like that kid. Omkar used to be really quiet, but he's finally coming out of his shell."

She didn't say anything but shielded her eyes with her hand. Her other hand lay in her lap, and she began drumming her fingers on her leg.

"Renee? You okay?"

"Why didn't you tell me you were back coaching Little League?"

I cleared my throat. "Um . . . they needed me."

She dropped the hand from her face and gave me a hard stare. "No, I didn't ask why you were coaching again. I asked why you didn't tell me."

I shrugged. "Didn't think it was important." But I knew better. Returning to coach Little League had been a huge decision, more difficult than I'd expected. Yet telling the woman I cared about—the same one I'd yelled at and belittled only a month ago at those same fields—would have opened me up to her judgment.

"It's really not that big a deal," I told her.

"Yeah. Whatever."

She was clearly upset, but I didn't understand why. All I did was coach my son, get hurt, heal a bit, then rejoin the team. She should have been happy.

Just then, the pager went off. I felt a sense of relief—saved by the bell. I showed her the flashing red lights. "Our table's ready."

She crossed her arms. "Can you just take me home?"

Chapter 33

"Give me a chance to explain," I said as I followed Renee to her apartment. She'd turned her back to me and was fiddling with the keys to her door.

"Jack, do you know how much you piss me off?"

"Can we just talk?"

"I don't know, can we?" she replied, her voice dripping with sarcasm. She sighed, gave me a sideways look, then motioned me inside.

I propped my crutches against the wall next to the door and took measured steps toward the sofa. My right shin banged against her floral chair and I almost tumbled forward onto the coffee table, but Renee, who'd been shadowing me, caught my arm.

"Careful, Jack. Pay attention where you're going." When I was safely resting on the sofa, she wagged a finger at me. "You wanted a chance. Talk."

"I guess I should have mentioned becoming manager again."

"Why?" Her tone was more curious than accusatory.

My mind was jumbled. I wasn't sure of anything anymore. Shouldn't Renee have been glad that I'd healed enough to teach my son how to play baseball? And why did I have to report in to her as if she were my boss?

Then I tried to think about things from her viewpoint. Maybe she hated surprises. Like the time I bought her the bird figurine and she didn't want to take it at first. But she'd also told me she loved it when her dad took her on a surprise vacation to Disney World for her tenth birthday.

I knew I was missing something important, and an inner voice told me it had everything to do with our lunchtime conversations. But we'd had so many. I remembered her telling me about losing her father, how she missed living in Florida, and how watching kids play baseball reminded her of annual trips to spring training games with her dad. And I had talked about my physical therapy exercises, Kellen's exploits, and Mom's coffee cake.

Then it suddenly made sense. I hadn't shared anything of consequence. Anything deep. "You're my friend," I said slowly. "And I should have told you."

"That's the first real thing you've said in a long time." She sat down beside me and tapped me on the chest. "I like being with this guy, not the one who shuts everyone out." She sighed. "Will you promise me something?"

"I guess."

"Promise that you'll be open and honest with me tonight. No games. No secrets. I want to know the real Jack."

I looked into her eyes, desperately wanting to be the man she hoped I was. "I'll try. Promise."

"Thanks."

"Now, Renee, don't think I'm trying to be cute here, but I gotta be honest with you."

"What's that?"

"Can we get some takeout? I'm starving."

I sat on the carpet with my back against the leather sofa and stared at the assortment of food spread out on the coffee table: skewers of chicken and beef with spicy peanut sauce, pineapple curry, and a large portion of Pad Thai noodles. It took all my willpower not to dive into the food while Renee was in the kitchen.

"What made you decide to become a manager again?" she asked as she placed two glasses of iced tea on the coffee table.

"You should have seen their faces, Renee. I think the team really knows how much baseball means to me. Even Kellen understands. Obviously, there's times the two of us don't get along." My mind flashed images of us at the ballfield, me yelling, him crying. "But baseball is something we have in common now. That's important."

"Then I'm glad you're back as manager. Isn't tomorrow the last day of the season?"

I nodded. "If we win, we get first place." I saw her frown, so I said, "It'd be nice for the kids."

"Yeah, right. The kids."

"Okay, okay. I admit it. I wouldn't mind taking first place. Then that Pirates manager can't hold up that trophy and gloat."

"Baxter. He's almost as bad as you." She poked me in the ribs. "Almost."

"Oh, you're hilarious." I took another bite from the skewer of chicken satay. "Excellent choice on the food."

"Glad you like it. You owe me forty-two dollars." She stuck out her hand. "Plus tip. Call it an even fifty. You asked me out, remember?" She maintained her poker face for a moment but couldn't hold it. "You're so easy to mess with. Hand me one of those spring rolls, would you?"

I held out a spring roll for her, then whisked it away when she reached for it. Smiling, I held it out again. And again pulled it away when she reached for it, like Lucy teasing Charlie Brown with the football. We were both laughing as I offered the roll once more and she grabbed for it. But she grabbed my busted fingers instead.

"Ow!" I yelped and dropped the spring roll on the carpet.

"Sorry, Jack."

I shut my eyes and bit down on my bottom lip, trying to will away the pain. Then I kneaded my ring finger and pinky. "Didn't mean to drop food on your carpet."

"Let me get you some ice and ibuprofen."

"Don't bother. Those won't help."

"You should really get that checked out. It's been going on quite a while, hasn't it?"

I clenched my hand into a fist and slowly relaxed it, then repeated the process. The last two fingers barely moved. "This is the only thing that even helps a little." I forced a smile. "See? Better. Come on, our food's getting cold."

Renee spooned Pad Thai and the curry dish onto two plates, then stacked two skewers of satay on top. "You gonna be okay?"

I nodded, my thoughts elsewhere. As I nibbled at the food on my plate, I thought about my numb hand and how it had impacted me through the years.

"Renee?"

"Yes?"

"You want to know the real me? Then I need to tell you a story."

❦

"I don't mean to brag," I said, "but I was a pretty good pitcher in high school. They called me The Cannon."

I steeled myself with a deep sigh, then reached back into the recesses of my mind to recall the last ballgame I ever played. It was our fifth game of the season, and I was penciled in to lead our team against our rival Smithville Tigers, who were favored to win the district championship.

With a fastball that had been clocked at ninety-three miles an hour, plus a curve that snapped off at seventy-five, I'd already become a bona fide star in Lee County. A dominant performance against Smithville would mean I was well on my way to scoring a full scholarship from UT. Jack Kennedy, Longhorn. I liked the way that sounded.

"That game was a total nightmare," I told Renee. "And it all began with a dropped popup."

After I'd struck out their leadoff hitter on four pitches, I was feeling strong. My fastball had good movement, and the only called ball was a curve that bit so hard that it struck the dirt in front of the plate.

I jumped up quickly on the next batter, the left-handed Johnny Luecke—I'll never forget his nickname, Lucky Luecke—with two fastballs in on his hands and a wasted pitch off the plate. I fired a curveball to finish him off, but he barely got a piece of it and lifted an easy fly ball up the third base line. I could have sworn my third baseman called for it, but as I drifted over to back him up, I realized he wasn't close to the play. At the last second, I stabbed with my glove, but the ball glanced off and fell to the ground, still in fair territory.

"Shit!" I yelled as I picked it up.

I saw the runner break for second and instinctively hummed it toward the bag, where it passed over the head of the shortstop into a vacant center field. Why my center fielder had roamed in behind second base was never clear, but the consequence was that the ball rolled to the warning track, under the Kauffman's Furniture sign in dead center field, more than a hundred feet from the nearest fielder. Lucky Luecke never hesitated, running to third and eventually sliding home without a throw.

I was angry—at my third baseman for failing to make the catch, at my center fielder for being woefully out of position, and at my catcher for not telling me to hold the ball.

The next Smithville batter was their scrawny pitcher, Tate Gillum, who looked like a younger version of Clay Baxter. He strode up to the plate in his pee-yellow uniform, acting all cocky. So I put the first pitch, a Kennedy heater, behind his numbers and against the backstop. That got his attention in a hurry.

He motioned as if to say, "Is that all you got?"

Fuming, I walked him on four pitches. I couldn't shake the fluke run and the confrontation with Gillum, and I subsequently lost my focus, surrendering a triple and a home run before finally striking out their puny second baseman to end the onslaught. The score was 4-0, and I seethed in the dugout. My teammates did nothing at the plate to help us crawl back into the game, and when I gave up back-to-back doubles in the top of the second, we trailed by five. I was close to being pulled for ineffectiveness for the first time in my high school career.

My initial at-bat was against Tate Gillum in the bottom half of the second inning, with two outs and a runner at second base. Gillum was a skinny senior with a crew cut and an almost-sidearm delivery. I'd faced him several times while playing as a freshman and on JV. He threw a decent breaking ball, but his fastball was below average. We should have been killing the guy.

As I stepped into the batter's box, I saw Gillum flip me off again, not so subtly rubbing the inside corner of his eye with his middle finger. I mouthed back a silent profanity, and Gillum responded by firing his first pitch high and tight, not enough to attract the umpire's concern, but plenty close to deliver his own message of intimidation. I stepped out and glared at him.

"Let's go, batter." The umpire motioned me back to the box.

Two foul balls put me down 1-2, and the catcher called time. He walked to the mound and conferenced with Gillum. Arriving back at the plate, the catcher shouldered me and whispered, "Time to get yours, hotdog. Watch out."

Gillum delivered, his arm somewhere between three-quarters and full sidearm, and the ball came straight at me. The jerk was throwing at my head! My knees buckled and I fell backward. Then the pitch turned sideways and dropped into the catcher's mitt. Strike three.

I lay on my back, looking up at the umpire. He tried to stifle a smile. The catcher and Tate Gillum had no such reservation. They ran to each other, slapped hands, and pointed at me, howling with laughter.

In an instant, embarrassment turned to rage. Someone tossed me my fielding glove, and I staggered to the mound for the third inning. My last inning. Ever.

Gillum stepped into the batter's box still smiling. I wiped the smile off his face with a pitch that slid above his shoulder and under his helmet, ricocheting off his left cheek and splattering blood everywhere. I should have pretended that the pitch slipped. Instead, I pointed and yelled, "Guess mine didn't break!"

My career might have been salvageable—there were certainly plenty of *take-no-crap-from-anyone* pitchers in the big leagues—but when a brawl broke out, I engaged with full fury. I was shoving and pushing, searching for Gillum.

Then I saw him, and he was close enough to hit. I reared back and punched in his direction. The Tigers catcher stepped between us while I was in mid-punch, and I felt the bones of my ring finger shatter against his helmet. My pinky got caught in the helmet's earhole and practically ripped off my hand when the guy jerked around.

"It still hurts," I said, turning my hand over so Renee could see the swollen knuckles and the way my little finger pointed in an odd direction like a defective compass.

"What did the doctor say?"

"I didn't see a doctor. Too embarrassed to tell anyone, I guess. Tried to tough it out."

"You probably tore some ligaments," Renee said softly, "and it sounds like you have nerve damage."

I'd damaged a lot, I knew that much. My fingers, my career, my reputation. My relationship with Dad.

"The worst part," I told her, "was facing my parents. No one needed to say that I'd squandered my chance for a scholarship, but my father made sure to remind me anyway. Mom told me I'd disrespected myself and the family. I think Dad disowned me then."

I shook my head in disgust. "I never played baseball again. Did you know that managing Little League was the first time I'd been inside the fence in more than twenty years?"

"Wow."

"I know. And of course, when I did get back on the field, my bad habits returned. Apparently my baseball instincts include being a total jerk."

She reached up and touched my face. "You can't hang on to those old regrets."

"You wanted me to be honest."

"And you have been. Now I know what makes you tick. When you care about something, you go at it one-hundred percent. Am I right?"

"But—"

"Jack, you're a good man. Everyone makes mistakes."

"You don't understand. I screw things up all the time. I'm not the best father, wasn't a great husband."

"You're human." She nestled into my side and wrapped her arms around me.

We sat next to each other and picked at the food on our plates. I was drained from reliving the past, yet comforted by the fact I'd finally told someone the whole story. Not just someone—Renee.

"I was afraid to tell you about my hand," I admitted. "But you make me feel like I can tell you anything." I leaned over and, with no sense of worry or self-doubt, kissed her on the cheek.

She turned toward me, smiling. "This is nice. Being with you like this."

As I gazed into her eyes, a wave of certainty washed over me, and I could almost feel my soul slipping back into perfect alignment. I wasn't going to be the guy caught looking at life anymore. I'd do whatever was necessary to become a better man.

I took her chin in my hands and met her soft, parted lips with my own, then drew her into a long, deep kiss.

Chapter 34

Kellen and I arrived at the Sugar Meadow fields at straight-up noon, slathered in sunscreen and ready for our final game. Even though I kept thinking about Renee and what the future might hold, I also knew I needed to concentrate on the task at hand—our final ballgame.

With the season drawing to a close, I knew I wasn't going to miss the whining about long practices, the heat, my lineups—and that was just from the parents. If another kid asked me, "Which one's right field again?" I was ready to park his butt on the dugout bench until Thanksgiving.

Four months of hitting fungoes, tossing batting practice, and coaching bases had exhausted me. Four months of watching Kellen whiff at practically everything, save the occasional dribbler to an infielder, had driven me crazy. Four months of thinking about nothing but baseball—actually, that had been the best part. Even with my injury and all the rehab, I wouldn't have traded my place in the dugout for one in the bleacher seats.

Kellen lugged his bat bag out of the trunk. "Who are we versing?" he asked.

"The Reds," I said. "If you guys can stay focused, we'll take first place."

"Corey said they give a big trophy to the champs."

I knew about the trophy. Harold Sanderson exhibited his, a three-foot-high monstrosity constructed of plastic and faux marble, next to an autographed poster of Craig Biggio. If this year's team trophy was anything like Harold's, I'd need to remove bookshelves just to make it fit.

A slow squeal came from my left, the unmistakable sound of car brakes in need of replacement. Stacy pulled up alongside and Mitchell hopped out. "I'll be back in time for your game," she told him through the open window. "Jack, I've got to run home and get my parents. I don't want them sitting out here too long in the heat. You need anything?"

I slipped my arms through the straps of my equipment bag and slung it over my shoulders like a backpack. "How about fifteen runs and some great defense?"

"Can't help you there. You down to one crutch now?"

"Yeah. And it might be the last week for that." She wished us luck and drove away. I turned to Kellen and Mitchell. "Let's rock and roll."

Half a dozen Dodgers were warming up their arms just past the outfield fence. Kellen and Mitchell raced to join them. At the batting cage, Captain Carl was feeding balls into the pitching machine. Omkar waved his bat as a ball zipped by.

"Smack one for me, Omkar," I said. I knew if the game came down to Omkar, Tyler, or Kellen needing to stroke a hit, we were in big trouble. But Pete's voice was in my head—*always tell the kids you believe in them.* "You're swinging great."

I hadn't yet made it to the dugout when I noticed Renee leaning against a tree. I rushed over and gave her a hug. "I'm glad you came."

"Wouldn't have missed it. I know how important this game is to you. By the way, I hear the kids are planning to dump the water cooler over your head if they win."

"That so?"

"I've heard it can be very refreshing." She gave me a wink.

I moved to the cyclone fence, rattled its chain-link panels, and whistled and waved to the outfield, where Coach Pete was hitting practice popups. "Bring it in, guys."

The boys squeezed together on the dugout bench as I addressed them. "Here's the deal. We should beat this team. But it's up to each of you. Dodgers, are you ready to play?"

"Yes, sir," they barked.

I picked up a bat and held it knob-up, as if wielding a microphone. I channeled my inner rock star and said, "I can't hear you, Dodgers. Are you ready?"

"Yes, sir!"

Then I took my bat microphone and, like a talk show host working an audience, asked each player if he was ready to step up his game. By the time I reached Kellen at the end of the bench, the decibel level in the dugout was insane. "What about you, Kel? Are you ready to give everything you have out on that field?"

"You bet your big hairy butt I am."

I grinned and checked my watch. Game time.

❧

The coach of the last-place Reds waddled toward our dugout and met me at the on-deck circle. "No umpires," he said. "League president told us to cool our jets until someone shows up."

"How long?"

"Could be fifteen minutes. My team's just going to find a tree and sit in the shade."

I didn't want to wait. Our team was primed to go. I looked to the bleachers and for a moment considered asking Renee to volunteer for one final game. But there was no way she'd accept, especially since she was rooting for us—for me. And there was this feeling I had, that I didn't want to think of her as an umpire anymore, that I didn't want a baseball game to come between us. "Well," I said, "I guess we don't have a choice."

I told the kids about the delay and told them to wait in the dugout. Then I found Corey's mom and handed her a twenty-dollar bill. "Can you get the kids some snacks? I don't know, maybe Sour Worms or sunflower seeds?"

While I waited for Corey's mom to return, I reviewed the game lineup. I'd scattered the strongest players around the infield—Corey at short, Mitchell at third, Appleton at first. Baker would anchor things behind the plate. As far as the batting order went, I wasn't taking any chances. I'd seen the Reds play. They couldn't buy a hit, so if Corey and my other big three could account for eight runs or so between them, that would be enough to win.

When Corey's mom showed up, she held out a bag of snacks and the kids attacked it as if it were a piñata, spilling its contents—Snickers bars and M&Ms. "One each," she said.

I went to find Renee.

As we sat on the bleachers, our fingers laced together, I thought about last night. I'd been telling myself that our date had simply been a natural result of all the time we'd spent together in the atrium. But I knew better. The date wasn't a culmination of our friendship; it was a beginning. She laid her head on my shoulder and I kissed her hair.

A loud commotion erupted from the dugout. Bats toppled to the concrete, clanging like an out-of-tune wind chime. Boys shouted—it sounded as if they were fighting.

"Gotta go drop the iron fist," I said with a smile.

I was ten feet from the dugout when Derek ran out, a wild look in his eyes. "Something's wrong with Mitchell!"

Screams rang from the dugout. A jolt of pain ricocheted down my right leg as I scrambled inside the fence.

Mitchell knelt on the ground, his hands clawing at his throat. His lips and eyelids were swollen. He wheezed a low whistle. I dropped to my knees and held him by the shoulders. He was trembling. "What happened?" I said.

He thrust a half-empty M&Ms bag at me. I read the bright red package: *M&M Peanut Butter.*

"You're going to be okay," I told him, not sure I believed it. I wasn't sure if Stacy was still at home, but there was no time to wait. "Renee!" I shouted. "I need you!"

Seconds later, she raced into the dugout. "What's wrong?"

"I think he's having an allergic reaction."

Renee laid Mitchell on his back. His arms were covered with hundreds of welts, as if he'd been attacked by wasps. She shoved a bat bag under his feet.

"He was holding this." I showed her the candy bag.

"He needs to go to the hospital. Someone give me a cell phone. Where are his parents?"

"I don't know."

Mitchell's breathing sounded like a tea kettle starting to boil.

"Male, eight years old," Renee said into the phone. "Difficulty breathing. Wheezing. Anaphylaxis. Looks like an allergic reaction to peanuts. Send an ambulance." She set down the phone.

"He needs an airway," she explained, "or he's . . ." She looked around. "Get everyone out of here. See if the league has a first aid kit. I need something sharp. And a tube. Maybe a ballpoint pen or a straw." She wiped her brow. "I haven't done an emergency trach in years."

"Holy shit. You're gonna—"

"Find his parents. See if they have Benadryl or epinephrine."

"Wait—there's a shot he carries."

"Get it. Hurry."

I spun and rifled through the bat bags hanging on the fence. Everything looked the same. Suddenly I noticed a bag monogrammed *Mitchell*. I pulled it from the fence, then ransacked its contents. I found his epi-pen beneath a pair of batting gloves. "Will this work?" I asked, handing it to Renee.

Mitchell had stopped breathing.

Renee slipped the device from its plastic cover, then jabbed the pen into his upper thigh, holding it firmly against his polyester baseball pants. The pen sounded an audible click as the needle auto-injected into his leg.

Within seconds, his muscles relaxed. A whistle pursed his lips.

"Don't move," she told Mitchell when he stirred. "Just rest."

"Who are you?"

Her eyes flicked to me and then back to Mitchell. She squeezed his hand. "I'm a doctor."

Chapter 35

The paramedics arrived quickly. They hooked Mitchell up to an oxygen mask and helped him onto a gurney. He was jittery from the medicine but stable. Mitchell disappeared into the rear of the ambulance, and Renee crawled inside with him.

The league president turned to me and said, "Take whatever time you need to get ready."

I thanked him, and then I gathered the team together under the canopy of the snack tree. "Dodgers, I know everyone's worried about Mitchell."

"He was shaking real bad, and then he just fell," Kellen said.

I leaned over and whispered in his ear, "What about you, Kel? You feeling okay? How's your breathing?"

Kellen took a calming breath. "I'm good, Dad. Really." Then he flashed a look of surprise. "I'm not squeezy!"

I gave him a reassuring pat on the head. "That's great, Kel. Listen up, guys, I'm sure Mitchell will be fine. I know the doctor who treated him. Now about the game. It seems strange to be talking about baseball after what just happened, but Mitchell and his mom both insisted we play. And that's what we're gonna do. I'll give everyone five minutes, and then meet me in the dugout."

As soon as the game began, I regretted the decision. The boys sat lifeless in the dugout and stood like zombies in the field. The parents were so quiet that I peeked over to make sure they were still there. I didn't want to be here, either.

Then the Reds hung four runs on us in the top of the first.

In our half of the inning, Baker and Appleton stroked singles to get things started. I stood with arms crossed in the coaching box, my mind elsewhere. I wasn't thinking about calling for the double steal; I was thinking about Mitchell. It was my fault he was in the hospital. I'd bought the snacks and forgotten to tell Corey's mom about his allergy. I'd been so focused on my lineup that I hadn't paid attention to what she handed out.

With one out, T-Bone, my dead-pull hitter, ripped a grounder to third. I shouldn't have been surprised, but I was. The third baseman fielded it, inadvertently stepped on the bag, and bounced a throw to first base for the double play. Normally, I'd have been pissed; this time I couldn't muster the energy.

During the next three innings, I watched as our boys played with no trace of enthusiasm. "Pete," I said, "Take over. I need to clear my head." I tossed my clipboard onto the concrete, then stepped through the dugout, past the hanging bat bags and the bench where Mitchell had lain not an hour ago. An equipment bag blocked the dugout exit, and I kicked it against the fence. I passed the snack tree, headed for the parking lot. Maybe I'd just wait there until the game was over.

That's when I ran into Clay Baxter. He wore a black t-shirt emblazoned with the skull and crossed-bats logo of the Pittsburgh Pirates, and he had a sickly *I'm-here-to-audit-your-taxes* smile on his face. "Just came by to see how your team's doing." He looked to the outfield scoreboard. "Five runs down? To those guys? That'll work."

"It's early."

"Keep telling yourself that. I've been around this game a long time. Your team's already given up."

Tate Gillum's face flashed in my mind, and I felt a familiar urge to knock this Baxter guy down a peg or two. I wanted to wag a finger in his face and brag about how we were going to come back and win the ballgame, win the championship.

But I also knew he was right—my guys had given up. Just like I had.

There was only one thing to do.

❧

I rushed back to the dugout as our team was coming off the field. "Take a knee, Dodgers," I said. "Let's talk about how we're gonna finish this game." Just then, my cell phone rang—it was Renee. I held up my hand for quiet.

"Hi, Jack," she said. "I wanted to update you on Mitchell. He's fine now. They'll probably release him in a couple of hours."

"That's great."

"How's everyone doing?"

I looked around at the team and told them, "Mitchell's doctor is on the phone. She said he's okay." The boys responded with cheers and high-fives. "She asked me how everyone's doing. You tell me. Are you ready to go out and win this game?"

The screams were so loud I thought Pete might hear them.

The pep talk translated into inspired hitting and aggressive baserunning, and we scored two runs in the bottom of the fifth, narrowing the deficit to three. In the top of the sixth, the Reds loaded the bases and sent their cleanup hitter to the plate, but he lifted a foul popup that Baker caught at the fence. Our fans woke up and went nuts. Going into our final at-bat, we still needed an unbelievable rally to crawl back into the game.

"We're only down by three," I told them. "Give me one more

inning. Look around—this is why you come to the ballpark. This is why we've been practicing. This is your time. Give me everything you got." I handed Baker a helmet. "Start us off."

When I turned around, I saw Kellen eating gummy worms out of his baseball glove. "Come on, Kellen," I said, "Cut it out." He wasn't listening and threw a piece at T-Bone, who ducked. The gummy worm struck me square in the face.

I grabbed Kellen by the arm and yanked him out of the dugout. "What's wrong with you?"

"I'm just having fun."

"Baseball's not about fun." When he looked up at me, bewildered, I told him, "It's about paying attention and working hard, not acting like a three year old."

"That's not what Mom told me."

"What?"

"She said baseball's supposed to make you happy." He crammed a fistful of gummy worms in his mouth; one dangled from his chin like fluorescent drool. "Aren't you happy, Dad?"

I had no answer.

Somehow I found my way to the coaching box. As Baker stepped up to hit, I reflected on the game I'd played for thirty-some years, the game that had doled out so much heartbreak, the game that had once made me happy. I remembered the story Coach Richter told me a month after he kicked me off the team, about a player who'd been beaned in consecutive at-bats. He had decided to quit baseball, couldn't overcome his panic. "I told that boy," Coach Richter said, "You have to face your fear, step in the batter's box, and deal with the outcome, positive or negative. Because baseball means disappointment. And it also means second chances."

I looked up. Appleton stood in front of the catcher, a bat in his hand. Then I glanced at the scoreboard. Baker had made an out; I hadn't noticed. When Appleton hit a comeback dribbler to the pitcher, we were down to our final out. I began to compose the post-game *we-gave-it-a-good-try* speech in my mind.

"Need a batter, here," the umpire said.

I checked my clipboard. "Omkar, you're up."

He trudged to where the bats hung, selected one, and said in a voice I could barely hear, "I don't want to make the last out."

"Hey, Omkar, no biggee. Like swinging in the cage."

Omkar slapped a one-hopper to the second baseman, who gloved it cleanly. I started walking toward the dugout, assuming the game was over. But the throw went wide and Omkar, who was one of our fastest runners, beat the first baseman to the bag.

"Way to hustle, Om!" I called, and a flicker of hope stirred inside me. Coach Pete and Omkar celebrated with fist bumps and a low-five. T-Bone banged the next pitch over third base, raising a puff of chalk and putting runners on the corners. Corey bounded to the plate as the potential tying run and took some hard practice cuts. A murmur rose in the stands.

"Rally cap time," I called, and turned my baseball cap inside out. In the dugout, it took mere seconds for twisted ballcaps and backwards jerseys to become the new uniform.

On the second pitch, Corey pounded the ball high into left field. It cleared the clueless outfielder by twenty feet and rolled to the fence. Omkar and T-Bone scored easily. Corey hustled around second base and legged it toward third. I threw up the stop sign, and he slid the last ten feet to easily beat the throw.

The crowd rose to its feet in anticipation. Boys stood inside the dugout fence like prisoners ready for a jailbreak, bouncing and yelling, their fingers curled around the wire. Two runs were in, and the tying run was at third. The winning run was coming to the plate. I pumped my fist. "Let's do this!"

And then I realized the batter was Kellen.

I sprinted to the on-deck circle. "I want you to bunt," I said.

"But I want to knock in Corey."

I didn't know if Corey could score, but I knew bunting was Kellen's only chance of reaching base. "Listen to me. Lay one down third base. It'll surprise everyone." I patted him on the butt and sent him to the plate.

As the pitch came in, Kellen's right hand slid up the barrel of the bat. He squared around and tapped the ball down the third base line. Corey took off for home. The baseball rolled along the dirt, through the chalk, and then slowly drifted away from the infield.

"Foul ball!" the umpire called, pointing toward the bleachers.

A collective groan sounded. Corey trudged back to the base. The third baseman crept close on the infield grass—he wasn't going to be surprised again. Kellen picked up his bat and looked hesitantly at me. I clapped to him. "That was a nice bunt. Good job, son."

Suddenly Kellen's face spread into a wide smile. And that triggered something in the recesses of my mind, an afterimage of me and my father walking home after pitching lessons, him telling me how proud he was, not of my pitching prowess but of how hard I worked at it.

I asked the ump for time and met Kellen down the baseline. "You still having fun?" I asked.

"Yeah. Isn't this awesome?"

"I want you to hit away."

"I can bunt it, Dad."

"I know you can. You're a great bunter. Look, we've already had three straight hits. Why not four? Give it a big swing. What does Coach Pete always say?"

"Don't make contact. Make impact."

"Then go do it." I raised my hand and Kellen slapped it with a high-five.

As I returned to the coaching box, Coach Richter's words about second chances flooded back. Kellen had endured so much—he needed a second chance. And I needed a second chance, too. "Be the one, Kellen," I chattered. "Little bingo now. Come on, son. Crush it."

Kellen unleashed a swing I'd never seen. He attacked the ball and slammed a line drive to the outfield, between left and center. Corey ran immediately; he'd tie the game. Kellen would be in scoring position, and if that ball rolled to the fence . . .

The center fielder came out of nowhere. He dove horizontally and snagged the ball before it hit the ground. It was an incredible catch. Just like that, the game was over.

The third baseman threw his glove in the air; it landed at my feet. The center fielder ran in with the ball held high in his hand and a rapturous look on his face. He was mobbed by his giddy teammates. Their parents hugged. Their coaches ran out to celebrate. I'd been right. The moment had been ripe for a second chance, but I didn't realize it would be seized by the other team. That was the Reds' first and only victory of the year.

I looked to Kellen, who trotted toward third base to join his teammates. I expected him to be devastated. He was grinning. "Did you see that, Dad? I killed it!"

"That was awesome, Kel. Sorry he caught it."

He hardly paused. "Yeah, that sucked. But I killed it! Smack-o-rama!"

I gave him a double high-five and chest-butted him. Then I lifted him into my arms and ran around the infield grass, tickling him as we went, listening to the sheer joy of his laughter. We collapsed onto home plate, giddy and out of breath, and moments later I felt the rush of ice water down my neck.

Chapter 36

When I was a kid, the long days of summer lingered. On a typical morning, I might have weeded the garden, sprayed away mud dauber nests from the eaves, and fired at soda can targets with my bolt-action twenty-gauge, all before noon. As afternoons grew unbearably hot, I usually retreated inside, helping Mom and Leah with chores around the house. But a little before dusk, when the oppressive heat relented for just a while, I returned outdoors, where the sky was wide and ripe with the promise of ten thousand stars. Larry Wayne lived three houses and several pastures away, and we'd join up and toss a baseball until darkness settled and we could no longer see the throws. Then we'd play a half-hour more, throwing only grounders.

This past summer, like most from my adulthood, slipped by quickly. Little League was through for the season. I was already missing it.

The anniversary of Melanie's accident came upon us quickly, but I didn't fear it as much as I thought I would. Kellen and I certainly didn't want to celebrate her death, but I thought it unwise—okay, Dr. Mike thought it unwise—to ignore the day.

That morning in early June dawned with a glorious sunrise. I sat on the deck in the backyard, wearing a pair of running shorts and sipping coffee from a *World's Greatest Dad* mug. I had been awake for three hours and had watched the sky turn from ebony to gold as another day dawned. Two large white birds—I pegged them as great egrets—glided over the greenbelt.

And I thought about Melanie.

Although I believed I was well on my way to accepting her death, time hadn't wiped away the sadness. As I reflected in the damp morning air, my mind flashed images of Melanie. She stood at the rear of the church, her arm crooked in her uncle's. She lay on a bedspread as we picnicked outside Austin, first waving away gnats and then slapping her legs as a swarm of mosquitoes took up residence on our lunch. She cradled our newborn son while he suckled her breast. She was gone, but the memories remained, like spots which persist after eying a bright light.

❧

Kellen woke and came down the stairs. "Today's Memory Day."

"Yep. And we're gonna try to remember all the good times we had with Mom. I bet you're hungry."

"Oh, yeah."

I opened the refrigerator. "I'll cook breakfast. What do you think Mom would've made?"

"Her favorite breakfast was poached eggs on toast. Oven toast. Not toaster toast."

"You're lucky. We have four eggs."

I plucked them from their container, and Kellen stood on tiptoes to oversee my preparation. "The eggs were always runny," he said. "Too runny."

"I remember. You want them a little firmer, I guess."

"No," he said resolutely, "I want 'em just the way she cooked 'em."

"You got it."

After breakfast, we changed into old clothes. Melanie had single-handedly nurtured our landscaping to a lush state, but things had languished during the past year. We spent two hours pulling weeds that had grown up through the azaleas and Indian hawthorn, and then I covered the beds with a layer of bark mulch. Finally, we planted a hibiscus that I'd chosen for its lavender flowers—Melanie's favorite color.

We drove to the place where our lives changed so dramatically a year ago. We parked at the nearby shopping center, bought a bouquet of flowers and a string of helium balloons from a floral shop, and walked across the street to the grassy median where Melanie had died.

"The tree looks different," Kellen said. The thick pecan bore an ugly scar along its trunk.

"See where the bark peeled away?" I said. "New bark won't grow back over the damaged area, but you can see the wound is healing. If we drive by here years from now, we'll still see that mark. But the tree will survive."

Kellen slowly rubbed his hands over the rough surface. "I was scared to come back here."

"Me, too."

He lifted his eyes skyward. "Do you think Mom's watching us?"

"I hope so."

Kellen sat on the cool grass and composed a note to his mom, the final time he wrote her a letter. My first thought had been that we would leave his note, the flowers, and the balloons at the base of the tree, but seeing the peaceful look on my son's face, I changed my mind.

"May I have some paper, too?"

I began to write my own letter of goodbye. Cars rushed by along the street, but I barely heard them. I told Melanie how much she meant to me, how she had made me a better person. I apologized for being self-centered and ignoring her and Kellen. I promised that I'd try to be a better man, a better father.

When we finished, we folded our notes, poked a hole in them, and tied them to the lavender balloons. As they rose into the sky, Kellen called, "We love you, Mom."

❧

In late June, I helped Stacy pack in preparation for her move. Her mom had suffered another stroke, this one more serious, and Stacy felt it important to be close by. School wouldn't start for almost two months, so Mitchell would have time to settle in.

"I don't need this big house anyway," she'd told me. "Reminds me too much of my ex-husband. Besides, I like the slower pace in Brenham."

Three days before they moved, Kellen and I took them to Miss Skeet's for a goodbye dinner. The boys immediately disappeared to the back, where they attacked the video games with a vengeance, spending quarters as if they were addicted gamblers at the slot machines. Stacy and I sat on the restaurant patio.

"I found something I thought you'd want," she said, then reached into her purse and extracted a present the size of a paperback book. "Open it."

As I tore the wrapping, the first thing I saw was Kellen's smiling face. He stood holding a paper certificate and wearing bright-gold honor cords around his neck. In the photograph, I stood to his left in a suit. And to his right, Melanie wrapped both arms around him. She was so proud of her son.

"Found the file on an extra memory card. It's from Kellen's graduation more than a year ago."

I stared at the framed print. "This was the last family picture we ever took. Thank you for this." I hugged her.

She raised her glass. "To friends."

"Good friends."

I placed my boot on the middle strand of the barbed wire fence and lifted the top wire. "Crawl on through, son. Watch your head."

Kellen crept deliberately between the strands of barbed wire. The field was thick with high grass. Parched blades crunched under my feet. The sun had only been up a couple of hours, but the dew had already burned off. I carefully stepped around a cluster of cow patties, thankful I no longer had to navigate my steps with crutches.

"This is where you played baseball as a kid?" Kellen asked, staring at the overgrown park. A dilapidated row of bleachers with faded green paint was the only indication that the land had ever been used for something other than grazing cattle.

"A little different from Sugar Meadow, huh?"

"Big time. Do you remember playing here?"

It was a fair question. Memories are such fleeting things. "I forget the names of most of my coaches and teammates, and I'm not sure what teams I played on, but I do remember moments."

"Like what?"

"I remember the first time I hit the fence in Little League. And I'll never forget one day—it was real wet after a morning rain. All us kids sat in the dugout, while a bunch of dads poured gasoline on the dirt. One of the coaches lit a match, and the entire infield turned into a four-foot-high fireball."

"Cool!"

"I thought so, too."

"Did you ever hit any home runs?"

"Not in Little League. But I did turn a triple play one time at third base."

"No way."

"Oh, yeah. It was a huge game, and all the bases were loaded. My best friend was the batter . . ."

As we sat on the old bleachers, I recounted the day I ate a mouthful of chalk on a line drive catch, picked off the advancing runners, and got mobbed by my teammates. Suddenly we were just two kids swapping baseball stories. My mind drifted back, past the ego-fueled, self-inflicted debacle of my last high school baseball game to the time where playing with my friends was the only activity I cared about. A time where I'd rush through my chores and homework so I could throw baseballs against a propped-up wheelbarrow. A time before other priorities pushed their way to the front of my life. Before driving a pickup, before drinking beer with Larry Wayne on Friday nights, before high school girlfriends, there was baseball.

"I bet you were awesome, Dad."

"Well, I had some good days, but I had my share of bad ones, too. Times when I struck out three times or let a grounder roll between my legs. You just have to remember the good times and let the bad slip away."

After a moment, Kellen said softly, "Like Mom?"

"Yeah."

"I wish she could've seen me hit that line drive."

"You know, Kel, I have a feeling that your mom was in heaven, sitting in a lawn chair and eating sunflower seeds, and she saw you smack that ball. She probably stood and cheered so loud that the other angels told her to quiet down."

He looked at me solemnly. "When I go to heaven, I want to tell her all about it."

"Kel, that's what I think heaven is. Angels just sitting around talking baseball."

We drove the several miles back to my parents' farm. My dad stood outside, in front of the family grill. Kellen ran into the house, leaving me face-to-face with my father, the man who'd busted my ass, who'd forced me to quit college when I flunked all my sophomore classes. "Stop screwing up your life," he had told me, "Be a man for once." Today he stood grilling hamburgers. He wore a white, u-neck undershirt covered by one of Mom's frilly kitchen aprons. Black socks covered his feet and stuck out of his sandals. My father, who had intimidated me growing up, wearing an apron. He looked like a nutty old man.

He caught me inspecting his outfit. "Wipe that goofy grin off your face."

"Looks good on you."

"Aw, hush," he said. "How was the park?"

"Grown over. What's it been, about twenty-five years?" Just after my final season in Little League, the old Schulze family gave twenty acres to Giddings to house the new city park. The complex was a huge improvement over the dilapidated place where I had played as a kid.

"Been a long time," he said. "I used to drive you to Little League games there. Do you remember that time you and—what's his name, Urbanowsky?"

"Urbanowich. His dad was the principal."

"Yeah, yeah, yeah, that's right. You pulled off the hidden ball trick at first base. I'll never forget that. The kid you got out was Floyd Peikert's son, you know, the guy from the co-op. Floyd was so mad that he ended up spitting on the umpire and getting run out of there." My father slapped his knee and laughed.

"I don't remember that."

"About as funny as the time you overthrew the first baseman and the fence and broke your coach's windshield. He was fit to be tied."

Clearly our memories of Little League were different. I vaguely remembered the windshield incident, although I thought I'd hit my coach's pickup with a foul ball. But what struck me was how my dad enjoyed talking about my old baseball games. I hadn't thought he'd paid attention or cared.

"You know, I was just telling Kellen about some of my old exploits."

"Did you impress him?"

"A little. But he's the ballplayer now. I'm trying to teach him like you taught me."

"Good luck. Did you ever learn anything?"

I chewed on a piece of charred hamburger as I pondered the question. My dad had taught me how to hit. How to keep my butt down on grounders. How to throw and not look like a girl. Hard tags, sliding, spitting. All the basics of the game. From the time I could walk until I was a teenager, my dad instructed me how to be a ballplayer.

But that's not all I learned. I discovered that I could handle setbacks like losing a game or getting tossed off the team. Or worse. Baseball had equipped me to be a man.

"I learned more than you could ever know, Dad. Thanks." I hugged him across his shoulders. "I want you to know that I love you."

"What brought that on?"

"Just thinking about baseball. And family."

He doused the flames rising from the grill with a splash of water from a plastic cup. Then he turned and looked me in the eye. "Jack, I know I've been hard on you through the years. But you've grown up. Made me proud." He unwrapped a slice of cheese and laid it across a patty. "You probably ought to get inside. Your mom's been talking to your girlfriend this whole time."

I entered the kitchen, where Renee and my mom stood on opposite sides of the island, preparing the final touches for lunch. They wore frilly aprons, duplicates of my father's, and looked like a mother and daughter.

"I've been telling Renee all these stories about you as a boy," Mom said without a hint of remorse. "I figure she needs to know what kind of person she's dating."

"I hear there's a picture of you in an Easter dress," Renee teased.

"Oh, thanks, Mom. You're a big help. The dress was my sister's idea."

"That reminds me. Leah called. She filed papers yesterday."

"That's so sad. I wonder how long it'll take Richard to figure out they're not coming back."

My dad appeared in the doorway with a pan of meat. "Burgers are done."

"Guess we're ready here, too," Mom said.

She unplugged the electric skillet. I could smell onions rising from her pan-fried potatoes. The fragrance mixed with the sugary-sweet scent of baked beans that Renee was stirring. The aroma didn't bother me, though—it smelled like home.

Chapter 37

The tall lefty gathered himself and fired the warm-up pitch, probably a two-seamer based on its movement. Luke Appleton had really blossomed over the past four years, developing into the league's most feared pitcher and most dominant power hitter.

Once again, April bluebonnets dotted the countryside; dewberries would soon appear in plump, purple majesty. Sugar Meadow Little League's season was in full bloom, too. The fields were teeming with kids. I sat on the bleachers, taking it all in.

Kellen settled into his position at shortstop, then drifted to his right and backhanded a practice grounder. He flipped the ball to Tyler Williams at second, who pivoted and fired a bullet to first. Years ago when I coached the Dodgers, I would have bet that neither of those boys would still be playing baseball, let alone become strong players.

"Hey, Coach K!" hollered a familiar voice, now deeper with the dawn of adolescence. Baker strolled by the bleachers, his Cubs jersey intentionally untucked. His hair was longer these days, and I saw the faintest hint of a mustache.

"Baker, how'd you guys do?"

"Lost nine to five. Charlie hit a homer over the trees, though."

"Good for him. Hope you win your next game."

"We play you."

"Oh. Then I hope you lose your next game."

"You're funny, Coach K. Good luck to you guys today." Then Baker disappeared to the concession stand. It didn't matter if a kid was five or twelve. They lived for the concession stand.

I turned to Renee. "You remember Ryan Baker."

"That's the kid who got ejected for yelling at the umpire last year, right? He played with Kellen that first year you coached."

"He's a good kid. Parents are nutcases, though. His mom cussed out his manager after the last game. We may have to take disciplinary action."

It was the part of the job I hated most. Two years ago Harold Sanderson talked me into serving with him as a Little League board officer. When I foolishly said I'd serve another term, a groundswell of support sprang up for me to lead the board. Someone even printed flyers and tacked them up. I guess it was my destiny—President Jack Kennedy.

"Can't believe this is Kellen's last year of Little League," I said.

Renee patted my leg. "You've done a good job with him."

"His defense is top-notch, that's for sure. Still doesn't hit like I think he's capable of."

"That's not what I meant."

I knew what she meant. We'd been married a little more than three years and understood each other perfectly. A year after we stood beside each other in Merciful Savior Lutheran Church, reciting our vows as my two best men—Pete and Kellen—looked on, Renee and I celebrated our anniversary with a picnic at the same place we'd honeymooned, Brazos Bend State Park.

We grilled hot dogs for lunch and then she presented me with a gift. I opened the box and lifted out a Sugar Meadow Little League t-shirt. She had taken a Sharpie and doctored the message, adding a letter and altering another. The message now read *SMiLE—Real Baseball.* It was a corny sentiment, but I appreciated it to a depth I'm not sure Renee could fathom. I wore that shirt every time I came to the ballpark.

As Kellen fielded another warm-up grounder, I considered how much he'd grown in the five years since Melanie's death. He was confident now. Strong. He was truly becoming a young man. How had it happened? Was it simply the passage of time?

I'd thought about this often. Part of the answer lay in the regenerative power of baseball. The game which doled out setback and taught humility also offered opportunities for redemption. When I first got involved, I thought Little League was simply a diversion, a glorified babysitting service. It took years for everything to make sense, but I finally understood the secret Pete revealed in a wacky demonstration with a grapefruit. Whether playing baseball, coaching kids, or raising a son—or dealing with the precious life that God gave us—don't settle for making contact. Make impact.

"Balls in. Coming down," the catcher said.

Luke Appleton threw his final warm-up pitch. The catcher fired it to Kellen at the second base bag. Kellen initiated a throw around the infield, and the umpire moved from the back fence toward the plate.

"Call a good game, Blue," I said through a smile.

The bald-headed black man turned around and wagged a finger at me. "I heard that!"

"Just checking," I said, then gave Pete the thumbs-up.

As Kellen returned the ball to the pitcher and settled into his place at shortstop, Renee scooted closer to me. She pulled the fingers of my right hand to her mouth and kissed them. Then she placed my hand on her tummy. I felt a kick under my fingers.

"The baby's excited about the game," she said. "Must be another baseball fan."

"Nothing wrong with that."

"Not at all." She gestured toward the field. "And just think, you'll get to do this all again one day. With your daughter."

I smiled, thinking about what it would be like to coach a bunch of pigtailed girls in tee ball a few years from now. Might even be fun. Renee handed me a bag of peanuts. The umpire brushed off the plate, pulled on his mask, and pointed at the pitcher.

"Play ball!"